The
COMANCHE
SCALP

The
COMANCHE
SCALP

William Colt MacDonald

Thorndike Press • Chivers Press
Thorndike, Maine USA   Bath, England

This Large Print edition is published by Thorndike Press, USA and by Chivers Press, England.

Published in 1998 in the U.S. by arrangement with Golden West Literary Agency.

Published in 1998 in the U.K. by arrangement with Golden West Literary Agency.

U.S. Hardcover   0-7862-1351-5   (Western Series Edition)
U.K. Hardcover   0-7540-3232-9   (Chivers Large Print)
U.K. Softcover   0-7540-3233-7   (Camden Large Print)

Thorndike Large Print® Western Series.

The text of this edition is unabridged.
Other aspects of the book may vary from the original edition.

Set in 16 pt. Plantin by Al Chase.

Printed in the United States on permanent paper.

British Library Cataloguing in Publication Data available

Library of Congress Cataloging in Publication Data
MacDonald, William Colt, 1891–1968.
    The Comanche scalp : a Gregory Quist story / by William Colt MacDonald.
        p. (large print) cm.
    ISBN 0-7862-1351-5 (lg. print : hc : alk. paper)
    1. Large type books.   I. Title.
[PS3525.A2122C66 1998]
813'.54—dc21   97-47175

For
CHRISTOPHER ALLAN MacDONALD

CONTENTS

CHAPTER I

Murder?

An hour after he had crossed the Mexican
Border, the downpour had completely
stopped, and there wasn't the ghost of a
cloud to be seen in the turquoise dome
above. But for a brief period there had been
a violent cloudburst, and Quist had been
forced to seek refuge beneath an overhanging
rock jutting from an abrupt bluff. From this
vantage point he had watched the surrounding semi-desert landscape change from dusty
grays and browns to vivid greens of mesquite
and prickly-pear and yucca, almost as though
some gigantic watercolorist had brushed a
full wash of viridian across the thirsty earth.
And then the storm had cleared as swiftly as
it had come, and Quist had once more
mounted the buckskin pony and continued
his journey. Now the sun beat down hotter
than ever, drawing steam from the damp-
ened shoulders of Quist's coat, while the surrounding hills and vegetation seemed ready
once more to assume their dusty grays and
dull browns.

Here and there a creosote bush or mesquite tree still dripped a few silvery drops as the rider passed, or the buckskin disturbed some tiny persistent rivulet before it disappeared swiftly beneath the sandy soil. There was no dust under the pony's hoofs now, and the air was clearer. That appeared to be the only change the rain had brought. It was definitely warmer than before, but the hot rays were fast broiling the humidity from the atmosphere.

Quist reined his pony around an upthrusting spire of sandrock, then again swung wide to avoid a still-glistening branch of lacy mesquite. It was impossible to hold to a straight course through the low trees and patches of brush and cacti. Occasionally the way would be clear for fifty yards or so, then a turn to right or left would become necessary. Quist grumbled at such delay. "Jeepers! If I hadn't had to take shelter when I did, even at this rate I could have been nearly to Corinth City by this time," he told himself, aloud. The spoken words welled up from his deep chest with something of the resonance of organ tones. "And a useless trip it looks to be. Stolen sheep! Goats! Jay Fletcher is getting to be more of an old woman all the time."

He considered removing his coat, then decided it would dry faster on his shoulders. He hoped the contents of the valise tied behind, on his saddle, hadn't become wet, and felt quite sure they hadn't. Some distance ahead, above the tops of the mesquite trees he could see a low range of hills, growing more rocky and mountainous as they ran toward the north. "That," he told himself, "would be the Trastorno Range. Not so high as some, but plenty rugged."

His gaze moved slightly to the right. Silhouetted against the blue sky, three buzzards soared and dipped and wheeled, wings practically motionless, like vagrant bits of scrap paper tossed to the breeze. As he watched, Quist noticed the birds moved nearer and ever nearer to the earth. He studied their flight a few moments, frowning slightly. "Could be something dead over that direction," he mused. "A man?" — shrugging of shoulders. "Maybe. More likely a dead coyote or jack rabbit. But I'd best take a look-see."

He changed course slightly and ten minutes later drew to a sudden halt. A surprised ejaculation broke from his lips. "I'll be damned! I knew it had been mighty wet hereabouts, but I never figured it was wet enough for anything like this. I'll be totally goddamed!"

For a distance of some sixty yards the way between the mesquites was clear, with nothing to obstruct the vision — just a clear stretch of sandy soil — but at the far end of the view, placed against a background of green foliage and spindling branches, was what appeared to Quist to be a rowboat, with an occupant bent at the oars, his back to the buckskin pony and the rider. Both boat and oarsman, however, were motionless.

Quist blinked his eyes. "Am I seeing a mirage?" he muttered. "There's not enough water hereabouts to float a boat, and I'd lay aces to two-spots there hasn't been either — not for a million years or so, leastwise. Either I'm seeing things, or there's something damn' funny going on around here."

He kicked his mount in the ribs and moved forward. Now the buzzards overhead winged their way to higher reaches in the atmosphere, though seemingly reluctant to leave. Within ten yards of the flat-bottomed skiff, Quist reined to a walk and lifted his voice, "Hi, there, pard."

There was no reply from the rowboat's occupant. The back, the head covered with a battered felt hat were motionless. There wasn't even a quiver from the extended oars, which Quist now saw were wedged in the sandy earth. Wondering if the man were deaf, Quist called to him again. Still, there was no reply. The pony was brought to a complete halt now, while Quist surveyed the scene. "This," he told himself, "is downright uncanny. A flat-bottomed rowboat in semi-desert country. I still can't believe it. And there's certainly no evidence of any volume of water around here." Now Quist noticed there was a bamboo fishing-pole in the boat, its end extending from the stern, as though the oarsman had been trolling, and from the pole ran a length of fishline which terminated some yards distant across the sand where it was attached to a scuffed and worn old cowman's boot.

Quist directed the pony wide to one side now and again halted. "I wouldn't want to scare away any fish," he told himself half-humorously before dismounting. "Maybe this *hombre* is just fishing for suckers and the laugh will be on me in a minute."

And yet he felt there was nothing laughable about the business, as he stepped down from the saddle. He gave a brief glance at the Winchester in its saddle-boot, then proceeded on foot toward the rowboat and its silent oarsman, his eyes alert for any "sign" that might have been left on the rain-packed earth. But there was none to be seen. Rain-packed. That was the answer. Any hoof- or footprints that might previously have existed, had been washed out by the teeming down-

11

pour. There wasn't a mark to be seen on the sand.

Still Quist kept looking as he neared the boat, which was flat-bottomed and about twelve feet long. An old boat it appeared to be, with the paint long since flaked from its sides. Pointed at the bow, and flat across the stern. Not watertight by any means; at some points the caulking had dropped from the seams between the light planking.

Quist spoke to the occupant of the boat again, but this time he scarcely expected an answer. The man was slumped over the oars which had been wedged at an angle in the sand, and between the oarlocks, the handles close to the man's chest, thus providing a support for the body and holding it in a sitting position on the foremost of the boat's two plank seats.

Coming closer, Quist stooped and peered into the face of the bent head. The man's eyes were partly open. Glassy. It was difficult to guess how long he'd been dead, but Quist felt quite sure death had come to him that day. There seemed to be no bone in the sprawling legs and bent knees in their worn overalls. One boot had been removed. The other was scuffed and runover at the heel. A matted gray beard hung to mid-chest. In the bottom of the boat were a worn faded coat, the near end of the fishing-pole and a forty-five-caliber six-shooter. Just above the buckle of the dead man's belt, with its empty holster, was a dark stain, and the planks in the bottom of the boat showed some evidence of the same color, though the rain had washed most of it away through the open seams.

"Gut-shot," Quist mused, frowning. "The slug caught him plumb center. But how, why? What's this crazy setup all about?" His frown deepened as he considered the situation, his gaze once more taking in the boat and its occupant. All clothing and boat had been drenched. The shapeless sombrero gave off thin wisps of steam in the heat. "One thing's pretty certain," Quist grunted irritably. "This happened before the rain came, or there'd be sign around some place." He touched one of the hands hanging over an oar. It didn't feel too cool or stiff. "So it wasn't much before the rain."

Quist shoved his flat-brimmed black sombrero to one side of his thick shock of tawny hair and scratched perplexedly at a spot over one ear. Then he reached down and retrieved the six-shooter from the bottom of the boat. A quick examination showed four cartridges and two empty shells in the gun's cylinder. One of the empty shells looked considerably older than the other, and was probably the one on which the gun's hammer had been carried. So it appeared quite evident that one shot had been fired recently.

Quist swore softly in frustration. "This is the damnedest setup. No sign to follow. One shot fired. Did you fix yourself like this, tie one boot to your fishline and then commit suicide? Only a crazy man would do a thing like that. Crazy! Maybe that's it. Offhand I'd say you're about seventy or past, old-timer. Maybe your mind got a bit touched. Though I'm not so sure it's suicide, if you were sane. What, otherwise? Murder? Fair gunfight?" He noticed now a rumpled burlap sack beneath the seat on which the dead body rested, and considered going through that, as well as the rumpled coat, to see if anything could be learned. "Probably just the poor old coot's belongings — might be some fishing-tackle. I'd best let it go until I've given a good look around. Could be, with a mite of luck, I'll find sign of some sort."

He replaced the six-shooter on the floor of the rowboat and started to move in ever widening circles, eyes searching closely every bit of earth that he covered. Here and there, mesquite bush or opuntia barred his path, but he continued doggedly at the job, a tall man whose breadth of shoulder seemed to detract from his height. He had thick, tawny

14

hair; in a country where most men wore beards and mustaches, Quist was clean shaven, with a wide firm-lipped mouth, and rather bony features. His eyes were good and of a deep topaz color. Or they might have been amber. His movements were lithe, half catlike, half lazy. Black corduroy trousers fitted his slim hips snugly and were cuffed widely at the ankles of his cowman boots. No holstered six-shooter showed beneath the bottom of his coat; that fact alone had fooled a lot of men who had had no idea of the speed with which Gregory Quist, special investigator for the T.N. & A.S. Railroad, could snap into action his forty-four six-shooter when circumstances warranted.

Only his own footprints showed in the sand as he worked farther and farther from the boat in his circling course, progressing in a half-stooping position, eyes alert for the slightest sign — a bit of rock kicked to one side, or a twig moved from its usual resting place; there were no horse droppings to be seen either. Quist swore a trifle bitterly. "Blast that rain, anyway. It's flooded out every bit of sign that might have been found otherwise. And I'm damn' sure there was some sign too. There had to be! That old codger never packed that rowboat 'way out here on his back. He'd have had to have had some sort of wagon to carry it. And where there's a wagon, there's horses. And maybe at least one rider. Blast that rain!"

He straightened up and glowered at the surrounding scene, finding he had moved nearly fifty feet distant from the rowboat by this time. "I might as well give up," Quist growled. "I'm just wasting time."

A clump of tall mesquites grew behind him. There seemed little use pursuing his way through those. No wagon nor rider would have been able to pass beneath their branches, and they grew so closely together that a passage between them wouldn't have been chosen at any rate. In addition, there were a great many loose chunks of rock scattered about beneath the branches. It was shady and looked even cool beneath those trees, some of which still dripped moisture.

Quist was just about to retrace his steps back to the boat, when off to his left, under one of the trees, a glint of something red caught his eye. It sort of shimmered and disappeared, then returned again. In a moment the shimmering-disappearing process recurred. "What the devil?" Quist grunted. After a moment he gave a short laugh as understanding came to him:

Beneath one of the trees was a flat slab of rock, its surface slightly hollowed to form a sort of basin that held a shallow pool of dripping rainwater. The pool wasn't more than a foot or so in diameter, and when still, reflected the green branches overhead, and some sort of red-colored object hung among the branches. Rain drops, dripping from the lacy mesquite foliage from time to time, splashed into the mirrorlike surface of the small pool and brought about the shimmering effect until the water had once more cleared in preparation for the arrival of succeeding drops.

A smile twitched the corners of Quist's mouth. "That really had me guessing for a minute" — he paused suddenly. "But what was that red thing reflected in the water?" He frowned, pondering. "Cripes! It's like's not a label off an old tomato can that blew out here. Still, with sun and all that rain and wear, it should be a faded red. What I see" — studying the reflection in the pool — "is plenty red. I reckon there's just one way to satisfy my curiosity, and that's to investigate."

Straightening his sombrero more firmly on his head, he made his way under the trees and through the lower branches. Arriving at the small pool in the rock he twisted around and glanced up. An exclamation of astonishment broke from his lips. "I'll be damned! This seems to be my day for queer setups."

Near his head, hanging among the branches, was what appeared to be an Indian scalp. Reaching up one arm he quickly disentangled it from the mesquite branches and pushed his way back to the open again, shaking raindrops from his sombrero as he moved. Once free of the trees he straightened and examined the scalp, with its dangling length of long blue-black hair.

"Jeepers!" Quist considered. "Whoever lifted the hair of this Injun sure took a chunk of scalp."

The scalp proper was roughly circular and about five inches across. Attached to its underside, someone had stitched next to the human skin a similarly-shaped section of soft dochide, and running around the circumference of the doehide was sewn an elaborate cylindrical piping of crimson beads traced with an intricate design in white beading of Indian workmanship.

"Somebody," Quist mused, "certainly must have valued this Injun topknot to fix it up in this fashion." He studied the beadwork piping. "I'm not sure, but this looks like Comanche bead-fixing to me." He turned it over. "Whoever it was even went to the trouble of braiding the hair, instead of just leaving it hang loose like most scalps I've seen."

The coarse black hair had been plaited tightly into a thick snakelike strand, about two feet long, which terminated in a red-and-white beaded sleeve from below which hung a short plumelike ebon tuft. Scalp and braid had been thoroughly drenched, but examining closely, Quist decided it hadn't been too long exposed to the weather.

"But where the devil did it come from — aside from some Injun's noggin?" he grunted puzzledly. "I can't imagine it's been hanging in that mesquite very long. But who'd want to hang it there? And why? I wonder if there's any connection between this scalp and that poor dead coot in his rowboat?"

Still frowning over the matter and studying the scalp in his hands, he started back toward the boat, walking slowly. And then, quite suddenly, it happened.

As though by magic a spurt of wet flying sand appeared a few feet in front of his course, even before his ears caught the far-off detonation of a six-shooter. A second slug tore out a chunk of earth some distance to his left, even as he sprinted for the Winchester on his saddle. And then, just as a third report sounded, Quist sprawled and went headlong to the earth, almost beneath the hoofs of his buckskin pony.

CHAPTER II

Rifle Fire

The instant he had started running toward his horse, Quist had thrust the scalp, with its long strand of black, braided hair, inside his shirt, next to his body. Then, when he had arrived nearly within reach of the buckskin pony, one booted toe had caught on a root concealed beneath the surface of the wet sand and he had tripped and gone plunging down, almost beneath the pony's hoofs.

Swearing disgustedly, Quist rolled catlike to his feet, jerked the Winchester from its boot and levered a cartridge into the chamber. The echoes of the shots were dying away as he dodged swiftly behind a tall mesquite bush, and through its branches surveyed the terrain in the direction from which the firing had come. But now the hidden gunman was apparently holding his fire.

"Come on, mister," Quist pleaded silently, "shake another slug out of your hawg-leg. Give me just one chance to return your compliment."

Only silence replied to the plea. Quist's topaz eyes ranged quickly above the treetops to a distant brush-covered hill. The shots may have come from there. "Except," Quist muttered dubiously, "that's mighty long range for six-shooter accuracy, and those shots certainly sounded like they had come from a Colt gun —"

Abruptly, his speculations ceased. Something resembling a wisp of black powder-smoke had drifted across the brush near the top of the hill. It was so faint as to be almost indiscernible, but Quist gambled on being right. Swiftly calculating the wind drift since the shots had been fired, he jerked the Winchester to his shoulder, his finger tightened on the trigger. Not one, but five forty-four-caliber bullets spurted from the long muzzle of the repeating rifle, as fast as Quist could lever them into firing position, covering a wide pattern over the vicinity from which he judged the shots had come.

He hadn't much hope of his shots finding a mark, but he did feel there was a slim chance of again drawing the hidden gun-man's fire, and he had shifted position somewhat after triggering the loads from the Winchester.

Smoke drifted from the rifle shots and vanished in sundrenched air while Quist waited. The silence extended to minutes. A slight breeze tossed the mesquite leaves.

Some sort of insect made humming sounds in the trees hear by. That was all. No more detonations were heard from the brushy hill-top.

Quist relaxed with a long disappointed sigh. "Damn! I wanted him to try something careless. Reckon I must have handed him a good scare, anyway. And he's too far off to catch up with, now, if he's got any sort of horse at all."

Still carrying the rifle at ready, Quist moved into the open once more and stood waiting. A minute passed, then two. Five. He became conscious after a time of the wet scalp within his shirt, and lowered the rifle long enough to fasten the buttons.

"That *hombre* must have high-tailed it the instant my slugs started arriving in his vicinity. Or it could be one of the shots found a mark. I'd best ride up that way and take a look-see when I leave here." His attention came back to the dead occupant of the row-boat and he bent his steps in that direction. "But what to do about you, mister? That's the question." He swore irritably and removing his sombrero waved it in the direction of the man's head where a swarm of black flies were droning greedily. It did little good. The flies scattered only to return immediately. Quist replaced the hat on his head of tawny hair and stood doubtfully regarding the still figure resting on the oars.

"Cripes! You should be taken into Corinth City, old-timer, but there's likely some sort of county law relative to touching a dead body found on the range. If I had a blanket with me I could spread it over you. That might keep the buzzards away. It wouldn't stop coyotes though." His puzzled gaze picked up the burlap sack beneath the seat. "I reckon I could empty that and draw it over your head, mister — blast those flies!"

Still holding the rifle in his right hand, he stooped and with his left retrieved the burlap sack. Then straightening up, he spilled out the contents on the bottom of the boat. There wasn't much to be seen: a couple of soiled denim shirts, one with a sleeve hanging by a thread; a tin box had fallen open to disclose some rusty fishhooks and lead sinkers of various sizes; there were two small sticks with old fishline wound around them; a pipe bowl with the stem missing; two dirty bandanna handkerchiefs. That was all.

"Not much in the way of worldly goods," Quist mused. "Nothing to identify you, either. Might be something in your coat. I'd best look before I leave here —"

Abruptly, he broke off his cogitations, stiffening slightly as some small noise at his rear reached his ears. Twisting his head he looked over one shoulder to see a man sitting a horse fifteen yards away. The man raised his voice just enough to carry that distance:

"Suppose you drop that Winchester, mister."

Quist swung farther around, his gaze taking in the rider, a tall man with good features and smoky-gray eyes, and with crisp black hair, slightly gray above the temples where it showed beneath the worn sombrero. The man was probably thirty-five years old; on his open vest was pinned a sheriff's badge of office. There was a holstered six-shooter at his hip, but he displayed no tendency to draw it. That, Quist mused, showed a hell of a lot of confidence in his ability. Quist decided he'd better drop the rifle.

The man spoke again "I don't like to have to give an order twice." The words were quiet, level-toned; no trace of anger there.

Quist dropped the rifle.

The man with the smoky-gray eyes gave a short nod of approval, and his gaze dropped to the bottom of Quist's coat. Then, "Don't you pack a six-shooter?"

"When circumstances call for it," Quist said quietly.

"Fair enough," the man with the sheriff's star said. He looked beyond Quist at the dead occupant in the rowboat. "Looks like a pretty *loco* deal of some sort. What's the answer?"

"You tell me and I'll tell you," Quist replied. He'd made no move to raise his hands above his head, nor had the sheriff ordered him to do so. The sheriff had confidence in his own ability, all right. Quist continued, "This is the way I found him."

"Dead?"

"Dead when I found him. I looked for sign —"

"And found it washed out, like's not. The fact remains I heard a hell of a lot of shooting over this way —"

"I can explain that," Quist began. "My part of it anyway —"

"Your explanation had better be damn' good, mister. Who are you?"

"Name's Quist. I —"

"I'm Hayes — Sheriff of Trastorno County. My friends call me Smoky. For the present I'm Sheriff to you. What brought you here?"

"I'm on my way to Corinth City — your county seat —"

"Why?"

"Business reasons."

"What sort of business?"

"Let's call it personal," Quist said tersely. He didn't particularly like such questioning,

25

but at the same time realized the sheriff was only doing his job, and doing it very efficiently. Usually in such situations, law officers kept their man covered with a six-shooter. Quist added, "And if it isn't purely personal, I'll be glad to explain further when the time comes right."

"For your sake I hope so. Now tell your story, Quist, and tell it fast."

As briefly as possible Quist told how he'd found the dead man in the rowing skiff and of the examination he'd made of the six-shooter in the boat. ". . . and then while I was looking around to see if there was any sign to be picked up, some bastard on that hilltop yonderly started throwing down with his six-shooter —"

"Hell of a long range for six-shooter accuracy," Sheriff Hayes put in. "And then you cut loose with your repeater. Yes, I heard the shots. That's what brought us over this way."

"Us?" Quist prompted.

"I'm not alone." The sheriff raised his head and gave a short, sharp whistle, then continued, "We were out looking for this man. Found his team and wagon drifting through the mesquite a short time before we caught the shots."

"You know him then?"

Hayes nodded. "Old Brose Randle. Sort of cracked at times. Nuts on the subject of fishing. His mind hasn't been right for a long spell as I see it. Probably drove out here, unloaded his boat and pretended to be fishing. Maybe with all that rain he really thought he was. Then, we'll never know why, he up and shot himself —"

Quist smiled. "So I'm exonerated."

Hayes shrugged his shoulders. "Looks that way to me, from what you say about his gun. There'll be an inquest, of course. You'd better be ready with your answers. And your explanations. But on the evidence so far — the evidence you give me —" He broke off. "I can't let you go on alone, of course. Not until matters are completely cleared up. There does seem to be something queer about the setup, but I suppose old Randle's mental condition explains that. You say you left Mexico this morning."

"Left Candelilla Wells shortly after dawn. Visiting some friends down there."

"And you don't care to say what business brings you to Corinth City?"

"Not at present."

"I'm sorry you take that viewpoint," Hayes said slowly. "Still, you know your rights. And you didn't find any sign, eh?"

Quist hadn't mentioned the scalp. "I've

told you what I know, sheriff. I was just trying to decide what to do about covering the body when you arrived. You move quiet, mister."

"It's saved my life on more than one occasion. On the other hand, this wet sand pads a horse's hoofs to some extent. And at the same time your thoughts were full of that *hombre* that shot at you and with the dead man."

"If you don't mind," Quist said, "I'd like to ride up to that hilltop and see what sign was left, if any."

"I'll send somebody up to take a looksee," Hayes said shortly. Before Quist could argue the point, the sheriff continued, "It won't do your Winchester any good to be laying in that damp sand. Better get it back in your boot."

Quist picked up the rifle, strode to his horse and after replacing the gun, climbed into the saddle of his buckskin which stood only a few yards from Hayes' mount. At that moment the squeaking of saddle leather was heard and the jangling of harness. Hayes smiled thinly at Quist. "Maybe now you realize why I came on here alone to investigate."

Quist nodded as four riders appeared through the mesquite, followed by a team drawing a light wagon, driven by a man whose own saddled mount was hitched to the rear of the wagon. The team horses were good-looking animals; the wagon itself was a dilapidated affair whose wheels creaked even though they must recently have undergone a good wetting. Considerable baling wire had been used for repairs on the vehicle at various points.

"Looks like you bagged somethin', sheriff," the foremost rider began, then stopped short with an exclamation of astonishment at sight of the dead figure in the flat-bottomed rowboat. Similar remarks were made by the others, and a good deal of surprised profanity. Hard looks were darted in Quist's direction, then were almost instantly drawn back to the dead figure in the boat. All the men wore cowpuncher togs and carried six-shooters. One of the riders, a stocky, broad-shouldered man with a heavy black mustache, was already scrambling from his saddle and running across the sand toward the boat, uttering some unintelligible shocked cry as he moved. The other riders now moved their horses nearer the dead man. The fellow driving the team jumped down and followed suit. They gathered about the boat, talking in low tones.

Hayes spoke to Quist, "That first *hombre*

is Jason Randle, foreman of the Rafter-S outfit. He's old Brose's son. The old man lived on the ranch. Jason is going to take this hard. I reckon maybe I should have shouted to him to stay back, until one of us could sort of break the news easy."

"Is there any easy way of breaking news of this sort — ?" Quist started to reply, then he paused.

Jason Randle had left the group and was stumbling back across the sand toward Quist and the sheriff, his features working convulsively. Wiping the back of one hand across his eyes, he pulled up between Quist and the sheriff, but now his blazing gaze was directed on Quist.

"By God, mister," he half sobbed, "if you can't explain this to my satisfaction, you'd better go for your iron —"

"Take it easy, Jason," Hayes cut in sharply, then softened his tone. "Look here, it's a blow, I know, but Mr. Quist isn't responsible. He's explained —"

"I want to hear that explanation," Jason Randle choked.

Quist felt sorry for the man. "Randle, I reckon it's pretty tough for you. You've got my sympathy. But I had nothing to do with your father's death. I had never seen him before. The whole setup is just as I found it

30

a short time ago. Now use your head. If I didn't know your dad, I couldn't have had any quarrel with him —"

"It's as Quist says, Jason," Hayes cut in soothingly. "This is just something you have to face. I hate like hell to say it at a time like this, but you know your dad's mind wasn't right. He was old and —"

"There wa'n't nothin' much wrong with his mind," Randle interrupted fiercely. "Sure, he was forgetful, at times, but he was never so far off that he'd shoot himself. Sure, I know he talked a lot about the old days, Injun fights and such, and he was always hopin' to get a chance to go fishin' in that old rowboat. Gawd A'mighty! It was just that sort of hope that would keep him from killing himself. What in hell reason would he have to do a thing like that?"

"It could have been an accident," Hayes pointed out quietly. "Maybe he was just trying out those oars, to see how it would be to sit in a boat. Mebbe he saw something to shoot at while sitting there and drew his gun, cocked it. Could be the gun slipped from his hand and went off. For all we know he might have had some sort of stroke."

By this time the other men had drifted away from the boat and were gathered around Quist, Randle and the sheriff. Hayes continued, "You want to remember, Jason, that Brose was well along in years. A stroke of apoplexy wouldn't be surprising —"

"I'll agree with that part," Randle grated, "but you can't tell me my father would ever take off one boot and fasten it to his fishline in such fashion. Only some bustard with a damn' funny sense of humor would fix him up that way —" He paused suddenly, then his angry eyes went to Quist, "By Gawd, mister, I want to hear your story —"

"You'll get it," Hayes interrupted. Briefly he related what had happened as Quist had told it. He ended, "Until we know something further to the contrary, I'm inclined to take Mr. Quist's word."

One or two of the other men asked questions. By this time Quist had picked up all their names: Bowen, Drake, Engle and Fuller worked for the Rafter-S Ranch, with Randle as their foreman. They were typical cowhands, leathery-faced, muscular; three of them wore heavy mustaches. All needed shaves.

"I still don't like it," Jason Randle said doggedly. "Mr. Quist ain't explained himself to my satisfaction yet. As far as being fired on from that hilltop goes, all right. I heard them shots myself. But I also heard Quist's shots from here —"

"All rifle shots," Hayes pointed out with weary patience. "Look here, Jason, use your head. There'll be an inquest on your dad, and the bullet will be probed out. If it proves to be a rifle slug, then maybe I'll go along with you." He paused, glancing at the sun. "Time's passing. We can take Brose's body back in the wagon. No use lugging that old boat back. I doubt it would hang together much longer. I'll explain to the coroner just how it was, and you fellows can back me up. Now, Jason" — to Randle — "I don't know just how you feel about it. Maybe you want to get back to town, soon's possible. On the other hand, if it isn't asking too much, I'd appreciate it if you'd take a *paseo* up to the hilltop and look around for sign. We do know some shooting came from that direction. See what you can turn up. On the other hand, if you don't feel like going, I understand. Somebody else can do it."

"I'll go," Randle said grimly, "but I'm still not —"

"Good," Hayes cut in, "and thanks, Jason. So I guess the rest of us had better get started back —"

"You letting Quist go his way?" Randle demanded.

"Mr. Quist's way is our way," Hayes re-

33

plied. "He was already headed for Corinth City."

The man named Bowen now asked a question: "Sheriff, could one of them six-shooter shots from the hilltop have hit Brose?"

"You should know better than to ask that, Hub," Hayes said tersely. "According to Mr. Quist, Brose was dead before those shots were fired. Cripes! You've looked at the body yourself. Does it look like one of those shots — ?"

"Yaah!" Jason Randle said scornfully. "According to Mr. Quist. But who's he that we should take his word? I figure, Smoky, you should at least put the bracelets on him. It's your duty."

The sheriff's lips tightened. "No man's telling me my duty. Jason, you're upset, so I'll overlook it. I just don't figure handcuffs are necessary. Mr. Quist won't be far out of my sight. Now, if you aim to ride to that hilltop, you'll oblige me by starting. Sign has a habit of getting cold sometimes."

Randle swore, directed another hard look at Quist, reluctantly climbed into his saddle and moved off through the mesquite. Hayes spoke to the others. Preparations were made to lift Brose Randle's body from the old rowboat to the wagon. The sheriff turned to

Quist, "I hate like the devil to do this, but in view of the circumstances —"

"Meaning," Quist cut in sharply, "that you're putting me under arrest?"

Hayes looked uncomfortable. "Dammit! Let's not call it arrest. But you saw the way Jason acts. I could see two or three of the others were right suspicious too. After all, you're a stranger hereabouts. Let's just say I'm holding you for questioning, until a few things are cleared up. After all, you're a material witness. I figure maybe, if things go right, it won't be too hard to arrange bail —"

"But I've already explained —" Quist protested.

"I'm not thinking about Brose Randle now," Hayes stated. "There's something else. Harlan Stewart, owner of the Rafter-S, was killed last night, under rather mysterious circumstances. We don't know who did it. And so, I'm just forced to hold for questioning, every stranger who comes within my reach." His gray eyes looked a trifle uncertain now. "I've got my job to do, Quist. Undoubtedly you can clear yourself, but for the present — well, I hope you won't mind — ?"

"Whether I mind or not doesn't seem to make much difference," Quist replied wryly. He forced a smile. "I must admit though that I admire the way you put it through."

Hayes relaxed; his lips twitched a trifle. "Mr. Quist," he said gravely, "I figure you and I are going to get along first rate. I'll tell you about Stewart on our way back."

CHAPTER III

Hideout Gun

It was shortly before suppertime when they entered Corinth City at the western end of town, and the descending sun was arching low over the rugged tops of the Trastorno Range. A brief halt was made before a rock-and-adobe building on the main street, where a faded sign, the width of the building, advertised: BARRY LOWE — Funeral Parlor & Fine Furniture. A crowd quickly gathered about the riders and wagon. Sheriff Hayes left it to the others to carry Brose Randle's body into the undertaking establishment, while he and Quist continued along Main Street, which had originally been known as Trail Street, the sheriff ignoring the questions from the crowd.

A few men in the gathering looked inquiringly after Quist as he and Hayes pushed on, but as Quist had no appearance of being a prisoner, their attention quickly switched back to the dead man being carried into the undertaker's. Quist's buckskin and the sheriff's gray mount walked side by side. "Corinth City's quite a burg," Quist com-

37

mented. "I've been through on the train but never stopped off."

"We're right proud of our town." Hayes nodded seriously. "Not so busy right now, but come beef round-up time, those cattle pens at the tracks east of town will be plenty busy. Oh, we're due to grow all right."

They had crossed a number of streets: Antelope, Crockett, Mesquite and Brazos, all crossing Main and running north and south. They were unpaved and were probably thoroughfares of sticky mud in the winter, though there were plank sidewalks running on either side. The rain hadn't appeared to hit to any extent, this far north, and the ponies kicked up small puffs of dust as they walked. South of Main and paralleling it, was Railroad Street, along which the T.N. & A.S. tracks ran. Beyond those were situated the local "Boot Hill" cemetery and a scattering of Mexican dwellings. The residential district proper lay north of Main.

Quist noticed several saloons, two general stores, two hotels — one of shabby frame construction, the other of faded brick. The Cattlemen's Commercial Bank was also of brick. There were a number of other structures of various commercial enterprise, many with high false-fronts. An almost unbroken line of hitchracks ran at either side of the roadway. Wooden awnings stretched to supporting two-by-fours at the edge of the plank sidewalks. Buildings were of frame, adobe, or rock-and-adobe. The sheriff's office, when they came to it, was of the last — a squat blocky structure, with a sign hanging from the edge of its wooden awning and reading in wind-and-sand blasted letters: Office of the Sheriff — Trastorno County.

"Like I say," Hayes commenced, as the two men dismounted, "I hate like hell to do this —"

"Are you always" — Quist smiled — "so apologetic with your prisoners, sheriff? Let's just say I'm co-operating."

"You're taking this pretty good, Quist."

Quist got his valise from the saddle and followed the sheriff inside the office. Hayes said, "It sure didn't look like it had rained much here." He sounded as though he were just making conversation to cover his embarrassment.

Quist nodded, glancing around. The office looked neat and clean. There was a desk near the window, with an unlighted oil lamp on it, and a stack of neatly piled papers beneath the open roll-top. On the left side of the room was a cot with folded blankets. A rack containing shotguns, rifles and handcuffs, stood at one side. On the walls were a couple of calendars from packing companies and a topographical map of the county.

". . . damned if I know where my deputy is," Hayes was saying uncertainly. "He'll likely drop in, in a minute or so —"

Quist chuckled. "You're stalling, sheriff. Maybe you should give me the keys and let me lock myself in."

"Oh, hell!" Hayes smiled sheepishly. "Come on. We'll get it over with. It won't be for long."

He pushed open a closed door in the rear wall and led the way to the cell-block, a more modern structure of solid cement which Quist judged had been built at some date later than the office. There was a narrow corridor, with six barred cell-doors on either side. Hayes produced a bunch of keys and opened the first door on the left side. "You won't be bothered," he said. "Nobody else in here at present."

"That sounds like a good law officer," Quist commented, as he stepped into the cell.

"Maybe I'm just lucky," Hayes said after a moment, a touch of gloom seeming to enter his tones. "Well, like I've said before, I don't like this any better than you do, Mr. Quist. It won't be long. I've got a coupla things to do, but I'll get back as soon as possible. Oh, yes, I'll take your horse down to the livery and see that he's taken care of." He smiled slightly. "Make yourself comfortable." He stepped out, closed the long barred-door and the lock snapped. An instant later the door to his office closed also.

"Well," Quist commented a bit wryly, when the sheriff's footsteps had died away, "things certainly happen to me." He set his valise down on a cot suspended by chains from one wall, and glanced around. The cell was clean, at any rate; a faint smell of sheep-dip hovered in the air. Two buckets, one filled with water, stood in a corner. High in the outer wall, was a small barred window. Quist strode across to the cell-door and tried it. It was locked all right. He returned to the cot, sat down on a straw-filled mattress, shoved a folded blanket to one side and started to roll a brown-paper cigarette. A match, lighted on one thumbnail, brought a spiral of gray smoke from his lips. "One dead man in a rowboat in desert country. A mysterious murder last night. And a sheriff, who appears capable as hell, being apologetic about shoving a suspect in a cell. Or some sort of witness, if not a suspect. Well, murder's been in my line of business before. I wonder if this mysterious killing — or the other one either — has anything to do with the T.N. & A.S. It's damn' funny Jay Fletcher would send for me to come here — but, hell! those two deaths hadn't occurred when he sent that message."

Quist glanced at his cell-window. He judged the sun was behind the mountains by this time. It would be dark in another hour. Stripping off his coat, he stepped to the pail of water and washed up. He had just finished and was drying himself on a bandanna, when steps were heard in the office, the door to the cell block opened, and a man appeared at Quist's cell-door, bearing a large tray.

He said "Howdy, Mr. Quist," and busied himself balancing the tray on one hand while he unlocked the cell-door with the other. Then he stopped inside. "Smoky said I'd better get some food to you. I'm Dyke Leigh — Smoky's deputy."

"You're more than welcome," Quist answered. "My stomach was beginning to think my throat was cut."

Deputy Dyke Leigh was a tall gangling man of twenty-seven or twenty-eight with a sandy complexion and rather tousled hair hanging on his forehead from beneath a tan sombrero. He was in Levis and denim shirt; a six-shooter hung loosely at his right hip, and he wore a badge of office on his open vest: his collar was open at the throat.

He placed the tray on the bed, after clanging the door to behind him and dropping keys back in his pocket. Quist's taste buds started working as he sniffed the steam rising from the tray. There was a thick steak, potatoes, a dish of corn, a thick slab of apple pie and a covered, tin pail of coffee. "This," Quist commenced gratefully, "is *muy elegante*, Leigh, and I'm mighty appreciative. Is this the regular jail fodder — ?"

"I'll be damned!" came the interruption. "I'll be doubledamned! Look here, Mr. Quist —"

The deputy's voice broke. He stood, mouth open, eyes staring at Quist. Quist said, "What's wrong?"

Deputy Leigh indicated the leather harness, equipped with an underarm holster holding a short-barreled, forty-four six-shooter, which was fitted to Quist's left shoulder. "Did Smoky know you had that contraption on?"

Quist smiled. "Probably not. I had my coat on, and it doesn't show under a coat."

The deputy grinned widely. "Damned if this isn't one on Smoky!" The grin suddenly vanished. "Lord! It would have been one on me, too, if you'd felt so inclined. I was so busy getting the tray in and unlocking the door, that I scarcely noticed you. Smoky said you weren't warlike nohow, so I reckon I got careless." The grin returned. "I sure got the laugh on the sheriff. He told me when he ordered me to take care of your horse to leave your rifle in the office. Wait until he learns what he missed?" Laughter bubbled from the deputy's lips. It was infectious and Quist chuckled, finding himself liking this lanky deputy. "Don't let me forget," Leigh chortled, "to tell Smoky he owes me a drink."

"Maybe he'll owe us both a drink." Quist grinned.

Leigh's attention came back to the underarm holster. "That's sure some hideout rig. I don't know as I ever saw one like it before."

"Probably not," Quist answered. "This happens to be my own design. Been using it a number of years now, and so far haven't found anything I liked better. You see how it works. When I draw, I just reach across and jerk the gun straight out through its open side, instead of up and out as you would with a belt holster. That dispenses with one movement, and there are times when a fraction of a second saved means the difference in beating the other man to the shot —"

"Sure, but what holds your gun in that open holster? I should think it would fall out."

Quist explained. "A flat steel spring, sewed within the leather, holds the gun in place until it's needed. For instance . . ."

Leigh didn't quite know just how it happened, but he caught a blurred view of Quist's right hand — then the butt of the forty-four six-shooter was filling Quist's palm, though the muzzle of the gun was pointed away from the deputy.

The deputy had backed a step and gone pale. Then as he saw Quist replace the weapon, his color returned. He gulped, "Thank God, you aren't feeling belligerent. What you could have done to me." His grin returned. "Or to Smoky Hayes today, if you'd been so inclined, and Smoky is right fast on the draw too."

Quist shrugged his shoulders. "Maybe I'd not been so fast, if the chips had been down and I was facing a killer. When the pressure's on, a man may get nervous and bungle a draw. All's I was trying to do was show you the advantage of this sort of gun. It's a sight more comfortable to wear than a hip gun, and — for me — faster."

"Whew! I should say so! But don't you wear a ca'tridge belt, Mr. Quist?"

Quist shook his head. "Too heavy. I carry a handful of loads in a pocket. If a man can't do his job with what's in the gun and an extra handful, he's got no business carrying a six-shooter."

"Cripes! I'm beginning to think you've got something there."

"Anyway, I hope so. And by using a forty-four-caliber six-shooter, I can use the same ca'tridges in my Winchester, if I'm toting a rifle." He broke off. "Shucks, I'm letting my supper get cold."

He sat down beside the tray and started to eat, finding the food good. The deputy sat at the other side of the tray, seemingly lost in thought. Once, Quist offered to share the coffee cup, but Leigh refused, mumbling something about having already eaten while this food was being prepared, then relapsed to silence again. Finally Quist put down his tools with a sigh of satisfaction, drained the coffee cup and started to roll a cigarette.

"By Cripes! I've got it!" Leigh suddenly blurted.

Quist lighted his cigarette and tossed papers and Durham to the deputy. "Not measles, I hope." He smiled.

"No, you don't get me. You're Quist —"

"I've admitted it."

"Gregory Quist, the railroad detective for

46

the Texas Northern and Arizona Southern Railroad."

"You could win a bet on that, Leigh."

"Hell's-bells on a tomcat! The papers were full of stuff about you, six months or so back. Something you did over in the Quivira country. Solved a murder case —"

"All right." Quist frowned. "Let's forget it."

"Just as you say, but I'm surprised Smoky didn't connect you up. Smoky knows just about everything."

"With two killings on his mind, I'm not surprised Sheriff Hayes failed to think of me as a railroad dick; or should I say one killing and one suicide?"

"Smoky thinks old Brose knocked himself off. But he hasn't said much. He'll wait until the coroner's jury acts, see what evidence comes out. But it's Harlan Stewart's murder that's got him down. Smoky and Harl were right close."

"So the sheriff was telling me." Quist nodded. "I gathered he was at his wits' ends trying to figure what happened and who did it. As I got it, he had been out to the Rafter-S, and about the time he returned to town, somebody threw a shot out of the darkness and finished off Stewart. And nobody at the ranch at the time except Stewart's wife, the ranch cook and old Brose Randle. And sometime that same night, old Brose took out, and wasn't located until today — dead."

"That's about it," Leigh said, then with a shrug of shoulders. "Could be Harl Stewart's better off at that. He was drinking himself to death as fast as possible. I figured him for a sick man."

"Did Stewart have any particular enemies?"

"That's exactly what Smoky would like to know. Sure, he's had small troubles with people here and there, but nothing that calls for murder."

"He had a daughter as well as a wife, I understand."

Leigh flushed slightly. "Did Smoky tell you about her?" the deputy asked self-consciously.

"Just mentioned her in passing, as you might say. Name's Eirene. Good-looking."

"Good-looking!" Leigh said indignantly. "Why — why, Mr. Quist, she's beautiful."

Quist's lips twitched. "I've got a hunch you're interested in that direction."

The deputy's flush deepened. "Maybe we'd better forget that. I'm trying to. I never did have any chance against Smoky —"

Anything more Leigh might have said was interrupted by a step in the corridor beyond the cells, and Sheriff Hayes appeared at the barred door. Leigh's keys jangled as he rose, thrust one arm through the bars and admitted Hayes.

"Mr. Quist," the sheriff said humbly, "is there anything I can say to make you realize I know I'm a fool — ?" He broke off, noting for the first time, Quist's underarm gun. "That really piles it on. I suppose you were wearing that when I took you in today."

Quist smiled. "You suppose correct, sheriff."

"For God's sake, let's forget that sheriff-business. I told you once today that my friends call me Smoky — though how I can ever expect you to be a friend after —" He paused, "Why didn't you tell me you were Gregory Quist, the T.N. & A.S. investigator? Good Lord, the whole country knows about you —"

"I think you exaggerate, Smoky," Quist cut in.

"The hell I do!" The sheriff swung on his deputy. "Dyke, I've always told you not to believe anything your eyes don't see. My eyes didn't see a gun today, so I figured Mr. Quist wasn't wearing one. That should be a lesson to both of us — especially me. I should turn in my badge and start playing with a string of spools. Sheriff Hayes!" — in self-scorn — "or maybe it should be Daze. Smoky Haze is likely better. That's me. Riding around in a haze."

"Don't be too tough on yourself, Smoky," Quist suggested.

"You're a mighty tolerant man, Mr. Quist," the sheriff said. "I'm just glad this wasn't one of my days to be harsh with anyone —"

"Looks like the drinks are on you, Smoky." Dyke Leigh chuckled. "And from now on, every time you see —"

"Drinks hell!" Hayes snapped. "I owe him a complete distillery. I only wish I could afford to pay such an obligation. Oh, I'll pay for the drinks, all right, but that will have to come later. Mr. Quist —"

"My friends call me Greg, Smoky."

"Thanks. I appreciate that, after what's happened. Greg, there's a man named Jay Fletcher down to the hotel raising particular hell —"

"Fletcher's a division superintendent for the T.N. & A.S." Quist looked amused. "What's Jay blowing off steam about now?"

"He claims he was to meet you at the hotel — Corinth City House — yesterday. When you didn't show up, he started kicking over the traces. When he reached the point where I was called in and ordered — ordered, mind you — to gather riders and go looking for you, well — anyway, that's when I learned who you were." The sheriff looked sheepish. "To tell the truth, I just lacked the guts to admit what I'd done, so I promised to start looking for you. So I'll be obliged if you'll run along *pronto* and let him think I'm on my job. You can tell him what a nitwit I am, if you care to. I didn't have the courage for it. He might have flayed me alive."

Quist laughed. "Jay's bark is worse than his bite."

"I'm not convinced," Hayes said ruefully. "You'd think he was the president of the railroad instead of just division superintendent, the way he talked."

"He damn' nigh could be. He owns plenty stock. He's turned down the general superintendent's job more than once, as well as other positions. But he likes it where he is. The T.N. & A.S. is his baby. He doesn't think any more of it than he does his right eye — both eyes and a couple of arms thrown in, I guess." Quist got into his coat. "Well, I'll be running along. I'll see you later, Smoky — Dyke — and we'll have those drinks. I'm going to hold you to that promise, Smoky."

"I sure as hell hope you do, Greg. I'm more than anxious to pay." He held out his hand. Quist shook with him, then with the deputy. They followed him to the door. There wasn't much light left on the street.

CHAPTER IV

Dangerous

There were fewer people on the street, when Quist left the sheriff's office, rifle and satchel in hand. The excitement over the finding of Brose Randle's body had died down and the town was returning to its accustomed suppertime activities. A faint afterglow still lingered beyond the peaks of the Trastorno Range. To the east, night was already seeping into the sky. Here and there along Main Street, a few lights shown a bit prematurely from store windows, competing but feebly with the day's light still remaining.

Quist chuckled softly. "Well, that's the first time," he told himself, "that I've been thrown into a cell the first day I arrived on a job."

At Mesquite Street he cut diagonally across the roadway and climbed the steps leading to the long porch of the Corinth City House. The side of the porch running along Mesquite showed one entrance to the hotel bar, and Quist eyed it longingly for a moment before deciding to go on into the lobby. A few men standing about the lobby eyed Quist curiously when he came in. Beyond the lobby a double-doored entrance showed the way to the hotel dining room from which came the clatter of crockery and table ware. An harassed-looking hotel clerk with gray hair and spectacles received Quist's name with an almost fawning gratitude, and pushed the register toward him. "Thank the good Lord, you got here at last, Mr. Quist," he chatted effusively. "We were all so worried for fear some accident had overtaken you. Your friend Mr. Fletcher has been most difficult."

"Yeah," Quist grunted, while he signed the register. "I know Jay. Don't let him upset you."

"I try not to," the clerk said. "We've put you in No. 19. Mr. Fletcher thought it would be all right. A nice airy room, with windows facing north and east. You won't get the afternoon sun, and, gracious, it's been so hot here the past two weeks. I understand there was considerable rain to the south, but we got scarcely enough to lay the dust. I sometimes wonder —"

"Yeah, so do I," Quist cut short the babbling. "No. 19 will be fine, I'm certain. I'll go right up."

"Right up the stairs and turn right to the corner," the clerk continued. "If you want anything, just let us know."

Quist shifted his satchel to the other hand and mounted a flight of stairs with a threadbare carpet, ascending from the lobby. Arriving at the second floor, he noticed a small skylight directly above the stairwell, though that was now dark. An oil lamp with shade was suspended from the ceiling, and glancing along a corridor to his left, Quist saw a second lamp. He turned right from the stairway and found No. 19 painted on a door, white paint on an oak-finished pine. Pushing open the door he entered and closed it behind him.

A thin, gray-haired man in gray "town" clothing, who had been staring moodily down at the street from an open window, swung around at Quist's entry. His tired eyes behind their rimless glasses showed an instant relief. "Greg! You're here at last. I've been worried sick. Where the devil have you been?"

But Quist paid the question no attention. Next to the oil lamp burning on a table, was a tray on which sat an opened bottle of whisky and glasses, and beside the tray was a metal bucket spotted with drops of moisture. Quist laughed softly. "Good old Jay! I figured you'd have my welfare in mind." Dropping his rifle and satchel to the bed, he tossed off his sombrero, and striding across to the bucket, lifted out a dripping bottle of beer from which the label was working loose. "A beautiful sight, Jay. *Menger Beer* from San Antonio. Nobody yet has ever brewed lager like old Charlie Degen, God bless him! You sure do cater to my tastes."

"Nonsense," Fletcher said stiffly. "I just happened to remember you liked beer. There was a shipment coming through, and I directed that a couple of cases be consigned to you, here. But the ice in that bucket is all melted — has been for some time."

"That's fine." Quist smiled. "Whoever got the idea that beer should be ice-cold is crazy as a bedbug." Picking up the opener he pried the cuplike stopper from a bottle and raised the beer to his lips. After moments he set down the empty bottle with a long sigh of satisfaction. "You'd better have one, Jay."

"You know mighty well I can't stand that slop" — impatiently. Fletcher came to the table and poured himself a modest whisky. "Where the Almighty have you been? I've been waiting since yesterday —"

"Just a minute, Jay. Let me catch my breath. You're lucky I'm here this soon. I was inclined to stop in the bar, downstairs, but then I figured, 'Jay won't let me down. He'll have beer handy. He always does when he wants something special.' " Laughing, Quist removed his coat now and opened a second bottle. "Not a bad room, Jay." He glanced around appreciatively. There was a bed and dresser; also a commode with wash bowl and pitcher, above which hung a flecked and spotted mirror. Two straight-backed chairs and a stand for hanging clothing. An open window with shade in the north wall; a second in the east wall overlooking Mesquite Street. But little breeze came through the openings.

"Naturally it's a good room," Jay Fletcher said stiffly. "The company believes in the best for its operatives —"

"Its detectives," Quist jeered. "Don't act so dignified."

"All right," Fletcher conceded tiredly. "Its private investigators."

"Buffalo chips!" Quist snapped. "I'm a railroad dick and a rose by any other name —"

"Greg, you're just too cynical for —"

"Hell, yes! How could I be anything but cynical in a job like mine?" He didn't wait for Fletcher to reply, but crossed to the back window, foaming bottle of beer in hand. "What's down below here?"

"A sort of corral. Rather a shelter for wagons and buggies. Horses, too, of course. A convenience for guests of the hotel. This room is just above the hotel bar, but it seemed to be the coolest of those available. The house is pretty well filled. I paid a man and his wife a premium to move down to the Drovers' Rest Hotel, so you could have the best possible here. I've got the room next to you." Fletcher added, "Now if you've got all that straight in your mind, I'd like to know why you weren't here when I arrived."

"So you moved a couple out of here just so you could show how powerful your railroad is," Quist half sneered. He sauntered back to the table, enjoying the slow flush that mounted to Fletcher's face and up into the man's thinning gray hair. Putting down the empty bottle, he opened a third and dropped into a chair. "Jay, sometimes I think you put the T.N. & A.S. above God Almighty."

Impatiently, Fletcher snapped. "You're entitled to your opinion. Right now I'm trying to learn where you've been while —"

"Look here, Jay, you knew I was visiting friends in Mexico. You know, or you should, that telegraph business is slower down there. I wasn't near a railroad either. Your telegram came by rider last night. This morning, very early, I got into the saddle and started —"

"Then you should have been here long before this."

Quist sighed. "Admitted, only I was delayed." Unbuttoning his shirt, he withdrew and tossed the Comanche scalp in Fletcher's direction. Fletcher caught it, then looked startled, as though he had caught a snake. Before he could speak, Quist continued, "I was delayed by a man sitting in a rowboat with a fishline rigged."

Fletcher sputtered. "Scalps! Rowboats!" His features reddened as he tossed the scalp disdainfully on the table. "Greg! This is no time to be funny. There're no fishing streams between here and — look here! I've waited patiently since yesterday. Neither the hotel clerk or the local telegrapher had word from you. Finally I did what I should have done in the first place — got in touch with the sheriff here — fellow named Hayes. Our road has influence. Hayes apparently has good sense. He didn't take my demands lightly. You're here."

"Now, Jay," Quist chided, "don't go pompous on me. Remember I've known you a long time. You're not impressing me." Deliberately, he rolled and lighted a cigarette. "Come down off your high horse."

Fletcher half shouted, "Will you in God's name tell me where you've been? Explain why you're not living up to your contract —"

"I'm trying to tell you," Quist said quietly.

"Just quit interrupting. I've been in jail —"

"Jail! Jail?" Fletcher's eyes widened behind their glasses. "How in the devil — ?"

"Remember what I said about interrupting. Now keep still. It all began when I found a dead man in a rowboat. . . ." From that point on Quist related the happenings of the day, from time to time raising one hand to stop Fletcher's interruptions. ". . . so that's the story, Jay," he concluded. "True, too, every word of it."

Fletcher just stared at him when he had finished. "Why, this is all unbelievable. In fact, it sounds downright crazy. Rowboat in the desert!" Abruptly, he remembered something else. "Blast that sheriff! He knew where you were, even when I was talking to him. Probably afraid to admit he was holding a T.N. & A.S. employee. Greg, when he arrested you, why didn't you tell him who you were? You carry credentials with you. He wouldn't have dared —"

Quist said slyly, "I was afraid he'd never heard of the T.N. & A.S.," then stopped the explosion with an uplifted hand. "Seriously, Jay, I wasn't worried. I wanted to size up the situation without anyone knowing who I was. As it turned out, Sheriff Hayes acted right reasonable. After all, he was only doing his duty."

"I suppose so," Fletcher conceded reluctantly. "You being a stranger to him, he could have acted up rough. However, all this has nothing to do with us, or the company. It's Hayes' affair."

"Which brings us to your telegram," Quist put in. "You mentioned something about sheep and goats, but didn't explain. And, Jay, sit down. No need of you pacing the floor like that. We've got all night to talk —"

"But we haven't," Fletcher contradicted, consulting his watch. "I'm catching the 10:49 back to El Paso tonight, now that you're here. About two months back a shipment of goats and sheep were billed here from California, consigned to a man named Auringer. There were two stock cars, fifty animals in each. Auringer owns the D-Bar-A cattle ranch here and is fairly influential. On the night the animals were due to arrive, the train was stopped at Borrico Pass, about twenty miles west of here, by a gang of masked men —"

"Anybody hurt?" Quist asked.

"No humans. The goats and sheep were driven out of the cars, then the train was allowed to resume its way. I learned later that the animals were driven over a bluff and killed."

"Fine pickings for buzzards and coyotes,"

Quist commented. "Looks like somebody doesn't want sheep in a cattle country. I don't understand this Auringer, a cattle man, going in for the woolly type of stock —"

"That's neither here nor there," Fletcher interrupted. "The fact remains that the company guaranteed safe delivery, and failed to make it. Auringer has put in a claim which we will pay, of course. But you can see, Greg, we can't afford to let things like that happen. Those masked bandits must be apprehended. It's up to you."

"Doesn't sound like too tough a job," Quist commented. "Cowmen don't like sheep. Therefore, some of them got together and decided to teach this Auringer *hombre* how they felt. Does he suspect any one in particular, do you know?"

"Since I've been here I've heard rumors that Auringer blames a man named Stewart, who owns the Rafter-S Ranch, but —"

"Jay, is that the Harlan Stewart who was murdered last night? You heard about that, of course."

Fletcher said reluctantly, "The same. I was afraid, Greg, that you might connect this sheep stealing and killing with that murder, and —"

"Why shouldn't I?" Quist demanded. "If

Auringer suspected Stewart, why isn't there a chance, at least, that Auringer had something to do with Stewart's death? Undoubtedly, he was mighty on the prod at the loss of his stock and —"

"Do you think he'd commit murder after two months, when he's had a cooling period?" Fletcher snapped. "Particularly when the road makes no difficulty about paying his claim —"

"I'll admit you've something on your side, but —"

"Pshaw! Stewart wasn't the type man who'd do a thing like that. I knew him slightly. He was an upstanding citizen. He owned quite a block of T.N. & A.S. stock —"

"Yeah!" Quist jeered. "So that makes him one of the untouchables, I suppose."

"Greg, I don't like your attitude. Your job is to get the men who held up that train. I don't want you messing into any outside affairs. You're too eager to run down murder mysteries —"

"Jeepers! That sort of thing is right in my corral. Jay, I'm going to do as I see fit in this business —"

"You'll get your head shot off one of these days, messing in things that don't concern you. It's too dangerous. I forbid —"

"Forbid and be blasted," Quist flared. "I'll do —"

"Don't take that tone with me, Greg. After all, I'm your superior —"

"In position only," Quist snapped. "Hell's-bells, you can have my resignation right now —"

"Your contract with us —"

"Do you want me to tell you what to do with that contract?" Quist demanded hotly. "Maybe you'd like me to explain it to you, too. My contract with the road states very clearly that I'm to have a free hand in all my actions on the company's behalf, and do things as I see fit, without interference from anybody. Not anybody! You know that as well as I do, Jay —"

"You can't ride roughshod over me this way," Fletcher snapped indignantly. "I'll take it up with the Board —"

"That bunch of fat-buttocked money-grubbers," Quist snarled. "What do they know about my job, except that it's my work that keeps them in their position — my work and that of others like me — much of the time? I'm sick of them and your stockholders too. Jay, I'm quitting right now —"

"Now, now, Greg," Fletcher said placatingly, "don't do anything hasty. Let's discuss this coolly and rationally —"

Quite suddenly Gregory Quist laughed and rising from his chair opened another bottle of beer. "By the Almighty, you do get hot under the collar, Jay. It seems every time we get together on some job, we get to scrapping. There's no sense in it." He poured a glass of whisky and handed it to Fletcher. "Here, drink up and quit arguing. You know I always do things my own way."

Fletcher sighed and accepted the glass. "Blast you, Greg," he said ruefully, "I think you just like to prod me into these arguments. All right, do it your own way, but don't take any risks. You're known as a hard, ruthless man. I know better, but this time at least, don't run any foolhardy chances."

"I think too much of my carcass to do anything like that," Quist smiled. "Tell me, did you pick up anything particular on Stewart's death?"

"Not much. There'll be an inquest tomorrow morning. I gather he has been in poor health the past several months, whether due to heavy drinking, or not, I couldn't say. He has many friends in Corinth City. It is said he has a beautiful wife as well as a very lovely daughter."

"So-o," Quist said softly. "I hadn't heard that about the wife being beautiful."

"Widow, rather. Stewart had married a second time, a woman much younger than himself. Greg, this seems to interest you." Fletcher smiled slyly. "I'd forgotten it momentarily, but now I remember you always did have the name of having a way with women —"

"If so, it was a name without the game." Quist's face reddened.

"Greg, you should have married long since."

"Hell's-bells on a tomcat, Jay! Now you know better than that. No man in my job has any business getting entangled with a woman."

They conversed a short time longer, then Fletcher said it was nearing the time to catch his train. Quist said, "I'll walk to the depot with you, Jay." He picked up the Comanche scalp, now quite dry from the heat of his body, and started to place it inside his satchel. On second thought he changed his mind, glanced quickly about the room, then placed the scalp behind the mirror hanging over the commode where it was suspended, out of sight, on the nail and wire that supported the mirror's frame.

"You afraid somebody will try to steal that?" Fletcher looked queerly at Quist. "It has no value I can see. These days you can find scalps in curio stores all over this country."

"I suppose so. I just remember that I was looking for sign around that skiff for a long time, and nobody shot at me. Once I had the scalp in my hands, however, the lead slugs started showering down. Something must have made the difference. I figure it must have had something to do with the scalp."

"But, why, Greg?"

"That I haven't yet figured out."

"Well, you know your business."

Quist said gloomily, "Sometimes I wonder if I do, when I run across a crazy deal like that one today."

"I imagine so. Well, whatever happens, remember what I said about taking foolhardy risks. It's dangerous, and you're too valuable a man for the company to lose."

"It's the company you're thinking about, of course."

Fletcher said reproachfully, "Oh, hell, Greg, you know what I mean."

Quist locked his door, after extinguishing the oil lamp. The two men stopped at Fletcher's room a few minutes, then side by side left the hotel in the direction of the T.N. & A.S. station.

CHAPTER V

A Lone Wolf

When Fletcher's train had pulled out, Quist left the depot and walked along Railroad Street, heading east. Most of the buildings here were dark; occasionally from some structure fronting on Main Street, light glowed through a rear window. Such establishments as had entrances on Railroad Street had been long since closed. At various points heaps of rubbish and tin cans were piled against rear walls. South of the T.N. & A.S. whose rails gleamed dully under the starry sky, Quist spied flickers of light, at widely separated points, and judged that they came from the Mexican adobes, built helter-skelter among the brush and mesquite.

He turned left at Bravos Street and just off the corner of Main and Brazos entered the sheriff's office where a lamp burning on the desk cast a broad rectangle of yellow light on the plank sidewalk. Hayes swung around from his desk and smiled a welcome as Quist pushed through the open door.

"Glad to see you, Greg. Sit down and take a load off your feet." Reaching into a desk drawer he produced a box of cigars and extended it to Quist. "Hope you got that Fletcher man pacified."

Quist laughed. "Jay calmed down after a time." He chose a cigar, cut one end with his pocket knife, then lighted it, first holding the match flame for the sheriff's weed. Blue smoke swirled through the office. "I wasn't sure but what you'd be closed up," Quist continued. "Still, come to think of it, it's only a couple of minutes after eleven. I was up so early this morning, that it seems like it should be later."

"I sent Dyke on home to his boarding-house. He was up all night, trying to see what he could learn about Stewart's shoot-ing."

Quist glanced at the cot against one wall. "I figured that cot was your deputy's."

Hayes shook his head. "That's my bed. I figure if someone comes in at night, looking for the sheriff, he don't want to run all over town trying to learn where he lives. When he wants the sheriff, he doesn't want one of the deputies. So, such as it is, this is my home." He broke off, changing the subject, "Greg, when I took you in today, why didn't you tell me who you were? There'd have been no trouble then."

"I wasn't troubled any, Smoky. After all,

put yourself in my place. It was a damn' funny setup to begin with. That sort of thing makes a man go slow in asserting himself. I was a stranger to you, and you were to me. I was just curious to learn what would happen. You know, a man never gets in trouble by keeping his mouth shut."

"Yeah." Hayes nodded. "I see your point and I can't say that I blame you. Anyway, it's a big laugh on me, and don't think this town isn't laughing either. I'll be buying drinks, left and right, for a week. The whole town knows you're here and who you are."

Quist frowned. "I'd rather they didn't, of course. I've got a job to do —"

"Don't blame me too much for that. After the fuss your Fletcher *hombre* raised —"

"I know — hell! I suppose I might just as well have been escorted in with a parade and a brass band."

"A man like you can't keep your identity secret, Greg. After all, your fame is pretty well spread. I remember reading an article in a magazine that mentioned several murders you'd cleared. The writer had a tag on each one, too — the Thunderbird Case, that business over near Gunsight. Then there was some sort of fuss down at Mascarada Pass — freight thieves, as I remember. Cripes! Within the past year there was that good job you did at Quivira City. And —"

"Let's forget it, Smoky," Quist said uncomfortably. "You know how some of those writers are — always making mountains out of molehills. The *Police Gazette* ran some stuff too — oh, hell, let's forget it. Right now, I'm here to see what I can learn about one of our trains that was stopped two months or so back, over near Borrico Pass —"

"I know what you mean. Stock cars, loaded with sheep and goats for Dewitt Auringer — we call him Witt. Sort of a low-down trick, if you asked me, even if sheep aren't popular here. I nosed around some on that business — still keeping my eyes open in fact — but I didn't find anything I could put my finger on. Then Witt told me the railroad was settling his claim, and I had other things to occupy me —" He broke off, scowling. "I've had Dyke Leigh snooping around on it —"

"That's not what you were going to say, Smoky."

The sheriff faced him frankly. "You're right, Greg, only I stopped because I didn't want you to get any wrong ideas. You see, there's a rumor around town it was Witt Auringer that killed Harl Stewart. Stewart hated sheep like poison. When he heard that

Witt was bringing some in, he gave Witt his opinion in no uncertain terms. The two men quarreled pretty bitterly —"

"But that's two months ago," Quist pointed out. "What's your opinion?"

"About Witt Auringer?" Hayes slowly shook his head. "I'd never believe it of Witt. He's hot-tempered, yes, but I don't figure he's the murdering type. If he'd been inclined to kill Stewart, he'd have reached for his gun when they were scrapping. He's no back shooter."

"But you haven't any idea who did it, eh?"

Hayes scowled. "Not one damned idea, Greg. Now that you're here, I've been hoping we might work together on the business. Ordinary crime — and there's mighty little of it in my county — I can deal with, but mysterious shootings sort of strain what I call my mind."

Quist looked dubious. "If I go messing into something that isn't railroad business, I'll have Jay Fletcher on my back again."

"But supposing Stewart's death was connected in some way with your business."

"Do you think it is?"

"Hell! I don't know what to think. But we've got to admit it's a possibility, I imagine."

"A possibility, yes," Quist conceded. "All

right, if it works out that way, you can count on me to try to bring Stewart's killer to justice. But I'll warn you, Smoky, I'm a lone wolf. I work in my own way, without interference. I believe in keeping my mouth shut until I'm sure in my own mind what's happened. I'd never tell my closest friend what I was doing, until I was ready to do it. Too many chances of a slipup somewhere. So you might not like my methods."

"I can understand them, Greg. I like to work that way myself. Right! If this Stewart killing does turn out to be railroad business, I'm going to call myself just plain lucky. As it stands at present it's just too much for one man's mind. I'll be mighty grateful for any help you can offer me — even if you do prove close-mouthed. And I'll tell Dyke not to act too curious too. Look, talking is dry work. I still want to buy you a drink."

"It's a good idea." The two men got to their fact. Hayes turned the lamp low and they stepped out to the small porch fronting the office. Quist said something about closing the door. Hayes shook his head. "Leave it open. I want as much night air to get in as possible — cool off the office. It'll probably be hot as Hades again tomorrow. Too bad that rain didn't hit here as well as south."

CHAPTER VI

Clues?

Except for lights from saloons here and there, most of the buildings along Main Street were dark. The bootheels of the two men clumped hollowly on the plank sidewalk. There weren't many pedestrians abroad, but scattered at hitchracks was a handful of ponies and waiting wagons. Quist asked, "Did Jason Randle find any sort of sign on that hilltop?"

"That I can't say," Hayes replied. Quist sensed rather than saw his frown. "I've seen not hide nor hair of Jason since he left us today. It's been sort of bothering me. 'Course, there's a chance that he headed straight for the Rafter-S, knowing he'd see me at Stewart's inquest in the morning. That reminds me, Greg, they'll be holding the inquest on old Randle right after they're finished with Stewart's body. The coroner expects you to be there, and tell what you know."

"The coroner's expectations will be met," Quist answered.

"You know, Greg, I'm still kicking myself

73

because I didn't let you ride up to that hill-top —"

"Forget it, Smoky. From what you tell me of Jason Randle, he'll probably pick up any sign that exists." He changed the subject, as they crossed Brazos Street. "Where we heading?"

"Best saloon in town — the Shamrock Bar. Shamus Maguire charges a nickel more per drink, and that keeps the riffraff out. The Shamrock is the one bar where I've never had any trouble. I guess Maguire was the first man to open a saloon in this town, when it was only a wide place in a cattle trail."

A moment later they had turned across a small porch and pushed their way through a pair of chest-high swinging doors, into the light from oil-lamps suspended from the ceiling. A mahogany bar ran along the right wall, at which stood two men in cowhand togs and three more in "town" clothing. Along the left wall were three round tables and straight-backed chairs. Five men sat playing seven-up at one of the tables; two of these were cowpunchers. Quist had never seen any of the men before. Maguire, a stocky, middle-aged man with a fringe of graying, brick-red hair running across the back of his skull and over the ears, was otherwise as bald as an egg. Shining pyramids of glasses and bottles were reflected in a spotless back-bar mirror.

As Quist and the sheriff approached the bar, Maguire wiped his hands on the white apron tied about his thick waist and moved up to greet them. "Shamus," Hayes said, "shake hands with Mr. Gregory Quist. He'll be with us for a few days."

Maguire studied Quist a moment with shrewd blue eyes, then his wide mouth opened in a grin beneath his one-time broken nose, and he thrust a broad hand, covered with a growth of red hairs, across the bar, meanwhile looking reproachfully at Hayes.

"Now, sher-r-riff," he said, "you'd not be after explaining who your fine fr-riend is. Is it stupid you think I am? And with all of Corinth City full of the talk of him this night?" There was a broad touch of Irish brogue to his speech. "Mister Quist, it's proud I am to shake the hand of you."

Hayes chuckled while the two men shook hands. "Greg, what were you saying about parades and brass bands?" He turned again to Maguire: "I don't know what Greg wants, but I'm taking a spot of bourbon, Shamus. And have one yourself."

Maguire turned to Quist, but before Quist could give his order, Hayes said quickly, "I'll lay you odds of two to one, Shamus, that he doesn't."

Maguire nodded and swung back to Quist. "Mister Quist, it's not me should be namin' your dr-r-ink, but could I be temptin' of you with some fine Irish whisky? It's the best stock of Burke's Finest I have." There was something pleading in his tone.

Two or three of the other men in the saloon laughed, and Quist knew he was the center of all eyes, for some reason or other. He smiled, "Well, Shamus, I've been eyeing that Heather Dew on your back shelf, but if you insist I'll try your Burke's."

Maguire beamed. " 'Tis a Daniel come to judgment, no less. It's the smart man you are, indeed, Mr. Quist. And I'm not insistin' at all, at all. But it's you who'll be thankin' of your stars for the blessed nectar in your thr-r-roat in a minute." Then proudly to Hayes. "You'll be payin' me for the once."

Bourbon was set before the sheriff, followed by a flat green bottle of Irish whisky for the other two. The three men poured their drinks, and lifted them. *"Slàinte!"* Maguire proposed. The drinks were downed.

"Now," Quist said to Hayes, "perhaps you'll tell me what all the betting was about?"

Maguire and Hayes laughed. "It's a bet with us every so often when I come in here and a new man is drinking here for the first time. You see, Shamus is trying to convert the town to Irish whisky, and the town insists on bourbon, despite his preaching. And so you lost the bet for me, Greg."

"Bourbon!" Maguire scoffed. " 'Tis a lack of education is responsible, no less. There is no finer drink then a prime noggin of Irish pot-still liquor."

Quist laughed. "I can't kick on your Burke's, Shamus, though I'm a Scotch man, myself, when I can get it."

"And a ver-r-ry good whisky, the Scotch. None finer-r — next to the Irish poteen 'tis my own preference. But would you be havin' another sip on me, Mister Quist?"

Another round was served. Hayes said, "That reminds me, Shamus. Due to some nitwittedness on my part I'm owing Mr. Quist a flock of drinks. So, anything he buys in here, just charge it to me."

"That I won't have," Quist protested firmly. They argued the matter until a third drink was proposed by Hayes. This, Quist refused, with the comment he'd had a long day. Eventually he and the sheriff left the Shamrock Bar, with the host's praises of Irish whisky still ringing with Celtic insistence in Quist's ears.

Outside, on the sidewalk, Quist said, "I've been wondering if that undertaker — Barry Lowe, is it? — has turned in yet."

"You'd like a look at Brose Randle's body, I suppose."

"And Stewart's."

"I imagine Barry will still be up. Doc Wakeman had me round up his coroner's jury, right after I left you at the jail, so I took the jurors around to view both bodies at the same time. That delayed Lowe's operations, so I imagine he'll be embalming tonight. Stewart is to be buried tomorrow afternoon. I should think Jason would want his father buried at the same time. Doubtless proceedings have been held up, too, by people coming in to look. Folks are plumb morbid about gun killings, it appears."

The two men reached Crockett Street where they crossed diagonally to the other side where the undertaker's was located. A light burned above a double-doored entrance, now closed. Next to the doors was a wide, plate-window where Lowe displayed his furniture stock, though this could be seen but dimly from the darkened street. Hayes tried one door and found it unlocked, then led the way in. They passed through a sort of display room of furniture and into a larger room where an oil lamp burned low. This Quist judged to be the room where "remains" were viewed. There were a couple of dusty artificial palms in pots and a row of folding chairs stacked against one wall. On another wall were two framed religious mottoes and a fly-specked reproduction of "The Rock of Ages," painting. Beyond was a half-opened door, through which a voice in the rear called something unintelligible.

Hayes pushed on through with Quist at his heels, into a large loft-like room where various pieces of furniture and caskets on wooden horses were arranged in helter-skelter display. Two men stood talking in the light from a big oil lamp near one wall. Quist recognized one of the pair as Jason Randle. The other man turned away and approached his visitors with, "Oh, it's you, sheriff."

"Right, Barry. And Mr. Gregory Quist." He performed the introduction. Barry Lowe was a tall spare man with squinting eyes and a beginning paunch that seemed out of place with the rest of his figure. He was about forty years old and his hair had a mussed appearance. At present he was in black trousers, white collarless shirt and carpet slippers.

After performing the introduction, Hayes had at once headed for Jason Randle. "I'm darned glad to see you got back, Jason. We were beginning to wonder if something had happened." Randle said something about getting back late, and then coming here after eating his supper. His voice dropped and Quist didn't catch what else he said.

". . . and Jason has been here all evening. We been making arrangements about his father," Barry Lowe was saying. "So you're the great T.N. & A.S. detective I've been hearing about."

"You can forget the 'great,' " Quist said shortly. "And I'm not even sure I'm a detective after finding Brose Randle's body today."

"A queer set-up all right, from all I hear. The boys were telling me about it when they brought old Brose in. Well, at least we can agree on the T.N. & A.S. part. Matter of fact, the railroad is right important to me too. If it doesn't bring the ice I ordered" — he broke off, then went on in rather delicate tones. "You see, my stock is nearly gone. Never figured on *two* bodies this way. And with the heat the way it's been. . . ."

Quist was glancing about while Lowe rambled on. Near the big shaded oil lamp, was a metal sink and some waterbuckets on a stand. On a long shelf were gallon jugs and bottles — embalming fluid and dyes, Quist suspected. Some small round boxes may have held rouge and powder. Rubber tubes hung over a nail driven in the wall, and below was a glass-doored cabinet containing equipment not unlike surgical instruments. Farther over, two long boxlike troughs were covered with canvas sheeting. Lowe now led Quist to the first of these and drew back the sheeting from a cold, naked body.

"This is Mr. Stewart," he announced in hushed tones.

Quist studied the body. Harlan Stewart had been a big man with iron-gray hair, though his once-muscular body now showed the ravages of extreme alcoholism. Quist's gaze ran from head to toe. There was no sign of any bullet wound, but the dead man's wrists showed the skin slightly lacerated, as though they might have been bound with rawhide, or something similar, quite recently. A small frown crossed Quist's forehead as he speculated as to what might have made the marks, if the man's hands hadn't been bound sometime before he was shot. And how had Hayes come to miss the marking on each wrist, slight as it was? Or had he? Anyway, he'd said nothing about it.

He touched one hand. It was rigid, cold. Well, that was natural enough, what with *rigor mortis* and the body packed in ice.

Hayes now came walking over. Randle hadn't left his place near the wall. Hayes said, "The bullet entered Stewart's back, beneath the left shoulder blade. Want the body turned over, Greg."

Quist shook his head. "I'll listen to what the coroner has to say, tomorrow morning. He'll likely trace the course of the bullet for us."

The sheriff nodded. "I see you've had experience of this sort before. Let's take a look at old Brose."

The sheeting was drawn back over Stewart's body. Next, Brose Randle's stiff form was uncovered. Ribs showed on the old wasted form, and below the ribs was a small dark hole, still showing some trace of congealed blood.

". . . and I ain't had time to properly wash it yet," Barry Lowe was saying. "Ain't done much about fixin' either body yet, matter of fact. Folks been pouring in here steady, till just 'bout an hour back. You'll never recognize 'em when I get finished up though. I got some rouge that makes 'em look just as natural as life. Come see 'em when they're laid out, Mr. Quist. You'll think they're just sleeping and ready to say 'hello' when they wake up."

"I'll bet you." Quist nodded. "You probably know your business all right. Well, thanks a lot, Mr. Lowe."

"Don't mention it, Mr. Quist. And I'll be glad to have your business, any time."

Quist winced. "I hope it's furniture sales you're referring to."

Lowe tittered and said, "Of course, Mr. Quist."

A few minutes later, Hayes and Quist left the building, followed reluctantly by Randle. On the street, Randle said, "This comes sort of hard, Quist, but I'm apologizing for my attitude toward you today. I was sort of wrought-up, about finding my father that way. I reckon I saw red for a few minutes."

Quist cut short the apology. "Let's drop it, Randle."

"Hell, if I'd known who you was —"

"Forget it," Quist said. "We all make mistakes."

Hayes cut in, "Jason, show Mr. Quist what you found on that hilltop — tell him about the sign and so on."

"I rode up there, like Smoky asked me to," Randle said. "There was some sign all right, but not too easy to locate. That rain had likely washed out a lot of stuff. Still it hadn't rained so much as farther south. I reckon we all got just the tail edge of it. But I could see there'd been a rider up there recent. Brush and grass was pretty high at that point. Scrubby cedar and piñon, but high enough to hide a horse and rider. Grass had been trampled. There was droppings. Dun hawss. Some hair caught in the brush. The pony had been shod on front hoofs only. Judging from such sign as I found, the rider had took out fast for some reason or other."

"You any idea why?" Quist asked.

Randle replied, "Dunno. Could be your Winchester slugs prodded the bustard on his way. One shot at least must have scared him witless. I know anything that close would have scairt me."

"I'm waiting to hear," Quist said quietly.

"Take a look at this," Randle said, producing an object from one pocket, which he handed to Quist. It was dark on the street and Hayes struck a match. The object Quist held in his hand was a curving chunk of walnut wood, well worn and polished smooth on one side, and with two dark notches cut in it. The reverse side was splintered and raw. Hayes struck a second match while Quist studied the wood.

Quist said softly. "Plumb interesting. Chunk off a walnut butt of a six-shooter. And two notches cut in it. Randle, do you figure that rider dropped this?" Hayes' match flickered out.

Randle said, "I couldn't swear to it, but I think it's likely. I followed up the tracks. That rider was movin' faster'n I could pick 'em up through the brush. When he reached clearings, he was headed toward Corinth City. The sun started gettin' low, so I gave up and headed for town. I'll leave the figuring out to you."

Quist speculated. "It looks as though I might have got in a lucky shot that struck the end of the bastard's gun-butt when he was leaving; and then glanced off. But the resulting shock of the bullet's impact splintered off one section, and it fell to the earth."

"Lucky for you, and him too, I reckon," Randle commented. "Anyway, I didn't see any blood-drippings, so I figure he wa'n't hurt. Likely scairt hell out of the bustard though."

The sheriff said, "I think you called the turn, Greg. As I see it, your first shot come too close for comfort, so he holstered his gun and lined out fast. Then, one of your other shots must have made a lucky hit and struck the bottom of the gun-butt, knocking a chunk off. It must have belonged to the *hombre* who shot at you. There's no evidence showing the raw side of that wood has been out in weather any length of time."

Quist nodded. "That's as good a guess as

any. As for Randle not finding any blood-drippings, it could be there was enough rain on that hilltop to wash 'em away. But I reckon I didn't hit anyone. Whoever it was, he was headed for town, so he must be local. Smoky, have you any idea who notches his gun hereabouts?"

"Damn' right," Hayes growled. "Joker Gaillard, for one."

"Who's Joker Gaillard?"

"Works for Auringer on the D-Bar-A. Considers himself a wit around town. Always playing pranks on somebody. Rides a dun horse, too, come to think of it. Sometimes he's damn' funny, if the joke isn't on you. Otherwise, he's a sort of pest."

Quist said thoughtfully. "Gunmen often notch their gun-butts, but I've yet to meet one who was much of a wit."

Hayes shrugged. "I've no proof that Gaillard is a professional gunman. Never been in any gunfights around here that I know of. Oh, he can shoot all right. Fast. At targets, tin cans and such. I figure gun-notching is just part of his act. A feller asked him one day if those two notches represented two killings. Without batting an eye, Gaillard told him very seriously 'no' — that he had started to carve a washboard and had only cut two ridges so far. Then he laughed fit to kill."

Quist chuckled. "That's enough to kill me, too. What do you aim to do about him, Smoky?"

Quist had a feeling the sheriff should grab Gaillard as soon as possible, and was somewhat surprised when Hayes said, "Gaillard will be in town for the inquest tomorrow. If he can't show me an undamaged gun, with two notches cut in the butt, he's going to have to answer some questions. I'll get the truth out of the pranky bustard, or know why. You want this chunk of gun-butt, Greg?"

"I don't know what I'd do with it, Smoky. Likely, you'll want to keep it for evidence of some sort."

The sheriff nodded. "I had something like that in mind, if you didn't want it. If I once get to fit this chunk of walnut to Joker Gaillard's six-shooter, he'll certainly be all through playing jokes on folks for a spell."

The three men talked a few minutes longer, before Quist announced he was ready for bed. They walked east along Main Street. Opposite the hotel, Quist said goodnight and crossed over, while Randle and the sheriff continued on. Except for the clerk who had registered Quist, there was no one in the lobby when he entered. The man put down his newspaper, said, "Good evening,

Mr. Quist," and turned to his key-rack. Then he gave a surprised exclamation.

Quist said, "What's up?"

"Your key seems to be missing from the rack, Mr. Quist. Are you certain you left it when you went out?"

"I distinctly remember leaving it. You should too —"

"Of course, I do, now you mention it. You were with Mr. Fletcher when he checked out. Well, now! Where could that key be?" He studied the rest of the rack, in hope the missing key had been misplaced. "Gracious! I don't understand this."

Quist asked quietly, "Could anyone have entered in your absence, stepped back of your desk and stolen the key? Have you been behind that desk all evening?"

"Yes, I have" — in troubled tones. "But, wait, I did step out once. Just for a few minutes. I had to go —"

"Maybe that explains it," Quist cut in. "Somebody just waited until you had to go. . . . Do you happen to remember who was in the lobby when you left?"

The clerk frowned. "Let me see. The dining room had been closed for some time. If I remember correctly the lobby was empty at the time. I could hear voices coming from the bar, and I think there were two or three men taking their ease on the porch —"

"I don't suppose it matters. You've probably got a master key, haven't you?"

"Oh, yes, certainly. I'll have to go up with you and unlock though. I'm not supposed to let the key go out of my keeping."

He panted beside Quist as they mounted the stairway to the landing above, where the oil lamps, now turned low, still burned. Then Quist said, "I reckon we're not going to need your key after all. The door's open."

Striding ahead of the clerk, he entered his room, struck a match, then crossed to light his lamp. Behind him came a frightened, squawking sound from the clerk. Quist turned and saw the man had gone white as a sheet. "Well," Quist said softly, and again, "well. I've a hunch you'd best put a new lock on this door, come morning."

"B-B-but — Mr. Q-Q-Quist," the clerk quavered, and looked about to faint. "Wha-wha-what in the world — ?" and could say no more.

The room was a shambles. Drawers had been jerked from dresser and commode. Quist's satchel had been pried open, though nothing had been taken. The mattress and bedding were overturned.

Quist said quietly, "Looks like you got mice in your hotel."

"M-m-mice?" Then a weak smile appeared on the clerk's face. "You take this very well, Mr. Quist. I'll get somebody up here at once to set this room to rights —"

"Don't bother. You just run along downstairs. I can set this bed to rights myself. Nothing else matters right now."

It required considerable persuasion, but he finally got rid of the clerk and quickly shut his door. Then he moved swiftly across the room and reached behind the mirror over the commode. The Comanche scalp was still there. A low breath of relief issued from Quist's lips, and he stuffed it back in place.

"Damn! I can't think of anything else a thief might want. Nothing has been taken. But why would he want an old scalp? He must have been a dumb bustard not to look behind that mirror. But such *hombres* always miss the obvious places."

He found a bottle of beer remaining in the bucket, opened it and sat down on the rumpled bed to think over the matter. He swore softly after a long draught from the bottle. "What could that scalp have to do with the skulduggery hereabouts? I reckon it's a clue of some sort, if I could figure it out. . . . And those marks on Stewart's wrists. Somebody sure as hell had him tied up. There's another clue. And still a third — that chunk of gun-butt off what was his name? Gaillard? — that's it. Joker Gaillard — off his gun. If it can be proved it's off his gun. I'd like to know what in blazes all this means."

After a time he put down the empty bottle and started to make up his tumbled bed.

CHAPTER VII

Inquest

Quist was awakened the following morning by a locksmith ready to replace the lock on his door. Quist shaved and dressed, then glanced out the window. Already it looked as though the day would be another hot one. Quist dropped the coat he had been about to don over his gunharness, and delved into his satchel for a vest, one that had been tailored specially to conform to the extra bulk of the underarm gun. This he slipped into and left unbuttoned. "Not that it makes any difference, I reckon," he mused. "Likely the sheriff and his deputy have mentioned it around that I tote a hide-out weapon."

Pushing past the locksmith at work on the door, Quist descended to the lobby. It wasn't yet seven-thirty. The clerk of the previous night was just being replaced by a younger day-clerk. The older man mentioned something about hoping the locksmith hadn't got Quist out of bed too early. They exchanged a few words, then Quist passed on into the dining room for his breakfast.

Half an hour later when he stepped into the street he noticed an unusual number of people about for so early in the morning. The hitchracks were lined with ponies, buggies and wagons. "Came in for the inquests I suppose," Quist told himself. He started toward the sheriff's office, walking east on Main, and was about to cross over at Brazos Street when Smoky Hayes hailed him from a group of men standing before the County Building and Courthouse across the street from the sheriff's office. The building was a two-storied structure of frame and adobe-and-rock. Smoke from cigars, cigarettes and pipes flouted above the group, ascending in the hot morning air to the blue sky above. The hot sun made black shadows between buildings.

"Hot again," Quist spoke to the sheriff, then nodded to Deputy Dyke Leigh.

"It's going to be hotter still when we get into the courthouse," Hayes said. "Seems like every man and his brother has come in for the inquests. Wait'll they start packin' 'em in, up there."

He introduced Quist to several men in the group, among whom was Dewitt Auringer, owner of the D-Bar-A, a rather good-looking man of around thirty years, with a heavy mustache and dark hair. He wore a weathered-looking sombrero and the usual cowman's outfit.

"Inquest's due to start at nine," Auringer commented. He seemed a trifle nervous. "I wish they'd get started, now."

"I'll go along with you on that," Hayes said seriously. "Harl Stewart and old Brose Randle are due to be buried at three — likely it'll be a heap later. I've got things to do: I've got to meet Eirene's train —" He broke off, speaking to Quist, "Harl's daughter. She was visiting friends up in Dallas when this happened. Then, soon's the inquest's over I've got to ride out to the Rafter-S and get Mrs. Stewart — bring her in for the funeral. And I don't relish that job any. Not even sure she'll be able to make it. Harl's death sure knocked her out. As is natural."

"Mrs. Stewart won't be at the inquest?" Quist asked.

The sheriff shook his head. "It's just too much to ask of her. She's told Doc Wakeman everything she knows. He'll testify on her behalf." After a minute, the sheriff drew Quist to one side, and said, "I hear somebody entered your room last night."

"How'd you know?" Quist said.

"The hotel clerk sent a message down to me shortly after it was discovered your room had been entered. He wanted I should come right along and investigate. I figured so long as there was no word from you it didn't amount to much. You'd had a long day; I thought you'd sooner get to sleep than talk to me."

Quist nodded. "There'd been nothing you could have done, anyway, Smoky. I'd not left anything of importance in my satchel, except the mate to the gun I wear. My Winchester was there, of course. I had my money and such with me. Shirts, underwear, handkerchiefs —"

"You didn't miss anything then?" the sheriff asked.

"Nothing was taken that I could see," Quist replied.

"Probably some of the scum around town figured you'd leave money there. Town this size always has its undesirables. I make 'em keep the peace, but I can't cover everything until it happens. Actually we don't have much crime here — until recently. There's folks are always ready to blame things on the Mexican element, but I can't see that. They're no worse than anybody else."

"I like Mexicans," Quist said. "Give 'em a square shake, and they'll meet you more than halfway. Some of us Anglos could take a lesson from 'em in courtesy too."

"That's pretty right, Greg. But I'll not forget that business. I've got two or three men around town will do some inquiring around, and maybe we can learn who tried some sneak-thievery."

Quist said, "How about this Joker Gaillard? You seen him yet this morning?"

Hayes shook his head. "Witt Auringer said he was still at the D-Bar-A when he left. Gaillard and the rest of Auringer's hands should be hitting town right soon though. Aren't many folks stay home when there's an inquest on."

A rather stoop-shouldered man with a short iron-gray beard and tired eyes spoke to Hayes. "Morning, Smoky. Got my jury on hand?"

The sheriff swung around. "Oh, hello, doc. Sure — jury's here, and a clerk to take down what's said, as well. Doc, shake hands with Greg Quist — Greg, this is Doctor Rush Wakeman."

Quist enclosed the doctor's bony hand in his own palm, and studied the tired, almost harassed eyes. The doctor's spare frame was almost as tall as his own, but Wakeman's indiscriminate gray clothing hung in rather baggy fashion on his bones. He looked to be the typical cow country doctor of that day — efficient, rushed to death with more cases than could be handled properly, sympathetic, withal a trifle crusty at times. He said to Quist, "I've been hearing quite a bit about you, Mr. Quist. If you're going to be here for a time, I hope you live up to your reputation. I know Smoky will appreciate any help you can give him." Then to the sheriff, "Come on, let's get up there and get this business over with."

He led the way into the courthouse, and up a flight of wooden steps at one side of the entrance. The sheriff spoke to various men and followed. Now the crowd commenced to push at the entrance. Above, the second floor was like a furnace; heat broiled down from the roof. It was a large room, with at one end, six chairs for the jurors and a table upon which stood a Bible, pitcher of water and a drinking glass. There were three straight-backed chairs arranged at the table. A few yards away from the table, more straight-backed chairs, in rows, reached to the back of the big room, with an aisle down the center. Hayes spoke an order, and tall windows around the room were raised. It didn't seem to be much cooler. Hayes growled to Quist, "Dammit-to-hell! I should have raised those windows when I was up here before."

People were still struggling up the stairway, to emerge panting and triumphant when they found a chair. The jurors and clerk were already in their seats as were various witnesses. Quist found a seat in the front row. The big room buzzed with conversation; now and then Quist heard his own name mentioned. The seats were filled quickly, but people still tried to get into the room. Hayes, seated next to Quist, spoke to Dyke Leigh and the deputy went to the back of the room to arrange some sort of order. There were but few women present. Pipes and cigarettes were lighted; tobacco smoke swirled near the rafters. An odor of perspiration soured the close, muggy atmosphere.

Doctor Wakeman raised his voice, calling for quiet. The clamor of voices continued. Swearing under his breath, the doctor borrowed Hayes' six-shooter and pounded on the table with the butt of the gun. That immediately brought quiet. Wakeman returned the gun, cleared his throat and stated that in his capacity as coroner he had called this inquiry to determine what information was possible about the deaths of Harlan Stewart and Ambrose Randle. He wanted to make it clear that an inquest was simply an inquiry, that was all. At the same time, he warned, witnesses would be speaking under oath, and any failure to give a truthful account, if discovered, could bring a charge of perjury with penalties provided by law, *et cetera, et cetera.* There were a few more preliminaries, then Wakeman called the first witness, Jason Randle, who spoke for the other punchers of the Rafter-S, as well as himself.

Randle took an oath on the Bible, after which the clerk prepared to jot down the testimony in a large record book. After giving his name, employment, etc., Randle, under questioning from the coroner, proceeded to give an account of certain doings the day Stewart had been shot.

Randle glanced uneasily over the room and began, "There's mighty little I can tell about the business. Like always on payday, Mr. Stewart gave us the day off and we came to town to get — er — some supplies and buy shirts and such —"

Someone in the audience guffawed, "Supplies is a good name for it."

Wakeman glowered at the man, wished he hadn't returned the six-shooter to the sheriff and pounded on the table with his fist, calling for silence. Laughter ceased. Wakeman said, "Mr. Randle, what time was this?"

"When we were paid off? I should say around nine in the morning. I figure we hit town before eleven."

"The whole Rafter-S crew?" the coroner asked.

"Not all, doc. Deacon Vogel, the cook, and" — he swallowed hard — "my father, Ambrose Randle, stayed at the ranch. You know how Deacon is — don't believe in drink."

"Was Mrs. Stewart at the ranchhouse when you left?" Wakeman asked.

"So far as I know. I hadn't seen her, but once I heard voices up at the house. I suppose she was there. She was there the night before."

Further inquiry brought out the fact that that same afternoon, Randle and one of the other punchers had encountered Harlan Stewart in various bars that day. Harlan Stewart had either nodded shortly when he met his men, or ignored them altogether. Yes, he was drinking pretty hard. And again, yes, Mr. Stewart had been drinking that way quite regularly for a good many weeks now. Randle seemed reluctant to disclose this fact about his former employer. No, he had no idea what had brought on the spell of drinking. It had come on right sudden, after Mr. Stewart seemed to be worried about something. His manner had changed and he seemed irritable most of the time. It was known that more than once friends had had to get him on his horse and see that he arrived safely at home. "Sheriff Hayes," Randle continued, "could attest to that. He'd helped Stewart more'n once to get home — most everybody knew that —"

"That," Wakeman cut in, "is something the sheriff can tell us about at the proper time."

There wasn't much more Randle could say. He and the other hands had hung around town until late that evening when word was received that Harlan Stewart had been killed. Then he and the other punchers had left for the ranch at once.

Various bartenders were next called on for testimony, among them Shamus Maguire. As he listened to their various reports, Quist gained the idea that Harlan Stewart had reached Corinth City shortly after noontime and proceeded to get liquored up as fast as possible. He had started at one end of the street and then crossed over and worked his way back, stopping at every saloon on the way. No, he hadn't talked to any extent, one barkeep testified, except to ask for another drink. He hadn't seemed to want conversation with anyone. He just stood slouched over his drink and glowered into space. It finally came Maguire's time to testify. After the usual preliminaries, Maguire told how

101

Stewart had come into the Shamrock Bar, apparently perfectly sober when he entered.

". . . but it was a thing in my mind," Maguire was saying, "that he was away on one of his toots, and I wasn't likin' the looks of it, at all, at all. After drinking of three bourbons — he wouldn't be touching of the good Irish whisky, you see — I gave him the refusal of fur-r-rther service, and tr-r-ried to talk a bit of sense into the man. But he'd not be listenin'. He'd have none of it. So sur-r-re and what does he do, but he stalks off indignant and out of my place, like I'd requested the loan of his right eye, instead of just askin' of the poor-r man to go aisy-like."

Here the coroner interjected a question. Maguire continued, "Sur-r-re it was late after-r-rnoon when next I got sight of the man, and says I to mesilf, 'tis the worst ever-r I've seen him, and it's hopin' I am he'll not be comin' into my place again. There was no one in my bar at the time, and I'd stepped out to the walk to breathe of a bit of fresh air, when I spied Mister-r Stewart just leavin' of the Red Mustang Saloon, which lies kitty-corner and across of the street from me. Now I'd not be tellin' you it was walkin' he was doing. How he stayed on his two feet I'd never-r be knowin'. He was like a man with a bad limp in the both of his legs, and them

102

trackin' him stiggerstagger all over the r-road. 'Twas only by the grace of God two ponies and a wagon wasn't runnin' him down."

"You'd say he was badly intoxicated then?" Wakeman asked.

"The wor-r-rst iver I see him," Maguire replied promptly. "He was carryin' of his coat across his shoulder, and how he'd hung on to that, I'd niver-r tell you. But 'tis a way of drunks to do the incompr-r-rehensible. And so he came into my place and when I followed on his heels, he asked for the dr-r-rink. But I told him right out, I'd not be lettin' him have it. His eyes was crossed when he give me a look, and I could see he had no idea if I'd sell him a drink or no. So I got a chair under him at one of my tables and sent wor-r-rd for Sheriff Hayes to come to be attendin' of his fr-r-riend."

Hayes rose and was sworn in. He told how he had had Maguire go to a near-by restaurant for hot coffee and sandwiches. They'd succeeded only in getting a small amount of coffee into Stewart before he became sick. "Mr. Stewart's talk became rather maudlin, unintelligible at times. It looked as though he might pass out, at any moment. I thought the best thing to do was get him home where Mrs. Stewart, once he was in bed, could take care of him. I sent Maguire to get his horse and have mine saddled, then we got him outside and on his horse's back. The outside air seemed to revive him somewhat, and he asked for a drink of whisky. Rather than argue I told Maguire to bring a small one. There was a crowd standing about, and I thought it best to get Harl away with the least argument possible."

The doctor asked a question. Hayes nodded, "Yes, he seemed able to ride, all right, once he was in the saddle. Second-nature to him, I suppose. We left town and had traveled probably five or six miles when I noticed him slumping in the saddle. The son was sinking fast by this time, and I wanted to get Harl — Mr. Stewart — home before dark. I spoke to him a couple of times, but he didn't answer. I was afraid he might fall off his horse, break his neck, so I took his rope and tied him into the saddle. Then I took a piggin' string and lashed his hands to the saddlehorn."

Quist sighed, saying to himself, "That's that. One clue shot to hell. I wondered why Smoky hadn't said anything about those marks on the wrists."

". . . and we reached the Rafter-S shortly before dark," Hayes was saying. "Mrs. Stewart had seen us and came out on the porch. Deacon Vogel, the ranch cook, saw us too.

I remember he saw me unlashing Harl from the saddle. He called and asked if I needed some help. Before I could reply, Mrs. Stewart called back that Deacon's help wouldn't be needed — that she and I could manage. Anyway, I got Harl down from the saddle. He muttered something about not needing help, but I knew better. Between Mrs. Stewart and me we got him into the house and on a bed. Here he seemed to rouse and become more coherent. He asked for some hot coffee. The fire in the kitchen was out, so Mrs. Stewart went to the cookhouse to get some from Vogel. When she returned, he drank some and almost instantly went to sleep. Figuring Harl was set for the night and would feel all right in the morning, except for a bad head, I got my horse and returned to Corinth City. I don't think I'd been back more than an hour when Vogel came pounding in with the news that somebody had shot Harl from outside, and killed him. I sent word to Doc Wakeman to come quick, then Dyke and I headed for the Rafter-S. Harl was dead, all right, and Mrs. Stewart was in no shape to give more than brief facts —"

Here Wakeman interrupted, "Perhaps I can take up from here on, sheriff. No use wasting time, now, telling how you and your deputy searched all night for sign, and how

you started out later on Brose Randle's trail."
Hayes nodded and resumed his seat. The
doctor swore to his oath, then started, "It
was unfortunate that I wasn't instantly available when Sheriff Hayes sent for me. I was
out on a call at Tom Breeder's Rocking-B
Ranch, delivering Mrs. Breeder's ninth baby
— a fine lusty boy, by the way." A snicker
ran through the audience. "It is unfortunate
too," Wakeman resumed, "that my col-
league, Dr. Veten, was also not available."

There was more snickering. Quist heard a
man back of him mutter, "That drunken
hawss-doctor."

". . . or maybe," Wakeman was saying, "it
didn't matter if neither of us was available.
Harl Stewart was beyond medical aid, within
moments after the shot struck him. I was
able to give a certain aid to Mrs. Stewart,
who was prostrated by the blow. The shock
was so great that I thought it best for her not
to try to testify today, and you'll have to have
her part of this inquiry through my lips. I
arrived at the Rafter-S to find her dazed,
almost in a fainting condition in one bed. In
the front bedroom, Mr. Stewart's body lay
sprawled across another bed. I examined him
and saw immediately there was nothing I
could do. I then gave my attention to his wife
— er — widow. I gave her a sedative and

was able to piece out, a little at a time, what had happened. Shortly after Sheriff Hayes had left the ranch, Harl Stewart had awakened. Mrs. Stewart told me that he stated he felt better and that he was going out on the front gallery for some air. His wife said he appeared fairly sober, so she made no objection when he left the front bedroom. She accompanied him to the doorway and he stood there a few minutes looking out into the night. He was fully clothed, except for his boots which the sheriff had drawn off before leaving. Mrs. Stewart remembered that he said something about the air smelling good, then as he turned to re-enter the house, a shot came from the outer darkness. Harl Stewart gave just one cry, then staggered back to the bedroom and collapsed across the bed."

A stir ran through the crowd, several looks were directed in Witt Auringer's direction. Auringer flushed and shifted uncomfortably on his seat. The coroner continued quickly, "Mrs. Stewart's memory of what happened next is rather disconnected. She knows she fainted, but has a dim recollection of hearing a horse, or horses, galloping off, though even of that she's not certain. Her next memory is of Deacon Vogel bending over her, as she lay on the floor, near the front door. He got her to a bed, then saddled and came to town for the sheriff. I talked to her again yesterday afternoon, and her repeated story was substantially the same. As you know, of course, Sheriff Hayes reached the house before I did, and the facts she gave him agree with the remarks I've just made. . . . Will Mr. D. K. Vogel come to the stand, please?"

Deacon Vogel, the Rafter-S cook, was a skinny-bodied individual, with a ragged "horse-tail" mustache, cavernous eyes, shaggy eyebrows and a doleful manner. He wore a tieless celluloid collar and what passed for town clothing. There was a certain reverence in the manner in which he placed his hand on the Bible and was sworn in. There were the usual preliminaries, before he got started with his testimony, under the doctor's prodding.

". . . and I can't say as to the exact time," he stated in his mournful tones. "It was gettin' nigh on to dark. At a guess I'd say around eight o'clock. I had fixed a snack of fodder for supper for old Brose Randle and myself. After supper we washed up, and then Brose went down to the blacksmith shop. He said somethin' 'bout tryin' to fit a pole to a gaff-hook — some sort of hook for fishin'. He was always preparin' for a fishin' trip, but he never got started. And so I'd settled in the peace of the bunkhouse to read the Good Book, while the hands was in town sniffin' the iniquities of sin and red liquor and a-consortin' with the jezebels whose feet lead down to brimstone and hellfire —"

Here, Wakeman interrupted. "No sermons, please, Mr. Vogel. I understand it was about this time that the sheriff and Mr. Stewart arrived."

Vogel looked slightly miffed, but nodded his head. "That is right, doc. I heard a sort of noise up near the back door of the house. Lookin' out, I spied Smoky Hayes and Mr. Stewart just pullin' to a halt. By the looks of the boss I seed he had been lookin' on the wine when it was red, again. Strong liquor is ragin', I says to myself, whisky is a mocker. It lays men low —" Catching a meaning look from the coroner, Vogel went on, "I went to the bunkhouse doorway and called to the sheriff, did he need any help. By that time Miz Stewart had come out, and she answered me back how she and the sheriff could manage. She could never have managed alone. The boss could scarce stand, what with Smoky supportin' him with one arm, while she pushed from behind. I rec'lect when they was gettin' him past an upright on that rear porch, his coat caught on a nail, and just that mite of interruption, dang nigh pulled the three of them down. But they made it inter the house, and I went back to my Bible."

Wakeman prompted with a question. Vogel went on, "In 'bout ten minutes, Miz Stewart come down to the bunkhouse to say that the boss wanted some hot coffee. I allus keep a pot a-brewin', so I gets a small bucket and fills it. While I'm fixin' the coffee, she allows as how it's a shame for a good man like Mr. Stewart to overdrink. Overdrink, she calls it. I told her flat out that them that lives by the bottle, must perish by the bottle." Vogel paused. "I don't figure she took to that much, but it's the truth. The Good Lord says —"

"Did Mrs. Stewart have anything else to say?" Wakeman cut in.

"Nothin' much. She asked where Brose Randle was. I told her I thought he was on another fishin' trip, down to the blacksmith shop. She got that joke and sort of smiled wan-like. Then she got the coffee and left. By this time it was dark. I got to thinkin' the boss' hawss should be took care of, so I walked up to the house and got it. Brought back the sheriff's pony too. Give it a drink. While I was at the corral, I noticed old Brose fussin' about inside. He had some harness and was gettin' two hawsses. I asked what he

110

was doin' and he allowed it was time to go 'way and get some fishin' done. I think 'batty, again, but it ain't my business, so I go back to my readin' of the Revelations agin. It wa'n't long 'fore Smoky comes down, tells me the boss is sleepin' good, climbs inter his saddle and heads back to town."

"This was at what time would you say, Mr. Vogel?" asked the coroner.

Vogel shrugged. "Ain't got no idea exact. It was dark — maybe startin' along toward nine o'clock, more'er less." Wakeman nodded and Vogel continued, "Tw'n't more than fifteen minutes — mebbe later — I heard old Brose drivin' the wagon up toward the front of the house on the way to the road. Thinks I, at last he's got that old wagon started some place. I'd never believe it. Likely drive to town and come back. I heerd him stop some place past the front of the house. Didn't pay him much 'tention. I was deep in that part of Revelations where —"

"It was about then the shot was fired?" Wakeman interrupted.

"C'rect, doc! It nigh yanked me outten my chair, the shock of it. Then I hear the wagon take out, hell-bent-fer-election, like the avengin' angel was in poorsuit. Then the screamin' started from the house. Now I knew there was hell an' brimstone to pay. I

111

thinks, old Brose has really gone insane this time. I left the bunkhouse in a leap and took out after Brose. But wa'n't no use. I wa'n't made to keep up with hawsses. So then I runs back to the house where I could still hear the screamin'. Before I got there, it had stopped. I found Miz Stewart layin' near the open front door. She was plumb out. I looks in the bedroom and sees Mr. Stewart, spread face down across the bed — blood on his shirt. Before I could get to examine him, Miz Stewart come alive and the screechin' started again. I worked to get her quiet. Got water. Tried to shush her. She had the high-steericks. Finally she gets hold of herself and says something about a shot comin' from outside. She tells me to go for the doctor. I hated like sin to leave her alone, but finally I saddled up and lit out for town to tell the sheriff."

"You didn't see who did the shooting?" Wakeman asked.

Vogel shook his head. "I can't believe it was old Brose. A murderer wouldn't have run off in sech open fashion. If you was to ast me, now that I've thought things over, I just figure Brose Randle saw somethin' or someone that just scared him plumb witless, and he didn't want nothin' to do with what was to follow."

112

CHAPTER VIII

Joker Gaillard

Vogel was released from the stand after a few questions that threw no further light on the inquiry, and before he could launch into some sort of Biblical oration. Doctor Wakeman said, "It's now time I gave my own testimony. It was past midnight when I reached the Rafter-S, and Sheriff Hayes was doing all possible in the way of searching for evidence. Later, as has been said, the sheriff gathered men and went on Ambrose Randle's trail. Meanwhile, I had Harl Stewart's body brought to the undertaker's, and probed out the bullet. It was of forty-five caliber, fired from a six-shooter. *Rigor mortis* had already set in, when I got to the ranch of course, and judging from the process it had made I'd say that Stewart met his death before nine o'clock, at least. It's pretty difficult to hit on the exact time. Weather conditions, the state of health of a deceased person before dying, all affect an analysis as to time. Any time I might state is subject to variations, one way or the other. But with what Mr. Vogel has told us, combined with

113

Mrs. Stewart's time and my examination, about the closest I would venture, is to say that Mr. Stewart was killed sometime between eight and nine that night. Without the testimony we have, it could swing an hour either way, too."

Wakeman paused. "Now, as to the course the bullet took . . ." Here he launched into a long definitely technical explanation that caused his hearers to shift uncomfortably on seats. "You people and the jury doubtless understand little of what I've just said, but it had to be said for the record," Wakeman continued. "In brief, here is what happened. A leaden bullet from a forty-five six-shooter entered Harl Stewart's back, just below the left shoulder blade, traveled upward somewhat and moved to the right, smashing through some bone on the way, until it came to rest just behind a point where the sternum — that's the breastbone — and the clavicle — you'd call it the collar-bone — meet. In striking bone, the bullet was badly battered and tore great holes on its way through the lungs. That's as clear as I can explain it to you. I doubt that Harl Stewart lived a full minute after he was shot."

The audience stirred. Wakeman went on, "That seems to be all the evidence, right now. It is my suggestion as it is nearing dinnertime, that we finish up and clear this room. Dinner can be sent into the jury and they can get on with their deliberations while we wait on the street, or near by." He spoke to the jury, "I hope it won't take too long. There's still the inquest on Ambrose Randle to get through."

Ten minutes later, the big room had been cleared. Accompanied by the sheriff, Quist crossed the street to a small restaurant. Neither man talked a great deal while eating. By the time they had concluded the meal and dropped into the Shamrock Bar for a quick drink, it was close to the hour when the coroner had requested witnesses to reconvene. The big room had aired out some; it wasn't any cooler. Chairs were again filled. After a moment, there was a rapping for order. The buzz of conversation died down.

Wakeman rose and asked the jury if it had reached any sort of finding. The jury foreman stumbled to his feet and, after consulting a paper in one hand, announced that they'd reached a decision. It was to the effect that Harlan Stewart had met his death as the result of a shot fired from a six-shooter by some person unknown, and Sheriff Hayes was directed to take immediate steps to apprehend the murderer. All of which was no more than Quist had expected. He stirred restlessly, when Hayes, seated by his side, drew a long sigh and said, "And now, dammit, it's in my lap. I'm sure going to need all the help you can give, Greg."

"I'd sooner be outside, moving around," Quist said irritably. "Maybe all this isn't quite a waste of time, but I'm not certain we know much more than we did before —"

There came more rapping on the table for attention. Wakeman thanked the jury and immediately launched into the inquest on Ambrose Randle. There were a few preliminaries bringing out evidence that old Randle hadn't been seen in town the day of his death or the previous evening. The coroner called on Jason Randle who reluctantly admitted that, yes, his father had been known to have "queer spells," at times, but his "bein' crazy about fishin' " had led some folks to take the wrong view of the old man. And that he felt mighty gawddam sure, his father hadn't killed Mr. Stewart —

Here, the coroner interrupted and sharply informed Jason Randle that the inquest on Harlan Stewart had already been concluded, and he, Jason, was to confine his remarks to such evidence as he might have on his father's death.

"In that case, doc," Randle said sullenly, "mebbe you'd best ask the great detective.

He was there first."

Randle was excused and Quist called to the stand. A stir ran through the crowd; necks were craned to see the T.N. & A.S. investigator. After taking the oath, Quist quickly got going and told as succinctly as possible of his finding of the dead body in the rowboat, and of being shot at later. He didn't, of course, mention finding the Comanche scalp. Amazed looks ran through the audience when Quist described how he had found Brose Randle, and of the fishline stretched behind the rowboat. When he had reached the point where the sheriff and other men had arrived on the scene, he suggested that Sheriff Hayes' testimony be heard for the rest of the story.

Quist dropped back in his chair, while Hayes took the witness stand, speaking for the men who had accompanied him, as well as for himself. He related how they had come upon Quist, of the conversation that had ensued, then added, "Right now I'd like to make a public apology for placing Mr. Quist under arrest. It was a blunder on my part, but Mr. Quist is good enough to allow as how it was an excusable blunder." People in the audience cast appreciative looks at Quist. A woman seated in one of the back rows fainted due to the heat. Time was lost while she was carried down the stairway to the open air.

Eventually, Hayes was allowed to continue. He told how he had sent Jason Randle to the hilltop to look for sign of the unknown man who had fired the shots at Quist. Certain sign had been found, but in the interest of law enforcement, he preferred, at this time, not to make public such findings.

At this point, the foreman of the jury interjected a question: in the sheriff's opinion, could the unknown man on the hilltop have been the one to kill Ambrose Randle? That, Hayes replied, was possible, but no evidence had been found to indicate it. On the contrary, in view of the state of Ambrose Randle's mind, it was also possible he had killed himself. The sheriff just didn't know, and he wanted to make it clear that his words weren't intended to sway the jury's opinion in any way.

There were a few more questions and Hayes returned to his seat, and again nothing new had been brought out, Quist considered. The doctor now took the stand and told of probing out the bullet and of the course it had taken when striking Ambrose Randle "plumb center." There was a great deal of technical language, all of which amounted to the fact that Randle had been shot through the abdomen, by a forty-five-caliber slug from a six-shooter, and that the bullet had stopped only when it struck the old man's spine. Death had occurred probably, in Wakeman's opinion, about nine o'clock on the morning his body had been found by Quist.

There wasn't much more. The big room was again cleared, and people poured into the street. Quist and the sheriff descended the stairs to await the verdict. "They'll not be long in that oven up there," the sheriff commented. "I think everybody's just about had their fill of inquests." He consulted his watch. "Damn! Time's aburnin'. Reckon I'll get Dyke to meet Eirene's train. There's the funeral yet and I've got to go 'way out there and get Mrs. Stewart. Don't know's I can ever make it there and back — hell! the funeral will just have to wait."

They waited in the shadow of the courthouse. Men stood in small knots on both sides of the street, discussing the inquest and awaiting word of the jury's latest findings. Suddenly, Sheriff Hayes stiffened. "There's one *hombre* we want to talk to. Spied him in the audience while I was giving testimony, then he slipped out before I could beckon to him." He lifted his voice, "Joker! Joker Gaillard!"

Quist followed the sheriff's gaze and saw a man just emerging from the Red Mustang Saloon, which was situated three doors east on Main and on the same side of the street as the courthouse. Gaillard swung around and grinned, "H'are yuh, Smoky," and started to approach.

He was a wiry-looking man of middle height in cowman togs and fawn-colored sombrero, with an acquiline nose, pale blue eyes and light brown hair. His mouth was wide, thin-lipped; a scar — made sometime by a knife, Quist judged — ran upward from the left corner of his mouth, giving his face a perpetual clownlike smile.

He came sauntering up to Hayes and Quist, laughing insolently. "What's on your mind, old law and order, limited?" His pale-eyed gaze shifted to Quist. "So this is the great de-teck-ative. H'are yuh, Quist? How come you ain't named Quest? More 'propriate. Quest — scorch! Get it?" He guffawed at his own joke.

"Very funny, indeed," Quist said caustically.

"Aw, now, Quist, don't be a sour-puss. Don't you know any jokes? I just try —"

Quist said, "Yeah. I just now met one."

Gaillard sobered a minute, then went into a paroxysm of laughter. "Not bad, Quist.

Damned if you ain't a card. I might get to like you, could you learn to mind your own business." He was still grinning widely when Hayes spoke:

"We can do without your comedy for a few minutes, Joker."

"Aw, Smoky, don't you like my comedy? You break my heart —"

Hayes snapped, "I'll break your neck in about five minutes!"

"I'll only need four to think up another good joke —"

Hayes swore, reached out and seized the man by the collar. Almost without effort he jerked Gaillard clear of the sidewalk until the man's feet were dangling free, then shook him violently. Quist's eyes widened slightly. It was like a terrier shaking a rat. When Hayes lowered the man to the sidewalk again, Gaillard was choking with laughter.

"Always showing off, ain't you, Smoky?" He grinned when he could catch his breath.

"Oh, hell," Hayes said impatiently. "Joker, where were you yesterday afternoon?"

"Me?" Gaillard asked innocently. "Don't tell me you're interested in what I do, Smoky." He started to burlesque the answer, "Oh, please, Mister Sheriff, I ain't done nothin'. It was those two sage-hens that committed the crime. They —" Hayes struck him a back-handed blow across the face. Gaillard grinned. "Aw, you went and spoiled a good joke, Smoky. All right, all right. Lemme see — where was you yesterday afternoon, Mr. Bones. Oh, yeah, well I was just around town, Smoky. In and out of a saloon here and there. Played some cards —"

"Got proof of that?"

"Likely I can dig it up." Gaillard laughed. "Gimme a spade —"

"See that you do," Hayes said tersely. "And bring it to me. Joker, they say you wear a gun with two notches cut in it."

Gaillard sobered momentarily. He looked uneasy. "We-ell, not always, Smoky. I don't remember as I strapped it on today —"

Hayes didn't give the man time to finish, but reached down and jerked the six-shooter from Gaillard's holster. He gave one look at the butt and his face fell. Silently he handed it to Quist. Quist looked at the walnut butt. There were two notches cut horizontally across the gun-handle. He handed the gun back to Gaillard and studied the man. Insolent laughter shone in the pale blue eyes. "Reckon I did strap it on, after all." He chuckled. "Funny thing 'bout those two notches. Folks asked me if they represent two gun killings. Matter of fact, I put 'em there when I was a baby: cuttin' my teeth on my pappy's gun-butt —" He went off into a gale of laughter.

"Go on, get out of here," Hayes said shortly. "You're flirtin' with a bruise, Joker, only you don't realize it. And dig up that proof like I said, too."

"I'll do that, Smoky," Gaillard said good-naturedly. He waved one hand lightly to Quist. "S'long, lawman. Take good care of the sheriff. Don't let him stumble over any feet but his own."

And he went swaggering, laughing, back to the Mustang Saloon. A crowd that had gathered about the sheriff echoed the laughter. Now it started to break up. Hayes spoke, low-voiced, angrily, to Quist, "What in hell you going to do with a bastard like that?"

"Ever try bending a gun-barrel over his head?" Quist asked shortly.

"I aim to do just that, if he ever gives me a real good excuse." He swore again. "If only he hadn't had that gun with the two notches cut in it. I felt sure we had something."

"Trouble is," Quist said slowly, "I somehow got an idea he was waiting to hear you ask for his gun. He was laughing at both of us." He drew a long sigh. "Well, we'll just have to keep looking. That *hombre* laughs a lot but I figure him as dangerous in a fight. He's just too damn' confident. I did admire, though, the way you picked him clear of the sidewalk and shook him like you aimed to jar all his teeth out of his head. That takes a good arm, Smoky."

Hayes nodded moodily. "I've got a mite of muscle," he admitted. "I get mad and forget myself sometimes, and then folks think I'm showing off. When I was a younker, I had ambitions to be one of these strong men you see in circuses. Got me some weights and practiced, month after month. Worked hard at it. My dad saw me tugging at some pulley weights one day, and he swore I was workin' 'em so hard, they were starting to smoke. He started calling me Smoky. The name sort of followed me around. Maybe I helped that too. My real name is Adelbert. I prefer Smoky to being called Addlepate."

Quist grinned. Hayes said quickly, "For God's sake, don't ever tell Gaillard my name." He took out his watch, swore softly. "Hell! I can't wait any longer. There's a buggy waiting at the livery for me. You can tell Doc Wakeman I had to go get Mrs. Stewart. Even now that funeral's going to be delayed like the devil. Make doc see why

I couldn't wait for that jury's decision. See you later, Greg."

The sheriff hadn't been out of town five minutes before the jury's verdict was turned in. Apparently the jury had found it difficult to arrive at a decision, as the finding was to the effect that Ambrose Randle had met his death due to a self-inflicted bullet wound due to some temporary mental derangement, or that he had been shot by some person unknown, and if the latter, the sheriff was directed to take the necessary steps, etc., etc. The jury had then retired to the nearest saloon to discuss informally the two deaths and what had really taken place as each man saw it.

Quist scowled, turned away from the courthouse and crossed the street toward the Shamrock Bar. This was definitely a good time for a couple of beers.

CHAPTER IX

Hired Gunfighter

In the Shamrock Bar, Quist met Dr. Wakeman, and relayed the sheriff's message. The doctor said, "I should probably have seen to it myself that Mrs. Stewart was able to come in for the funeral." He sighed. "Jeepers! I can't be everywhere at once though." The doctor was drinking bourbon, entirely regardless of Shamus Maguire's look of reproach.

Maguire looked hopefully at Quist. Quist shook his head and said firmly, "Beer, Shamus. But have one yourself."

"It's that I'm intendin'," Maguire said. "And are you forgettin' entir-r-rely, Mister-r Quist, that you cannot be payin' for the drink in my place? You'd not be for-r-gettin' of the sher-r-riff's orders?" Quist scowled and voiced some protest. Beer was set out. Maguire poured himself a neat glass of Irish whisky. He said, *"Slàinte!"* and downed the drink. Quist poured some beer into a glass.

Wakeman said, "You going to the funeral — funerals — Mr. Quist?"

Quist shook his head. "Can't think of any reason why I should, doc."

"Don't blame you. Barbarous affairs, funerals — throwback to the middle ages."

"Could be." Quist seemed lost in thought. He swirled some beer around in his glass, gazed moodily into the depths.

Wakeman lifted a small black bag from the bar. "Well, I've got to get caught up on my calls." He nodded to Quist and made his way to the street.

Five minutes later, Quist finished his beer and also departed. His first stop was at the undertaker's. Here, disregarding Barry Lowe's efforts to persuade him to come to the back room and view the two bodies, see how "lifelike" they were, Quist asked to see the clothing of the deceased that was removed when they were brought to the undertaker's.

Lowe nodded. "If I hadn't been so busy, they'd have been burned by this time. But I'll go get 'em for you —"

"Burned?" Quist said.

"Folks never want such clothing, after their dear departed have well — er — departed. It's customary to burn 'em, after we get permission. I already asked the sheriff and Jason Randle. They both said go ahead. 'Course, we always empty the pockets first."

"I'd like to see what was in the pockets too," Quist said.

He waited until Lowe had returned to the front room with a big bundle of clothing and two envelopes, and stood impatiently near while Quist examined things. There was no question which clothing had belonged to Stewart and which to Brose Randle. Clean, good condition, in one instance; shabby in the other. But there were similarities. There was the stained front of Randle's denim shirt; a dark brown streak ran down the back of Stewart's white shirt. The same crusty-feeling brown stain was found on the waist-band of Stewart's broadcloth trousers as well as on Randle's faded overalls. There were shabby run-over boots and boots of neat hand-tooled leather. Quist turned to the two envelopes, containing the contents of pockets: money, handkerchiefs, tobacco, two cigars, two pocket knives. The usual small accessories a man carries around with him. But in both cases, no letters, though there was a receipted bill made out to Harlan Stewart by a hay-and-feed store. Quist sighed. Not much there. He thanked Barry Lowe and took his departure, not heeding the undertaker's complaints relative to the lateness of the day, and with two funerals to be concluded, too.

For the next hour and a half, Quist went from saloon to saloon, listening to conversation here, asking questions there. He found to his annoyance that nobody would accept his money for drinks. "Sheriff's orders, y'know, Mr. Quist." Generally, Quist left his beer unfinished and strode on. At the hotel bar, he procured four bottles of beer and an opener, and went to sit on the long gallery that ran on two sides of the hotel. Along the Main Street side and around on Mesquite. Here the railing was lined with straight-backed chairs for the convenience of guests.

There were a few men scattered along the railing. Quist briefly answered their nods and made his way to a far chair where his thinking wouldn't be interrupted. Tilted back in his chair, booted feet on railing, bottle near to hand, he sat in the shadow, almost unseeing the passing of pedestrians, riders and wagons, in the dusty white glare of the street. Out there it was hot; here he was relatively cool. He drew out brown papers and Durham, twisted and lighted a cigarette. A scowl creased his forehead; he shoved the flat-topped sombrero to the back of his head, revealing the lighter streak across his forehead, generally covered by the hatband, in strong contrast to the deep tan of his features.

He twisted his head around at sound of a

step to his left, then said, "Hello, Dyke. Rest your feet and try some beer."

"Thanks, no. I just had one." Deputy Leigh dropped into a seat at Quist's side, propped his feet on the railing. "Well, I met Eirene all right. Took her down to Mrs. Emmons' place — she was an old friend of the first Mrs. Stewart, Eirene's mother. She'll wait there until Smoky drives Mrs. Stewart in. The funeral's going to be late as hell."

"Stewart's daughter taking it hard, I expect?"

The deputy nodded. "As is natural. Hardly knew what to expect when she got off the train, but she had her chin up. No weeps. I told her Smoky had had to drive out for Mrs. Stewart. She scarcely appeared to hear me. But she'll hold up; Eirene's a thoroughbred." He changed the subject. "What did you think of the jury's verdicts."

"About what I expected." Quist took a sip of beer.

"Do you agree with 'em?"

Quist shrugged. "As to Stewart's murder — sure, he was murdered. I don't know enough to say more. But I'll never believe old Brose Randle committed suicide." Leigh asked a question. Quist explained, "Look here, Randle was gutshot — plumb center.

130

That hurts like hell. Any man aiming to kill himself, shoots at the head or heart, where it will all be over fast. No man with sense shoots himself that low —"

"Did old Brose have good sense? Was he in his right mind?"

"A man could be crazy as a loon, Dyke, and I still think instinct, his former training and so on, would direct his shot to head or heart. Nope, I figure Randle was murdered too."

Leigh frowned. "You didn't say that at the inquest."

"I was giving facts. I told what I'd seen," Quist replied shortly, then, "I suppose Smoky showed you that chunk of gun-butt Jason Randle found on that hilltop." The deputy nodded. Quist went on, "Probably you didn't see Smoky before he left. Anyway, we talked to Joker Gaillard. He still has a six-shooter with two notches cut in it."

"The hell you say." The deputy looked disappointed. "Then it couldn't have been Gaillard who shot at you —"

"Dyke, what does Gaillard do around the D-Bar-A? He doesn't strike me as a working cowhand — he's more like a hired gunman."

"Y'know, Greg," Leigh said earnestly, "I've thought that more'n once. Gaillard comes and goes about as he pleases. Been working on the D-Bar-A about four months now, if you can call it working. There's some think Auringer should have been put on the stand today, considering the argument he had over sheep with Stewart." Leigh briefly mentioned details regarding the argument. "There's been rumors, but Smoky figured, and doc, too, that there was no sense blackening a man's character, just to satisfy rumors. Smoky said Auringer had a solid alibi to cover the time when Stewart was shot." Quist said he was inclined to agree, but pointed out that Auringer could have hired the job done.

The deputy stiffened. "You mean he hired Joker Gaillard to do the job?"

"I didn't say that at all." Quist sounded irritable and had recourse to his beer bottle. "Just the same, Dyke, I wish you'd snoop around and find out where Gaillard was that night." The deputy said he would. Quist went on, "Gaillard sure has a good opinion of himself."

Leigh chuckled. "Typical practical joker, do anything for a laugh, regardless who gets hurt. His ideas aren't always funny, but sometimes — well, like once he got into the hotel kitchen and put machine oil in the syrup. Then there was the joke he played on

Charley Otis — he has a general store here. Sometimes he works late and if Mrs. Otis goes out in the evening, she leaves the key to the house on a piece of cord hanging on a nail under the front porch. Well, Otis — he's a sort of pompous duck — comes home late one night, and reaches under for the key. But the cord seems longer than usual, with no key. He keeps yankin' on the cord, there seems something holding it back — when suddenly, *swoosh!* there's a mighty lively skunk at his feet. You can guess what happened. Otis didn't show up at his general store for a couple of days. Gaillard had put that skunk with the cord around its neck, in a closed box that could be opened by a strong pull on the cord. Dam'd if I know how Joker ever handled that skunk without getting sprayed himself. Probably tail-lifted the critter —"

"Could be the skunk recognized its own breed," Quist offered.

"The whole town near died laughing, of course. Charley Otis made threats but nothing came of it. Then there was the time Fat Joe, down to the barber shop, broke his arm. Joker had sawed the legs off a chair and then replaced them with tiny brads to hold 'em in place until Joe sat. There was the night he changed saddles and hitchrack places on a couple cowhands' hawsses. One gets into the saddle and rides off. Then Joker tells the other, his hawss has been stolen. The chase was on, and after accusations was made, the exchange was discovered. But it nearly led to a gunfight." The deputy related various other examples of Gaillard's brand of humor. Another beer bottle was emptied. "So you see," the deputy concluded, "it's hard to believe Joker's a gunfighter. He's plumb deceiving."

"Maybe," Quist conceded, and changed the subject. "Who else might have a motive for killing Stewart?"

"I can't think of anybody else, aside from Auringer, and I can't believe he had anything to do with it. Stewart was liked by most everybody. Trouble is, after his second marriage he started discouraging visitors to his place. As is natural, men around here were anxious to meet the bride — and they seemed to keep returning for more meetings. Mrs. Stewart is a looker, no doubt about it, and I suspect Stewart, being much older, could have been jealous. Then, just about six months ago he took to drinking hard. He'd get plastered day after day, until somebody — generally Smoky — poured him into his saddle and started him home. Sometimes he'd have to be accompanied. This last time was the worst I ever saw him though."

"I've been talking a bit around town," Quist said. "Folks been saying just about the same as you do. I —"

"Oh, yes," Leigh interrupted. "I've been meaning to ask. That day you found Brose Randle, you didn't happen to see a scalp laying around any place, did you?"

"Scalp?" Quist queried.

"Yeah — Injun scalp."

Quist chuckled. "Cripes, Dyke, I haven't even seen an Indian for some time now. Why you asking?"

"Didn't think you had. Why, Jason Randle was asking me about it. Seems old Brose had an old Comanche scalp he was right fond of. It hasn't been found at the Rafter-S, and neither was it with his belongings in that rowboat."

"I was thinking about that rowboat," Quist said. "Don't often see one in this country."

"As I get the story," Dyke said, "old Brose showed up from Oklahoma one day, driving that old wagon with the boat on it. He had a skin-and-bones hawss and a mule drawing the wagon — both long since dead. I'm damned if I know where he got the boat, but he claimed to be on his way to California to fish and just stopped off to visit his son for a few days at the Rafter-S. The upshot was that he hung around so long that Harl Stewart put him on the payroll as a sort of handy man — though I reckon he never did enough to be handy. Likely Stewart felt sorry for him. And that old boat set out in the weather, on that old wagon, down near the corral, ever since. And it's nigh three years since Brose come to visit. The old coot was getting sort of senile, too, though most of the time he's bright enough." The deputy rose. "I've got to get back to the office. There's an expense account to be made out. I can save Smoky that trouble. Like's not, after the funeral, he'll take Eirene and Mrs. Stewart home and then stay the night. He hasn't seen Eirene for going on two weeks."

Quist said "so-long," and watched him leave, then shifted his gaze across the street where a man had been standing, apparently waiting, for some time. Now Witt Auringer started to cross over. He reached the sidewalk, then clomped up the gallery steps on his high-heeled boots, his manner rather uncertain. Quist was opening another bottle of beer as Auringer drew near. Auringer said abruptly, "I'd like a word with you, Quist."

"A dozen if you like," Quist said genially. "Have a beer to clear your throat? There's a bottle handy —"

"Don't like beer," the man said ungraciously.

Quist's face tightened as though the man had committed sacrilege. "Have a chair, anyway," he said with cold courtesy. Auringer, instead, lowered his frame to the hotel railing, meanwhile tugging nervously at his heavy mustache, his dark eyes studying Quist. Quist said, "Well, what's on your mind?"

"It's like this, Quist, there's rumors around that I had something to do with Stewart's killing. I want to make it clear, I didn't."

"Go ahead" — shortly — "make it clear, Auringer. I'm listening. Always glad to have one less suspect. I'm listening."

Auringer's eyes widened. "Hell, I was right in town here, when it happened. I proved that by a dozen men who saw me. Smoky Hayes will tell you —"

"He's already told me, or his deputy did. But you can't deny that you and Stewart had a pretty hot scrap about something."

"Hell, that's months back. He was sore when he heard I was bringing in sheep. What's wrong with sheep? There's money in 'em. Sure, I know cowmen don't like 'em. I'm a cowman, too, but if I see a chance to make some quick money, why not sheep?

But any argument I had over sheep, wouldn't make me kill a man. Now I talked to Mr. Jay Fletcher when he was here and he allowed as how you'd find out who killed my stock when the train was stopped. Those sheep and goats cost me good money — fifty Rambouillet breed — good stock. Those Angora goats I was figuring to experiment with — figured maybe I could cross 'em with some of those Mex goats hereabouts. If things worked out, then I could increase my flocks. Mex goats come cheap, too. But to hear cowmen talk 'round here, you'd think I was aiming to go slaughterin' women and little children, or turn tigers loose on the range."

"You got to admit sheep don't mix with cattle," Quist pointed out. "They eat the grass down to nothing, then chop up the roots with their sharp hoofs. When the roots are gone, so is the grass."

"That's neither here nor there," Auringer said doggedly. "There's money in 'em for the man who raises 'em. If my scheme worked out, I'd get rid of my cows in time. But, hell" — bitterly — "until you find out who killed my stock and put 'em in prison, I don't dare bring in any more sheep and goats. I figure that's costing me money. So you just forget this murder business and do like Mr. Fletcher said —"

"Just a minute, Auringer," Quist said testily, "do you think Stewart was back of those masked men who did away with your sheep?"

"Who in hell else could it be?" Auringer demanded aggrievedly. "Everybody talked against sheep, but he talked loudest — why, cripes A'mighty, Quist, he as much as said, right to my face, that I'd never succeed in bringing sheep in here. Advised me not to try it."

"And you were just itching then to go for your gun, I hear."

"So was Stewart," Auringer half shouted, eyes blazing.

"But Smoky Hayes stepped between you and broke it up, before anybody got hurt. Yeah, Smoky told me about it. Since then, the more you thought on it, the madder you got. So night before last you sent somebody out to kill Harlan Stewart —"

"My Gawd, Quist! Don't say that. I swear it's not so!"

"*You* say! Auringer, how long ago did you let it be known you were going to bring sheep onto this range?"

Auringer frowned. "Couldn't say, offhand. Been talkin' about it a long time. Then maybe five-six months back, I come to a definite decision. Right away cow folks started jumpin' down my throat."

"And so, you figured trouble was coming," Quist cut in, "and soon's you could locate one, you hired yourself a gunfighter, Joker Gaillard by name."

"Look here, Quist, you got me all wrong. Sure, I hired Gaillard. A man's got to have some protection, and —" He broke off, perspiration dotting his forehead.

"Has Gaillard an alibi for the night Stewart was killed?"

"We-ell, I can't say right now where he was, but I swear —"

Quist held up one hand. "Sure, we're all swearing about this business, but nothing's solved. Meanwhile, until I find a better suspect, I'm going to keep digging into your affairs, Auringer."

"Dammit, why pick on me? There's other men —"

"Meaning just what?" Quist cut in.

"Why don't you talk to Rupe Chandler —"

"I don't even know him."

"He runs the Golden Spur — bar and gambling. Stewart had a fight with him, too, one day last week. Knocked him down on the street. Later Stewart told us he'd kicked the man off the Rafter-S. Stewart was drunk, but not too drunk to catch Chandler off-guard. The punch smashed Chandler 'most to the middle of the street —" He broke off suddenly. "Look here, maybe I talked too much. Maybe —"

"It's sometimes good for a man to talk, Auringer. So now I've got two suspects. Yes, you're not clear yet."

Angrily, Auringer whirled up from his seat and went striding from the gallery. Quist followed him with curious eyes, musing, "I can be an awful bastard at times. But maybe it works. Maybe I've found something out."

CHAPTER X

Warning

The sun was lowering in the west, the town filling up. Quist, still seated on the hotel gallery, trying to put together a puzzle that refused to be solved, glanced at his watch. It was already well after three o'clock. The funeral would be late all right. Below him, on the sidewalk, Quist heard Joker Gaillard's voice. Gaillard was just passing with another man, a swarthy rather slovenly looking individual, with a week's growth of coarse black beard, sombrero pulled low over one eye, and a well-worn six-shooter at his right hip.

Quist replied civilly enough to Gaillard's greeting and waited for him and the other man to pass on. Gaillard said, "Now that ain't no way to solve crime, railroad dick, sittin' on your can. Bet you get paid good money for it, too. Ain't you ashamed of yourself, taking money for loafin' all day. But I reckon" — he grinned widely, the pale blue eyes glinting with laughter — "that's how you get the dough. Loafin'. Get it? — dough — loaf." He howled with laughter. His companion stared steadily at Quist, beady eyes dark and sullen.

"Funny as a crutch, you are," Quist said caustically.

"Wait — wait," Gaillard said. "There's a connection there. Crutch! Hold-up! Looking for bandits, ain't you?" More laughter.

Quist said, "I didn't know the circus had come to town."

Gaillard paused. "Circus? I don't —"

"I always look for a circus when I see a clown," Quist chuckled.

Gaillard grinned. "All right, I'll admit I bit. But look, lawman, there ain't room for two funny men in Corinth City. Does that tell you anything?"

"Tells me you'll be leaving soon," Quist said, smiling thinly. "Maybe feet-first."

Another guffaw. "That's the funniest thing you've said yet, Quist. Dam'd if I ever see your beat. You're good for a laugh every time I meet you — and I'll still be laughing when you take off."

"And," Quist said, "you might as well shove along right now — providing your pal has had a good enough look at me."

"Who? Oh, Tonkawa. Pay him no attention, Quist." Gaillard chuckled. "Probably he's never seen a funny specimen like you. I'm just taking him around, showing him the sights. Ain't that so, Tonkawa?"

But the other man just grunted and started to move off. Gaillard followed, saying over his shoulder, "Well, *adiós*, Quist. Don't choke on any beer bottles. It might give you the hops!" And shaking with merriment he strode off after his companion.

Quist glowered after the pair. "Damned if that Gaillard isn't just about the most irritating *hombre* I ever ran across," he growled. "Just spoiling for a fight, too, or I miss my guess. Well, maybe the bustard will get it, too, before I'm through."

A party of riders passed, walking their horses, and led by Jason Randle: the Rafter-S hands arriving for the funeral. Quist rose from his chair and craned his head over the railing to look down the street. There was quite a crowd waiting now in the vicinity of Barry Lowe's place. Buggies and horses were crowded at hitchracks. A number of people stood talking on the sidewalks. Faces had been freshly shaven; boiled shirts donned, boots shined.

Quist sat back in his chair. "Damned if they don't dress up just about the same as they would for a wedding," he mused. He reached for his final bottle of beer, finished that and then rose and headed down Mesquite Street in the direction of the T.N. & A.S. depot. Here he sent off a telegram, then left the depot and made his way back to Main Street. As he neared the hotel, he saw Deputy Leigh standing on the corner. Leigh said, "I'll buy you a beer."

Quist shook his head. "Been drinking beer all afternoon. I've reached the point where I gurgle every step I take. What's on your mind, Dyke?" He started to roll a cigarette.

"I saw Joker Gaillard and asked him where he was at the time Stewart was shot. Well, you know how Gaillard is — has to stall around with some funny stuff before he'll talk sensible —"

"I know how the bustard is, all right," Quist growled.

"Anyway," Leigh resumed, "I finally got it out of him. Gaillard claims that he was in the Red Mustang Saloon, at the time the news arrived about Stewart being shot and old Brose running off with the team and wagon. And the boat."

"Do you reckon Joker can prove that?"

"He already has. The whole Rafter-S crew was drinking at the Red Mustang too. I saw Jason Randle about ten minutes back and asked him for corroboration. Randle remembers well that the Joker was there, at the time, because he'd just dropped a dead mouse in Randle's beer, when Randle wasn't looking, and everybody else was laughing fit to kill. It was just at that time the news about Stewart and old Randle arrived."

"Then what happened?"

"The laughing halted mighty *pronto*. There was the usual excited talk for a few minutes that accompanies news like that, then the Rafter-S mounted and took out for the ranch."

"Jason Randle told you this, eh?"

Leigh nodded. "Not that I doubted Jason's word, but just to have a double-check I asked Johnny Drake about it, too. Drake's probably as level-headed a cowhand as there is on the Rafter-S payroll. Naturally, he remembered the dead mouse. He told me that Randle had just started to bawl out Gaillard, when the news come about Stewart and old Brose. Oh, it all checks. Gaillard's alibi is watertight."

"How'd Jason Randle take the news?"

"Johnny Drake tells me he just sort of acted stunned for a minute, but it struck Johnny that Jason was more concerned about his father running off with the wagon, than he was about Stewart. Then he started talking to Gaillard again, like mebbe he was still bothered about that mouse. Eventually the crew got mounted. Johnny said that Jason was last to mount. He stood talking to Gaillard about something or other, until one of the hands — Johnny thinks it was Gus Fuller — called to Jason they'd better get going; then they all left." Leigh shook his head. "A dead mouse! That Gaillard!"

"Dyke, who do you know named Tonkawa around here?"

"Tonkawa Talbert. Why? What — ?"

Quist told him of the conversation he'd had with Gaillard some time before. "This Tonkawa *hombre* just stood and stared at me all the time. What do you know about him?"

"Nothing good," the deputy frowned. "Don't understand him going around with Gaillard. They've never been chummy. Tonkawa Talbert is just one of the riffraff around town. Been in jail several times — drunkenness, petty thieving, rolled a drunk one time. He carries a gun but I never heard of him shooting anybody. Probably has, though. He did a short term for breaking and entering one time — few years back. I can't understand him and Gaillard —"

"Don't try to. Here's something else. Right after you left me on the hotel gallery today, Dewitt Auringer braced me —"

"What did Witt want?"

"He set out to convince me he hadn't shot Stewart, and wanted me to concentrate on finding out who did away with his sheep and goats. In order to get suspicion off his own shoulders, he dropped a hint I should check into a fight that somebody named Rupe Chandler had with Stewart one day last week. Know anything about that?"

Leigh laughed shortly. "I doubt that amounted to much. Neither Smoky nor I heard anything about it until a couple of hours later. Somebody said Stewart was liquored up, as usual. Neither Chandler nor Stewart made any complaints so we just forgot the matter."

"Auringer told me that Stewart caught Chandler offguard and knocked him nearly into the middle of the street."

The deputy laughed. "It must have been a lucky punch. Chandler considers himself something of a fighting man. Hell's-bells! Stewart wouldn't have a chance with him. Somebody must have stepped in and stopped it, or Chandler would have put Harl in the hospital."

"Either that," Quist pointed out, "or this Chandler *hombre* had some good reason for not fighting back. Who is he, anyway?"

"Came here about a year back. Took over the old Crystal Castle and renamed it the Golden Spur. Bar. Gambling. Good-looking jasper. I reckon he fancies himself as a lady's man."

Quist nodded. "I remember the place

now. Big frame building. I remember thinking the sign, Golden Spur, looked like
fresher painting than the rest of the building.
It was closed last time I passed it."

"Chandler doesn't generally open until
middle afternoon, then his games run practically until daylight. Look here, he'll likely
be open now. Why don't we take a *paseo*
down that way?"

Quist agreed. The two men swung around
and started along the sidewalk. By the time
they neared the undertaker's there was considerable of a jam there, vehicles and people.
Quist and the deputy pushed through the
crowd, and three buildings farther on, arrived before the open double-doored entrance of the Golden Spur.

There weren't many people in the place.
A long bar ran along the right hand wall.
Scattered through the rest of the room were
the various games-of-chance — so-called.
Faro tables, dice layouts, roulette, chuck-a-
luck, poker tables, most of which at the present moment were draped with oilcloth
covers. Five men sat playing at a corner
table, cards in their hands, poker chips
stacked before them. At the back of the
room, a stairway ascended to a balcony running around three sides. There were a
number of rooms, with closed doors, up

there. Quist wondered. For private games? Possibly games of some sort. He didn't see any women about the place. Later, maybe.

"Too early for much activity, yet," Leigh said as they started across the room. "Tonight the place will be jammed. There's Rupe Chandler at the far end, talking to his bartender. There'll be three bartenders tonight."

There weren't half a dozen men ranged at the bar, which was long enough to boast two mirrors above the back bar of shining glasses and bottles. An oil painting — a reclining nude — was hung between the mirrors. Typical barroom art. A masterpiece of bad foreshortening and limbs looking like bloated pink sausages. But to the patrons of the Golden Spur it passed for the ultimate in draughtsmanship and color, design and composition. Though the building had been recently swept, Quist's nose wrinkled at the odor of stale liquor, perspiration and old tobacco butts. His yellow eyes ranged along the bar, passed the few customers, to the tall man who called himself Rupe Chandler. A tall man with rather handsome features and a thin blond mustache, but with eyes placed too closely together. Beneath the tilted-back sombrero, slicked-back hair was plastered closely to the skull. Chandler was in shirt sleeves and fancy vest; striped trousers. He wasn't wearing a gun at the moment, though Quist knew he could handle one.

"Calls himself Rupe Chandler now, does he?" Quist observed to the deputy.

"You know him?" Leigh asked.

There was no time for a reply. They were at the bar now, and Chandler was approaching from the other side of the long counter.

"Well, it's good to see you, Quist," he spoke with assumed heartiness, thrusting one hand across the bar.

Quist was engaged in rolling a brown-paper cigarette, and failed to see the hand. "Is it, Rupert?" he asked quietly.

"Sure as hell it is," Chandler said, withdrawing his hand. "H'are, Dyke? What you gents drinking? I've been expecting to see you in, Quist."

"Have you? Why?" — shortly.

"Well, hell —" Chandler paused, then concluded lamely, "Cripes, I figured you'd hear I was in Corinth City. Smoky Hayes came in and requested that any drinking you do should be charged to him. So, naturally —"

"So, naturally," Quist said coldly, "you've been shivering in your boots ever since."

Chandler flushed. "Aw, now, Quist, you don't want to be like that. I —"

151

Quist snapped, "How in hell should you know how I want to be? And I'm not drinking, so don't call your barkeep. I come in to have a talk with you."

"You ain't got anything on me," Chandler said defiantly. "That business in El Paso was all cleared up. I had witnesses —"

"Quit it!" Quist half snarled. "Who said anything about El Paso? I'm thinking about Corinth City."

There was no one else near, at the bar. Deputy Leigh was listening in wide-eyed surprise. Chandler asked, "What do you mean — Corinth City?"

"Rafter-S, rather," Quist said bluntly. "Why'd you kill Harlan Stewart?" Chandler gasped and went white. Quist added with a thin smile, "If you did kill him."

Chandler mopped perspiration from his face and forced a weak laugh. "Same old joker, ain't you? Come in here, scare hell out of a man. For a minute there I thought I was under suspicion —"

"You are, Rupert. Chan Rupert, wasn't it? And now it's Rupe Chandler. What do I call you now?"

Chandler swallowed hard. "Folks around here know me as Rupe Chandler. I decided to break away from the old life, make a new start. Nobody's got anything on me. I haven't had any trouble. There's no reason for suspecting I had —"

"Wasn't there a fight between you and Stewart one day last week?"

"Oh, that. Cripes A'mighty, Quist. That wasn't anything. He was drinking — as usual. That was quieted down. Hell, Harl Stewart was a good friend. I visited at his ranch —"

"What was the fight about?" Quist persisted.

Chandler shrugged. "I don't remember now —"

"Don't lie to me!" Quist snapped. "You remember all right."

"It wasn't much really, didn't amount to anything. Dyke, here, will tell you Stewart got sort of quarrelsome sometimes when he was in his cups —"

"Dammit! Quit stalling, Chandler!" Quist snapped.

"All right, all right. He'd been playing roulette and lost some money. Claimed I had a lead fret on my wheel —"

"And of course you didn't," Quist said caustically.

"Certainly not. I'm running my games straight. Hell, you know as well as I do, Quist, games don't have to be crooked. The house percentage will show profits —"

"Some tin-horns get greedy, Chandler. All right, so it was just a gambling argument, and it's too late now to prove you're wrong."

"Just a gambling argument, that's all." Chandler breathed easier. "You know how those things come up from time to time —"

"And I suppose it was just a gambling argument the night Stewart kicked you off the Rafter-S, eh?"

"Nobody kicked me off —"

"All right, told you to get out and not come back, then. Stewart did some talking you know."

"Gambling argument there too," Chandler said sullenly. "We'd been matching cards and when he lost, Stewart claimed my deck was marked. He got mad. But, hell, Quist, we settled all that. Would I be liable to kill a man just because I won his money? Even if I'd lost —"

"You swear that's all there was to it — gambling arguments?"

"S'help me God, Quist —"

"You'll need His help if I find you've lied to me. That's a warning, Chandler. You know I don't run bluffs, so if you know anything pertaining to Stewart's death, you'd better make a clean breast of it."

"So help me I don't," Chandler said nervously. "Just because I had a little trouble back in El Paso is no sign you should suspect me of murder. There's other men —"

"Who?" Quist snapped.

"Well" — lamely — "I don't want to accuse anybody."

"You've said too much or too little, Chandler. Am I going to have to beat the truth out of you? Maybe that's an idea. I can borrow a cell in the jail and —"

"Oh, for God's sake, Quist. I haven't done anything —"

"Who were you set to accuse?" Quist demanded sternly.

"We-ell, I wouldn't want it to go any farther" — Chandler's eyes weren't meeting Quist's — "but I overheard Harl Stewart tell Jason Randle, one day, that if he'd spend more time in the bunkhouse and less in the ranchhouse —"

"What in the devil you hinting at?" Quist interrupted.

A smirk crossed Chandler's face. "You're forcing it out of me, remember, but now that Stewart's dead, Mrs. Stewart's due to inherit a whale of a lot of money. And everybody with an eye knows she's a looker. I can't say I blame Randle — hell, anybody that saw Jason when Mrs. Stewart was around, would guess he was plumb sweet on the lady."

Quist swore disgustedly, and swung abruptly away from the bar. "C'mon, Dyke," he growled, "let's get out of this place. It stinks to high heaven as does its proprietor." He spoke to Chandler, "And don't think I'm through with you, either. You're still a suspect."

Chandler stood glowering nervously after them, as Quist and Leigh headed for the street. Quist said irritably, "Cripes! What a skunk!"

"And talking about Mrs. Stewart that way," Dyke Leigh said angrily. "Melinda Stewart of all women. Why, Greg —"

"He didn't actually say anything against Mrs. Stewart."

"He hinted like the devil that —"

"It's all in the way you look at such things, Dyke," Quist said, more quietly now. The deputy asked a question. Quist explained, "I knew Chandler in El Paso, couple of years back. He killed a man during a card game, claimed the other man went for his gun. I happened to know that the other man rarely toted a gun. But Chandler had witnesses — all friends. Chandler got off scot free."

At the hotel, the two men parted. Quist mounted the steps to the hotel gallery and sat down, his forehead knotted with thought-wrinkles. He was scarcely aware of the fact when the funeral got under way. It came to him later that there were a great many riders and buggies in the procession that turned down Mesquite Street and headed out toward the cemetery.

When the last buggy had passed from view, Quist rose and walked down to the undertaking establishment. He entered and found no one there. When next he emerged, he came out the rear door, strode thoughtfully along Railroad Street, and eventually wound up back at the hotel, where he ascended immediately to his room, thinking, *Maybe things are coming a little clearer, but not much. It's still a puzzle.*

CHAPTER XI

A Nocturnal Visitor

It was after eight that night. Quist sat at the
table in his hotel room, writing a letter to Jay
Fletcher. Had it been to any other railroad
official, Quist would have called it a report.
To Fletcher, an old friend, it was a letter.
The kerosene lamp at Quist's elbow cast
highlights on an empty beer bottle, a partly
full one and two unopened bottles on a tray.
The shades were lowered on the two windows, but now and then a vagrant puff of
warm night air caused them to move slightly.
Quist had removed his gun harness which
lay on the bed. His open satchel stood on a
chair.

. . . so that's the way it shapes up, Jay, he
wrote, *and I can't tell you much more than
you knew when you were here. Everyone
seems ready to suspect everyone else, and
I've not even had time to dig into that
sheep and goats business, yet. I feel sure
that scalp is mixed in the business, but can't
figure how. Got one lead today that might
take me up to Oklahoma, if our operative*

*there doesn't uncover something for me.
Both Stewart and Brose Randle were
buried this afternoon. Hell of a big turn-out.
Of course, Stewart was a pretty big man in
this section —*

Quist paused, lifted his head, listened.
Again came the knock on the door. Not a loud
knock by any means. Quist rose and moved
silently over to his bed, sat down, right hand
not far from the gun butt in his harness holster. The knock sounded a third time.

Quist called, "Come in."

The door opened and shut again. A girl
stood there. Quist got quickly to his feet,
bowing, saying, "This is a surprise — a
pleasant surprise."

"Mr. Quist? — But then, it must be. I'm
Eirene Stewart."

Even while Quist was placing a chair for
her, he was thinking he'd not seen many
girls so lovely. Black, glossy hair, gathered
in a knob at her nape; good eyes; nose
slightly turned up, full lips and a determined
chin. She wore a dress of some very dark
material with a tight bodice; there was a bit
of lace at throat and wrists.

Quist waited for her to explain the visit.
She seemed somewhat at a loss how to begin. Quist mentioned the funeral, and hoped

it hadn't been too much of an ordeal. The conversation was rather halting at first. Quist learned that both Eirene and Mrs. Stewart had decided not to return to the ranch until the following day. They were staying at a friend's house, a Mrs. Emmons. Smoky — Dyke — everybody had been very kind.

"I hope I'll be able to be placed in that category too," Quist said. "If there's anything I can do —"

"Oh, there is, I'm sure of it," Eirene Stewart said. "Melinda — that is, my mother — stepmother — Dad's wife," stammeringly, "intended to come with me, tonight. At the last minute she decided against it. She's actually in no condition to go out. Dr. Wakeman came and gave her something to make her sleep. It's been an ordeal for her —"

"And for you also," Quist put in.

The girl studied him a moment. Were his eyes really yellow? No, the color was topaz. They could be amber. "An ordeal for me, too, yes," she admitted finally. "But a thing like this that happened to Dad — well, it hits some people differently from others. Maybe I'm still too numbed by the shock. Perhaps, later, I'll feel as Melinda does now. In another way we're different. I've always lived on the ranch. I'm more used to hearing of shootings. I've known the rougher, outdoor life. Melinda's city-bred. Too, you must take into consideration that Melinda was — was there when it happened. The shock of that, alone, is enough to knock her out. The news, when it came to me, terrible as it was, was softened somewhat by friends. I've had a chance to think things over. I've listened to Melinda. She seems to be living them over, hour after hour. All my tears won't bring Dad back. I realize that. Right now, I have to keep on the move. I want to do something about this — this —"

"Exactly what do you have in mind doing, Miss Stewart?"

"I've come to ask you to do everything possible to uncover the man who killed my father. Smoky and Dyke tell me you're here on business for your company and that will undoubtedly have to come first. They've told me of your reputation, and that they could have no better help than you can give. They're counting on your assistance."

"I've already told Smoky I'd do all possible, so long as it didn't interfere with my job. But I have to work my own way, you know."

"Isn't it possible for you to just postpone your job for a time, Mr. Quist? I'd be willing to pay nearly anything you ask. You see, before he remarried, Dad settled quite a sum of money on me."

Quist said, "We won't talk about money. My company pays me well — probably more than I'm worth. Anything I'd do would have to be done my own way, and I couldn't accept anything from you. And now, I'd like to ask you a few questions, if you can stand it. Some of them may hurt. And you can answer or not as you see fit."

Eirene's chin came up. "I can stand it. Ask anything you want."

Quist nodded. "What sort of will did your father leave?"

"None, so far as I know. He was always against writing wills, he said, because it made him feel old. He didn't want to feel old. He wasn't really. Though he was near sixty, he didn't look it —"

"Then the bulk of the estate will likely go to your stepmother — Melinda Stewart?"

"Very likely. I don't know much about the law, and if you think that bothers me, Mr. Quist, you're wrong." Her words commenced to sound heated.

Quist smiled, raising one hand. "I didn't say it bothered you," he pointed out mildly, "not right now. But, tell me, how did you feel when your father remarried?"

Eirene Stewart hesitated, looking away. Then her gaze came back and she said frankly, "I didn't like it. Not one bit. Immediately I received the telegram saying he had married, I moved into town. My mother had died when I was young, but I still couldn't imagine anyone replacing her in Dad's affections. Dad came to see me when they got home. We quarreled bitterly. Later I got to thinking things over. I realized there were times when he must have felt lonely for a wife. He was still relatively young, even though Melinda is nearing thirty. I was very selfish. At first I refused to even meet her. I should have had my face slapped — or my — my —" she smiled slightly, "— or something worse. Eventually Dad got us together, and I realized what a fool I'd been. No one could resist Melinda. I couldn't blame Dad a bit. It was Melinda who persuaded me to come back to the ranch and live. We had some good times."

"How long ago did Mr. Stewart marry Mrs. Stewart?"

"A little less than two years ago. He'd gone to Tucson on business and met her while there."

"What did Mrs. Stewart do before she was married?"

"I don't know exactly what it was. She was a dealer in some sort of small business of her own. I think stationery. Dad said something like that, once. I remember they were laughing at her being a business woman. At that, I'll bet she was capable."

"Miss Stewart, I'm going to be rather blunt. Your father has been drinking a good deal the past six months. Have you any idea why?"

The girl bit her lip. "You know, if you care for someone as I did Dad, you see his faults and pass them over. Dad has always done a lot of drinking, but never like he has the past months. What brought that on, I don't know. Maybe his business affairs at Tucson went wrong. He never said. I was at school at the time — in Austin. I remember Melinda writing me that she was going there to visit friends, and that she'd tried to persuade Dad to go with her. But he was busy at the ranch at the time. Later he did make the trip to bring her back. I noticed a difference in him when I returned from school. He was moody. He lost weight. And, as you say, he was drinking too much. Before that, he always welcomed company. Somebody was always riding out from town. Finally he became quarrelsome. I wanted him to go see Dr. Wakeman, see if something was wrong, but he refused. There were times when he was even pretty short with Smoky — Sheriff Hayes — when Smoky would ride out to visit with me. And I don't think he had a closer friend than Smoky Hayes. I've sometimes thought that Dad was jealous of other men. It could be he got to thinking about the difference in his age and Melinda's."

"Do you plan to marry Smoky?"

The girl's cheeks crimsoned. "Is it necessary I answer that, Mr. Quist?"

"Not at all, Miss Stewart. The question just popped into my head."

"You're thinking that Smoky is about fifteen years older than I, aren't you?" The girl smiled slightly. "All right, I'll admit we've talked that over. But nothing has been settled definitely yet —"

"We can drop the subject," Quist said. "Tell me, did you know anything about Brose Randle?"

"That reminds me," Eirene Stewart said. "After the funeral today, Jason asked me if I'd look around the ranchhouse and see if his father's Indian scalp — but I don't suppose you know —"

"I knew he had an old scalp that was missing. Heard something about it. Have you ever seen it?"

"I'd like to have a dollar for every time I've seen it. Old Brose used to take me on his knee when I was a small girl, and tell me how he got that scalp. He was a pretty rough old codger, and had been quite an Indian fighter at one time. He'd 'lifted' that scalp himself in a fight with the Comanches. Later he got some Comanche squaw to fix it up with beadwork. I've heard it rumored that it wasn't an Indian battle at all, but something personal between Brose and the Comanche brave, both of them wanting the same squaw. But young ladies weren't supposed to hear that sort of story."

Quist smiled. "You've known the Randles a long time, then. I'd heard that Brose came from Oklahoma."

"They're Texas, both of them. Jason even punched cows for Dad, years ago. Then both Randles went away. About three years ago, Jason returned, said he'd been in New Mexico and Arizona. Didn't know where his father was. Jason's a good cowman. A foreman was needed and Dad gave Jason the job. Later, old Brose showed up with a rowboat on an old wagon — but I suppose you know that."

Quist nodded, changing the subject, "Miss Stewart, do you know of any enemy your father had — a dangerous enemy?"

The girl slowly shook her head. "He's had trouble with various men, particularly the last six months — Witt Auringer, Rupe Chandler, two or three other stock raisers.

Auringer wanted to bring in sheep. Some of the cowmen wanted him to take drastic action of some sort against Auringer. I know Dad refused and that brought on some quarreling. And Dad hated sheep like poison too. But he believed in letting the law handle troubles. But I can't think of one person who would want him dead."

Quist and the girl talked for fifteen minutes more, then she prepared to take her departure. He liked the warm hand clasp she gave him on leaving, and he promised to visit the ranch some day soon.

After the girl had left, Quist reseated himself at the table and quickly finished the letter to Jay Fletcher. Once it had been put into an envelope and sealed, he sat a long time frowning over a bottle of beer. "Just one more little nibble on a big knot," he told himself, scowling. "Now what in hell happened in Tucson to upset Harlan Stewart and start him drinking like that? It looks like I'll have to ask one of our operatives to see what he can run down over in Tucson."

He rose, donned his gun-harness, coat and sombrero, extinguished the light and descended to the street. Ten minutes later, at the T.N. & A.S. depot he was engaged in writing a lengthy telegram to a man named Kittle, in Arizona. After showing certain credentials to the telegraph operator and asking that the message be sent off at once, Quist retraced his steps to the hotel and once more mounted to his room. He undressed in the dark, after raising the shades at the two open windows, hung his gun-harness near at hand on the corner of the bed, and stretched out.

For a long time sleep eluded him as he lay thinking. The harder he thought the more wide awake he became. Now and then slight noises drifted up from the streets below. A rider dismounted in the fenced-off area at the rear of the hotel. Now and then voices sifted up from the hotel bar. A door slammed somewhere, and two drunks went singing maudlinly down Mesquite Street. Then silence again, and quiet settled on Corinth City. Quist finally dropped off to sleep.

How long he'd been asleep he wasn't certain, when something awakened him. Moonlight now poured into the room from the Mesquite Street side, casting a broad beam of silver light across a good third of the floor and part of the rear wall. Quist listened intently, raised up on one elbow. There, the sound had come again. A faint scraping sound beyond his open rear window.

Slipping silently from the bed, Quist quickly arranged his pillows beneath the blankets to make them appear to be a sleeping form, then lifting his six-shooter from holster, he moved with the stealth of an Apache to a far corner of the room, deep in shadow, and waited.

Now there wasn't a sound to be heard. A minute passed, and then two more. Quist began to think he'd been mistaken. The hotel bar must have closed long since. There were no noises from the street. The whole town seemed wrapped —

Quist tensed, half crouched behind a chair near the door. Again had come that scraping sound — a boot drawn across wood. Now Quist could hear the heavy breathing of the climbing man, just beyond and below the window in his rear wall.

An arm appeared at the opening, then fingers closed over the window ledge, followed by a second hand. A sombreroed head appeared cautiously. Then shoulders. Here, Quist's visitor paused a moment and peered intently into the room, in the direction of the bed. The bed, fortunately, wasn't reached by the moonlight; in the gloom, there seemed to be a man sleeping there.

Quist held his breath, watching. The man came farther into the room, shoulders and half his body silhouetted against the window opening. It was no one whom Quist recognized; the man's hat was pulled low on his face. Now one leg was thrown over the sill, and the man drew himself into the room. Here, he straightened a moment, his gaze never leaving the bed. Quist caught the long breath the man exhaled.

Now the man started to move across the room. A board creaked under foot, and the fellow stiffened. Waited. Gaze never leaving the bed. After a minute, the man breathed easier. He studied the form on the bed a moment longer, then continued on toward the commode, casting looks back over his shoulder as he moved. Bracing one hand on the commode, Quist's visitor lifted one arm toward the mirror, and reached behind it, groping for something next to the wall.

Things were coming clearer to Quist now: this must be the same man who had entered his room the previous evening. Now he had remembered — or someone had reminded him — of a hiding place that had been over-looked on the other visit, say behind a picture, perhaps, or a mirror.

The man had just withdrawn the scalp from behind the mirror, when, from his darkened corner, Quist asked quietly, "Find what you were looking for, mister?"

CHAPTER XII

Powdersmoke

A quick indrawn breath answered Quist's question. Nothing more. The words had sounded unusually loud in the quiet room, with moonlight flooding one side. The man at the mirror had stiffened without turning, then slowly, cautiously, his gaze swerved toward the bed. A sort of baffled groan came from his mouth as he realized he'd been deceived. Still he didn't turn around.

Quist said tersely, "Drop that scalp, mister, and lift 'em high."

No reply. No movement. The man stood as before, back to Quist, the scalp dangling from one hand.

"I don't want to have to tell you again," Quist said sharply.

Almost too late, Quist realized his visitor was stalling, playing for time until the exact point from which Quist's voice had come could be located. There was a soft thud as the scalp struck the floor. The man spun around. Swiftly-drawn gunmetal rasped against holster leather. Flame and smoke lighted up the room.

Even as Quist shifted position, he heard the leaden slug chamfer the edge of the chair behind which he'd been crouching. Quist fired once, then threw himself sidewise as the heavy forty-four jumped a second time in his fist, the powerful detonations shaking dust from the ceiling.

There came another shot from the other man, but it flew well wide of his mark, as he pitched abruptly to the floor. Quist heard the fellow's head strike the commode on the way down, then the clatter of the six-shooter as it went flying from the weakened grasp. A moment's silence. There came a long tired sigh. That was all.

Powdersmoke swirled through the room, stinging eyes and nostrils, bringing a dryness to a throat already dry. Quist waited a moment longer, then rose from his half-crouching position. There had been no further movement from the man on the floor. Quist strode to his coat on the clothes stand, fumbled in one pocket for cartridges and reloaded, then reholstered his gun. He got a match and lifted the glass chimney from the lamp, lighted it.

He became suddenly conscious of an uproar in the hall beyond his door. Other doors banged. There were excited voices, running footsteps. Feet pounded up the stairway.

Someone knocked loudly at his door. "Mr. Quist! Are you all right?" Something frantic in the hotel clerk's voice. "Mr. Quist! What has happened — ?"

"I'm all right," Quist called back. "Be there in a minute."

He went to the silent form, sprawled face down on the floor, one outflung arm, fingers stretched wide, reaching toward the six-shooter a couple of feet away, on the carpet. Quist stooped down, peering at the face. The one eye he could see beneath the oily black hair, was already glazing. Knowing it was useless, still Quist felt for a pulse in the outflung arm. There wasn't any. Quist studied the dead features a minute. "Now, why in the devil," he muttered, "did Tonkawa Talbert want that scalp? Or did someone hire him to get it?"

The scalp lay on the floor where Talbert had dropped it, before reaching for his gun. Quist retrieved it and replaced it behind the mirror. Then he went to the door and flung it open. A small knot of men, most of them in night attire, crowded behind the night clerk, peering into the room. The excited voices rose again.

"Are you having some trouble, Mr. Quist — ?" the clerk began. The words ended in a choked gurgling sound as he saw the dead man on the floor.

Quist said grimly, "Is this room always this unlucky?"

"S-seems to — to be that way, doesn't it?" the clerk quavered. He forced a wan smile. "A-anyway, Mr. Quist, it's not m-mice, this time. Is — is that man dead?"

Quist nodded. "He's all through breaking into hotel rooms — or any other kind. When I questioned him, he started to shoot. I — look here, you'd best send for the doctor and Sheriff Hayes. *Pronto!*"

"Y-yes, sir, Mr. Quist. I'll get right to it."

The clerk left the room. Other men would have remained, but Quist put them out, then closed his door. Outside, in the hall, the voices continued. Quist pulled on his trousers and sat down on the bed. After a minute he rose again, went to the window through which Talbert had entered. Below, a small roof jutted above the steps of the hotel-bar's back entrance. Next to the steps was a stack of empty beer cases and a couple of whisky barrels. Reaching Quist's second floor window hadn't been difficult. Quist returned to his seat.

Sheriff Hayes arrived sooner than Quist had hoped for. Quist let him into the room, closed the door again, shutting out the crowded, peering faces. Hayes said, "Good

Lord, Greg! What now?" He stooped at the side of the dead form, then rose. "Tonkawa Talbert. I'll be blasted! What the devil happened?"

Quist related briefly what had taken place. "I couldn't do anything else, Smoky. He nearly caught me offguard as it was."

"Hell, yes," Hayes agreed. "I see your point. When a man starts throwing lead your way, you don't have time to ask his intentions. It's a clear case of self-defense. But what did Tonkawa want in your room? Have you ever had any trouble with him"

"Never saw the man before today — no, it's yesterday, now. He came along with Joker Gaillard while I was sitting on the hotel gallery. Gaillard and I pushed some smart talk back and forth — most of it from Gaillard — and Talbert just stood and stared at me all the time. Maybe he wanted to see what I looked like. Could be he already had this stunt in mind. I don t figure it."

"By God, I'll bet Gaillard is back of this some way. Tonkawa never had sense enough to cook this up on his own. I just reckon I'll grab Gaillard and —"

"It wouldn't do any good, Smoky. Gaillard would deny all connection with this, and you couldn't prove different. Talbert can't talk. Let Gaillard ride a spell. Maybe if we give him a long enough rope, he'll hang himself."

"I guess you're right," Hayes said reluctantly. "But I still can't figure what Tonkawa was after. Oh, sure, he was a dumb ignorant bustard. Hell, he couldn't even read and write. I've had him in jail two or three times. Petty crime. Signed an X for his name; couldn't even write that. He's not in Gaillard's class, yet you say you saw them together. Sure, he'd likely steal from anybody, but why pick out you? Was it just money he was after?"

"I don't think so," Quist said slowly. "I figure Talbert is the same one who broke into my room before. He didn't find what he was after. Later, somebody pointed out a hiding place he might have missed — behind a picture, or a mirror say." The sheriff's eyes ranged about the room, came to rest on the mirror. Quist went on, "Talbert made a second attempt to get what he missed the first time."

Quist crossed to the mirror and took out the Comanche scalp which he handed to Hayes. "I'll be damned!" Hayes exclaimed. "This must be old Brose's scalp. Sure, I think it is. He showed it to me one time. Set a lot of store by it for some reason or other. I remember, Jason was asking if anybody had seen it in that boat. I reckon he wanted to keep it?"

"But, why?" Quist asked in turn.

"Jeepers! You've got me." The sheriff examined the scalp, then shrugged his shoulders, looking at Quist with puzzled eyes. "Now, why should Talbert, or anybody else, risk his life, or imprisonment, to steal a lousy Injun scalp? That's the craziest idea. Greg, can you understand it?"

"No more than you do," Quist replied. He took the scalp from Hayes' hands and replaced it behind the mirror. "Let's keep this a secret between you and me, Smoky. If Randle knows I have it, he'll come around bothering me. Tell Dyke if you like, but tell him to keep his trap closed."

"You think that scalp has something to do with Harlan Stewart's death?" the sheriff frowned.

"Somehow, I can't help thinking it has — but don't ask me in what way. I just don't know, Smoky." He paused, then, "Would you have any ideas on the subject?"

Hayes shook his head. "Hell's-bells! I don't even know how the scalp came into your hands. You haven't said, and knowing you like to work your own way, I didn't want to ask."

Quist smiled. "I wish I could always get

this kind of co-operation from law officers. To tell the truth, it was an accident I found this scalp, the day I ran across old Brose's body in the boat. I was casting around, looking for sign, when . . ." From that point he related how he'd come to find the scalp. ". . . and then when I walked out into the center of that clearing, somebody started shooting at me from that hilltop. Shortly after, you and the Rafter-S punchers arrived."

"That setup gets queerer all the time," Hayes said perplexedly. He scratched his head, cogitating. "You don't suppose that old Brose hid the scalp in that place, do you?"

"Why should he do that? I want to hear what you think, Smoky. I've got my own idea. Could be our thoughts will run in the same channel."

"We-ell," Hayes said slowly, "supposing some other person was after that scalp and Brose didn't want him to get it. Maybe it was that bustard that shot at you. We'll say he come after Brose, and Brose hid it in the mesquite — or could be the feller was closing in fast, and Brose just tossed it wild into those trees. Then the feller caught up with Brose —" The sheriff paused.

"You're giving me confidence in my own solutions now, Smoky," Quist said. "Keep going."

"We-ell, I don't know" — more thoughtful scratching of his head — "it could be the feller demanded the scalp from old Brose and threatened to shoot him. Old Brose goes for his gun, but the bustard shoots first —"

Quist dryly interrupted, "Didn't the coroner's jury more or less favor the theory that Brose killed himself while temporarily insane. Of course I know that —"

"By God, Greg! The more I think of it, the more I'm inclined to think Brose was murdered. I've been mulling it over in my mind. A man shooting himself, would naturally tend to aim at his head or heart — not his middle —"

"Exactly the way I figured, Smoky. You and I will yet make a team if we continue to agree this way. But we still don't know why anyone should want this scalp — murder for it — get killed for it. Got any more ideas?"

"Not a damn' one," Hayes said irritably. He looked again at the dead man. "You go through this *hombre*'s pockets, Greg?"

"Knowing the law, I haven't touched the body," Quist said. "Figured you'd get here fast."

"Well, I haven't much hope, but we'll see." Hayes stooped down, turned the body over. His hands went into pants' pockets.

Knife, dirty bandanna, some small change amounting to nearly two dollars. Then the sheriff started on the coat pockets. Cigarette papers, Durham, a gnawed plug of tobacco, in one pocket. The other revealed a second bandanna, in the same condition as the first, three blue poker chips and an ancient tintype showing a younger Talbert wearing a derby hat. The picture was scarred and scratched almost beyond recognition.

"Tonkawa had enough money to dress up once, anyway," Hayes grunted, as he replaced the articles. Next, thrusting his hand to the inner pocket of the coat he drew out various papers and cards: the cards were from saloons, gambling houses and fancy parlors; there was a folded bill announcing the coming of a circus three years before, on which someone had drawn in lead pencil an obscene sketch; there was an old receipt for the repair charges on a six-shooter, and something that looked like a folded check. Hayes unfolded the check, then swore suddenly.

Quist said quickly, "What is it?"

Before Hayes could reply, there came a knock at the door and Dr. Wakeman's voice. The sheriff started placing the papers and cards back in the coat pocket. Quist stepped to the door and admitted the doctor.

Wakeman set his bag on a chair and said "Howdy, Quist — Smoky." He scowled at the dead man on the floor. "And now this means still another inquest, blast it."

"Already know he's dead, without an examination, eh, doc?" Hayes said.

"Can tell that without an examination," Wakeman said shortly. "Anyway, the clerk told his messenger that Quist said he was dead. Quist's word was good with me. I figured there wasn't any hurry. Stopped off and roused Barry Lowe out of bed. Told him he could come down and get another dead man. Likely be here soon." He stooped near the body, asking questions. Quist told him what had happened. Wakeman said, "Hmmm! Two shots eh? So close together I thought at first there was just one. That's good shooting, Quist."

"Lucky shooting," Quist said laconically.

The doctor said suddenly. "This body been moved? The way some of this blood ran across the shirt —"

"Yeah, I moved it," Hayes cut in. "Turned Tonkawa over." He described how the corpse had been lying. "I wanted to see if there was anything in the pockets to tell us anything."

Wakeman snapped, "Smoky, I don't like my corpses moved."

Hayes said imperturbably, "I'm sheriff of Trastorno County, doc. I like to work my way too —"

"As coroner . . ." the doctor bridled, then halted, and got to his feet. "Nothing here for me to do. Inquest at nine tomorrow morning — no, it's this morning now. I forgot midnight had passed. Round up a jury for me, will you, Smoky?"

"I'll do that. But how about setting the inquest for this afternoon. I doubt Greg has had a decent sleep since he came here."

"Afternoon it is," Wakeman snapped. "Try to get some intelligent jurors. Not that I expect any trouble for Greg. Clear case of self-defense. But an inquest's necessary." He nodded to both men and left the room, without closing the door after him.

Men in the hall kept peering in. Quist was about to shut the door when Barry Lowe and another man arrived for the body, carrying a stretcher between them. They studied the corpse a moment. Lowe's assistant said, "Looks like that carpet got spoiled some," Lowe said. "Well, this is the way it goes — here today and gone tomorrow. Mr. Quist, you should be interested in seeing Tonkawa when I get him fixed up. You got a personal interest, I might say, and if you'll —"

"Will you, for God's sake," Quist snapped, "finish up and get out of this room?"

Lowe looked reproachfully at Quist, then motioned to his assistant to get busy with the stretcher. A few minutes later, Talbert was carried out. The undertakers had scarcely left when the clerk came bustling in, full of apologies: "So sorry, Mr. Quist, but we're full up. Not another room to give you." He displayed a section cut from an old piece of carpet, which he spread over the dark stain on the floor. "There! You won't have to look at it, anyway."

And in a moment he, too, had departed. Quist slammed the door, turned the key and then swung back to the sheriff. "What was it you took from Talbert's pocket, Smoky? It looked like a check."

"It was a check," Hayes nodded. "And I didn't put it back in Talbert's pocket. I figured this was something we might keep between us and not talk about it. If doc had seen it, or that blasted ghoul that calls himself an undertaker . . ."

He didn't finish but handed the slip of paper to Quist. Quist seized it and his mouth fell open at the written words. It was a check on the Cattlemen's Commercial Bank for one thousand dollars and drawn to the order of Tonkawa Talbert. It was signed by Harlan Stewart. Quist glanced again at the date, frowned at the sheriff, then swore disgustedly, "This business gets crazier and crazier, Smoky."

Hayes nodded. "It's got my brain riding in circles."

"But," Quist insisted, "how in the devil could Harlan Stewart write a check on the same day he was buried? This just doesn't make sense."

"I know," Hayes agreed. "It doesn't make sense, but there it is, Greg."

Quist drew a long breath, looked again at the check, then back to Hayes. "Sometimes," he said irritably, "I think old Brose Randle had the right idea. Smoky, why don't you and I get a boat and just go fishing? It'd be a lot easier on a man's mind."

CHAPTER XIII

Evidence

It was shortly after nine the following morning, when Quist emerged from the hotel dining room, after a breakfast of eggs, ham, biscuit and three cups of coffee. He stood frowning through the lobby window a minute. Men, wagons and horses passed on the street. Two women sailed past, marketing baskets in one hand, sun parasols in the other, long gingham dresses stirring the dust on the plank sidewalk. The day-clerk at the desk behind him said, "I understand you had a mite of trouble in your room last night, Mr. Quist."

Quist shook his head with some irritation. "You're wrong." And at the clerk's look of surprise, added, "It was early this morning."

Understanding broke on the clerk's face. "We're ordering a new carpet for your room, Mr. Quist."

"That's fine," Quist said. "Please don't put it down until after I've left. There's been so much activity up there so far, I'm beginning to think I took up residence in the middle of a round-up." Without waiting for the

185

clerk to reply, he mounted the steps to his room. Five minutes later he had descended again, empty satchel in hand, and moved out to the shadow of the hotel gallery. A few men sitting in chairs at the railing spoke to him. Quist nodded good-morning in a manner that spoke plainer than words that he was in no mood to talk of Tonkawa Talbert's shooting. He paused a moment at the top of the steps leading to the sidewalk, feeling the hot glare of sun that welled up from the dusty street.

His gaze strayed across Main where a horse and buggy had just emerged from the wide doorway of the Bluebonnet Livery Stable. Dyke Leigh was in the driver's seat, with a feminine companion beside him; Quist judged her to be Melinda Stewart. Behind the buggy came a horse with Stewart's daughter in the saddle. Walking beside her was Sheriff Hayes. The horse was halted a minute while the sheriff made some adjustments in Eirene Stewart's stirrup leathers. They had moved out to the center of the street when the sheriff spied Quist. He said something to his companions, and buggy and saddled horse stopped before the hotel. Quist moved down and rounded the hitchrack, doffing his sombrero as he answered the others' greetings. Hayes performed the introduction, and the next instant Quist felt Melinda's small warm hand in his own.

There was a certain magnetism in that hand he was thinking, even as she withdrew it. Her slim form, in its tightly-fitting suit with short jacket, was rounded in the right places. Quist had a glimpse of a small shined shoe, buttoned at the side. There was some sort of hat, but the veil was of sufficient transparency not to hide her large gray eyes with their unbelievably long lashes, and finely-chiseled nose and full lips. The hair beneath the hat was of a shining chestnut, containing a certain golden glint.

"It's a pleasure to know you, Mr. Quist," Melinda Stewart answered his appropriate words. Her voice held a husky sweetness that made Quist's heart beat a trifle faster. "Sheriff Hayes has already told us so much about you, that — that — well, I almost feel we're friends. I hope so, anyway."

"No more so than I, Mrs. Stewart," Quist replied gravely. "You have my sympathy, of course" — and mentally kicked himself at once, seeing tears well behind the long dark lashes.

For a moment, Melinda Stewart turned her head away, while Dyke Leigh shifted uncomfortably on the seat beside her. Then she regained her voice, low and husky, just reaching Quist's ears. "Mr. Hayes — Sheriff Hayes — has told me — well, it's good to know you plan to help us. I won't say more now, Mr. Quist, but in the next few days, sometime, I'd appreciate your calling, at the ranch. Right now, I'm not quite ready to talk to people. Oh, I'm foolish, I know, but it has been a blow and — and —"

Quist bowed quickly. "Of course, Mrs. Stewart. I understand."

She forced a wan smile. "It is agreed then, that we'll see you one of these days. Until then, Mr. Quist —" She left the words unfinished. Quist bowed again and stepped back from the buggy. The others prepared to start. Eirene Stewart gave Quist a short wave of one hand as they were leaving. "We'll be expecting you to come out to the Rafter-S, Mr. Quist," she seconded Melinda Stewart's invitation. Quist and the sheriff stood side by side at the hitchrack, watching them depart.

". . . and I'd intended to drive her home," Hayes was saying, "but with this inquest on Tonkawa Talbert coming up this afternoon, I thought I'd best stay in town. There's no doubt about you being cleared, but sometimes folks act ornery. You never know what a jury will do. One of 'em will get to feeling his own importance, sometimes. If that happens, it will make it easier for you if I'm here." Quist said thanks, and the sheriff went on, "Eirene's riding Dyke's horse. I told him to take his time coming back. He jumped at the chance, of course. He used to be pretty sweet on Eirene. Still is, for that matter. I don't know . . ." The sheriff's face clouded.

"What's bothering you?" Quist asked.

"Sometimes," the sheriff said slowly, "I feel like a skunk, cutting in there. Eirene and Dyke were school-day sweethearts. Then again, when my head's not in the clouds, I get to thinking of the difference in our ages — Eirene's and mine. Lord, Greg, I'll be pushing the fifties around in another fifteen years, and the older you get the faster those years pass. Then I think of Harl Stewart, and how much older he was than his wife. I'm not sure he was happy, after the first bloom wore off —"

"You can't blame him for marrying her, though," Quist put in. "She's a mighty handsome woman."

"I suppose." Hayes nodded. "There's a lot of men think so. I guess that bothered Harl, too, though he never let on much to me. He was always one to keep his own counsel. I'd not say this to anyone but you. Dyke was telling me that Rupe Chandler made some snide remarks yesterday. I aim to have a talk with that bustard. With what Dyke says you know about him, I shouldn't have any trouble persuading him to leave town."

"Don't be hasty, Smoky," Quist said meaningly. "I'd sooner have him here for a while, where we can lay hands on him."

"I reckon you're right." A couple of men passed and nodded to Quist and the sheriff. Smoky said, "Good-mawnin'," absent-mindedly, then continued, "Eirene tells me she had a talk with you last night."

"Yeah," Quist said. "Something she said got me thinking. Maybe you can help. Eirene said that it was about six months ago, after a trip her father had made to Tucson, to fetch his wife back from a visit, that he started drinking heavily. Do you have any idea what could have gone wrong about that time?"

Hayes frowned thoughtfully. "Now that you mention it, it was just about that time that Harl started acting odd and began licking up the booze. But damned if I can help you, Greg. I'd taken a leave of absence from office, to go up to Colorado — Cripple Creek. There's a mine up there I've got an interest in. I wasn't in town when Harl and his missus returned here. It could be some mining trouble over near Tucson that upset Harl. He had wide mining interests in Arizona."

"Do you happen to know if he's been pressed for money?"

"I don't think so. I've checked with our local bank. He was well fixed. Big balance on hand. No outstanding debts. No mortgages on his properties — that reminds me. That check I took from Tonkawa's pocket last night. It's not Harlan Stewart's signature — it's a forgery. I didn't have much recollection of his writing. Showed the check to Eirene and Mrs. Stewart this morning. They both stated immediately the writing doesn't resemble Harl's at all. To be sure, I showed the check to Banker Tillman. He agrees — said if Tonkawa had ever presented the check for payment at his bank, he'd have immediately sent for me to arrest him."

"How do you figure it?" Quist asked, scowling.

"Dammit, I don't! All I can think of is that somebody who didn't know Harl was already dead, did that forgery."

"But who could that be?"

"Whoever the man is who wants that blasted scalp so bad," Hayes growled. "Looks like he offered Tonkawa a thousand bucks to steal it." He paused, then, "I wonder could it be somebody in Tucson, or from there? I'll check with the hotel and see if anybody came here from Arizona."

"Might be an idea," Quist agreed. "I believe in checking on everything; then eliminate the impossible. Sometimes, it works."

"It's a good method." Hayes gestured toward the satchel in Quist's hand. "You figuring on going some place?"

Quist shook his head. "That night it was pried open, the lock got out of whack. I noticed there was a locksmith here. Figured to get it repaired."

"Old Wolcott can do it. Good man on locks — and guns too. Is it getting near your drink-time, Greg?"

"Mite too early for me. And that reminds me of something, Smoky. Will you for cripes' sake call off your barkeeps, and make it clear I'm capable of paying for my own drinks? Everyone of 'em insists on charging my liquor to you, wherever I go."

Hayes chuckled. "Hell, I owe it to you, Greg."

"I don't want it. They'll get to thinking I'm a poor relation or something. That can't go on. Either you call off that idea, or in self-respect I'll have to quit drinking altogether."

An expression of mock alarm crossed the

sheriff's features. "Lord, you sound drastic, Greg. Now, don't do anything hasty. All right" — face relaxing in a grin — "I'll call 'em off."

The two men parted. Quist strolled east on Main, then crossed over at Brazos Street. Three doors past the sheriff's office, a faded blue sign over the doorway of a hole-in-the-wall establishment, carried the words: EZRA WOLCOTT — Gunsmith — Locks and Guns Repaired.

Quist entered. Wolcott was elderly, with tangled, iron-gray locks and bushy eyebrows. He wore a heavy mustache that drooped below his lower lip, and rimless spectacles. A long, oil-smudged apron hung below his tieless collar, and there was a smear of gunpowder grime on one cheek. He lowered the stockless barrel of a rifle through which he'd been squinting, when Quist opened the door, sized up his visitor, then said cordially, "Bet yo're Gregory Quist."

"You win your bet." Quist smiled. The two men shook hands.

"Heerd about you. Reckon there ain't nobody in town whut ain't. What can I do for you, Mr. Quist?"

Quist showed him the damaged lock on the satchel. "Needs a mite of repairs."

Wolcott examined the lock. "Sho', ain't

nothin' to that. Fix 'er up jim-dandy. You in a hurry for it?"

Quist shook his head. "I expect to be here a couple of days yet, anyway."

"That's plenty time. You just drop in, tomorrow or next day." Wolcott looked disappointed. "Was sorta hopin' you'd have some gun repairs fer me. I'd admire to boast I done work for the great detective —"

Quist smiled wryly. "You can forget that 'great,' Mr. Wolcott. Like to fix guns, do you?"

"Ain't no business more pleasurable. I gets work sent me from all over. Look at this." He handed Quist a six-shooter.

Quist examined the gun. "Cock-eyed hammer, eh?" The prong of the hammer slanted off to the left at an angle. "Right-hand gun-slipper's weapon, eh?"

"You know your business, Mr. Quist. Personally, I don't see this slippin' and fannin' and such. All's a feller needs is the sure judgment to cock his gun and pull trigger. 'Tain't how fast a man can shoot, sez I, but how accurate. Now that there weepon — feller come ridin' clear through from Phoenix to bring me his business. I'd been recommended t'him. Ridin' on up to some place in Oklahoma. Left his weapon here yesterday. Says he'll be comin' back in 'bout a month. Pick it up then. Name o' Hawkins. Wants his action loosened up. I'm the man can do it. Like I say, I gets work from all over. Fixed a gun fer one of the Earps once. 'Nother time Dallas Stoudenmire gave me some business —"

Quist's eyes were wandering around while the oldster rambled on. The place was a boar's-nest, no doubt of it, with equipment, guns and locks scattered helter-skelter about. There was an oil-soaked, scarred work-bench, with a couple of vises bolted to it. A rack of second-hand six-shooters bore a penciled notice: For Sale Cheep. There were shotguns and rifles, muzzle-loaders and breech-loaders, ancient cap-and-ball pistols and modern six-shooters, assembled and in parts. Chunks of fine-grained wood for stocks were stacked in one corner. A table, rickety, and with one short leg braced with a piece of rock, held work awaiting repairs: more guns and locks. Now, still talking, Wolcott tossed Quist's satchel on top of the damaged equipment. The satchel in its flight knocked a six-shooter from the table.

Quist stooped to retrieve the gun, and saw that the wooden butt had been entirely re-moved. There was only the steel frame for a handle. Quist said, "It appears you're due to whittle out a new butt. Looks like a pretty good gun, Mr. Wolcott. Should make a nice hawg-leg when you get it fixed."

"When I git 'round to it." Wolcott nodded. "That idjit, Joker Gaillard brung it in. You'll never guess whut he wanted?"

"Probably not," Quist said evenly. "When was this?"

"Uhmmm . . . lemme see . . ." Wolcott considered, then, "Evenin' before last. Jest before my closin' time. You know whut he wanted?"

"I'm curious," Quist admitted.

"Said he'd found this gun, with the butt missin', on his way to town. Wanted I should fix it up with a rubber bulb for a butt, stick a tube through the barrel, so's he could squirt water at folks. Nacherly, I refused to take on any sech nonsense, as he should've dang well knowed. Why people puts up with his tomfoolery, I'll never savvy. Tried muh best to show the idjit I could put a brand-new butt on the gun, and he'd have an extra weapon. No good. Wouldn't lissen to me a-tall. Said it would take too long. We *habled* some and then he asks what I'll give him in a trade on another forty-five. Got a couple of bran'-new weapons here, but he 'lowed they'd be too expensive. Wanted a used gun, he insisted. Finally we made a dicker for a hawg-laig what was in prime condition. I

196

didn't get much best of the deal. Joker knows his firearms all right."

"What sort of gun was he toting in his holster when he came in"

"Never noticed," Wolcott replied. "Likely his reg'lar forty-five with the two notches cut into it. Like I say, it was gettin' dark and I only had the one lamp burnin' — fixin' t'close up when he come in. Now he'll like's not start totin' two hawg-laigs like some gun-fighter."

Quist shrugged. "Could be he just wanted a spare." He looked at the buttless gun. "How much you want for this six-shooter?

"You want it?" the oldster asked eagerly. "Mr. Quist, for fifteen dollars I can put you on thet gun the finest butt —"

"No, just as it stands. Maybe later I'll bring it in and get a butt put on."

Wolcott considered. "Twelve dollars too much?"

Quist thrust the weapon in the waistband of his trousers. "You've got yourself a deal, Mr. Wolcott." He counted out twelve dollars and a few minutes later strode out of the shop in the direction of the sheriff's office.

Hayes was standing slouched moodily against one of the uprights that supported his porch roof. He glanced up, saw Quist approaching. "All right, Greg," he smiled,

"You can get that bright light out of your eye. I couldn't learn a thing. Asked the clerk at your hotel, inquired at the Drovers' Rest Hotel, and even snooped around at the Mex flophouse, out at the west end of town. Not a one of those places has had a guest from any part of Arizona for nearly two weeks."

"Maybe he didn't stay at a hotel," Quist said. "A rider from Phoenix passed through here yesterday. Name's Hawkins. Left a gun with Ezra Wolcott to be fixed up. Says he'll be back in about a month. Now —"

"Hmmm! Hawkins, eh?" Hayes frowned. "I'm afraid you're still on the wrong track, Greg. I don't know the man personally, but Hawkins is a deputy-marshal up to Phoenix. So, once more, you can get that light out of your eye."

Quist smiled. "Not yet, Smoky. Got that chunk of gunbutt that Jason Randle found up on the hilltop."

Hayes studied Quist's face, then nodded. "Yeah, it's inside. I'll get it."

Quist followed him into the office. The sheriff produced the splintered chunk of walnut. Quist took it, drew the buttless six-shooter from his waistband, and fitted the two together. Hayes swore excitedly. "Greg! Where'd you get it?" Quist told him in terse words. Hayes said, "I'll be damned! Then it was Joker Gaillard on that hilltop — Joker Gaillard who shot at you. Do you suppose he had a hand in Brose Randle's death — wait!" His face fell. "I don't know, Greg. Maybe we're going off half cocked. These butts are standard equipment and will fit all six-shooters of this model. Lots of men just send to the company for a complete walnut butt —"

"Sure, I know that, Smoky. I also know that to have definite proof, we'd have to find the rest of the walnut chunk and fit the two chunks and the gun together. Not to mention the screws that Joker likely tossed away, with the rest of the butt. But can you honestly say we haven't got some definite evidence? Don't you feel it in your own mind?"

Reluctantly, Hayes shook his head in the negative. "I sure wish I could go along with you, Greg. But you forget we examined Joker's gun. He still had the gun with the two notches."

"That was the gun he got from Wolcott. I told you he insisted on a used gun —"

"But, the notches —" Hayes persisted doggedly.

"Had been fresh cut, if you'd noticed closely," Quist pointed out. "The edges of the notches were sharp, not worn from handling. Hell, I could still smell the oil and grease Gaillard had rubbed into those notches to take off the new look. But the color of those notches weren't the same as the rest of the butt."

"You sure?"

"Absolutely."

Hayes drew a long sigh, cursed his own stupidity, then turned admiring eyes on Quist. "Cripes A'mighty," he said. "You don't miss much, do you?"

"I miss a hell of a lot sometimes, Smoky. You forget I've had more training in this sort of thing than you have. Don't praise me too much. Maybe I'm just lucky in noticing things —" He broke off. "Where you going?"

Hayes was halfway through the door. "Gaillard's in town. I'm going to put him under arrest —"

Quist caught the sheriff's sleeve. "Let's not, Smoky," he suggested. "Let the bustard run loose a spell yet. Maybe he'll make another careless step. We still don't know what his connection is with Brose Randle. Or that scalp. If any."

Hayes turned slowly back into the office. "You're right, Greg. We've just got to wait a spell. Meanwhile, I reckon I can grab Gaillard most any time, if needed. But there's one thing that won't wait. I want to buy a drink for the man who's giving me the sort of help I want on this job."

Quist chuckled. "Now that you mention it, Smoky, it is just about first beer time. But get one thing straight. *I'm* doing the buying."

CHAPTER XIV

The Red Mustang

During dinner, at the hotel, Hayes discussed with Quist the advisability of entering, as evidence in the Tonkawa Talbert inquest, the finding of the thousand dollar check on the dead man's body. "I had aimed to withhold it," Hayes was saying, "but so long as Banker Tillman knows about it — and knows it's a forgery, I think I'll admit to taking it from Talbert's coat pocket."

Quist nodded. "Might as well. Perhaps if the news gets nosed around, somebody might come up with something. Certainly, you and I are stopped on the proposition — we don't know who forged Stewart's name."

"I'm glad you agree, Greg. I hate like hell to hold out any sort of evidence."

The inquest, an hour later, produced no fresh evidence. Talbert's bad reputation in Corinth City brought him little sympathy, and his action in entering Quist's room was credited to further proof of the man's thieving tendencies. The jury suggested that the sheriff endeavor to learn who had forged Stewart's name to the check. It was at first suggested that Talbert himself had done it, until it was brought out the man could neither read nor write. As to the verdict, Quist was completely exonerated from blame; it was considered he had acted in self-defense, and the sheriff was directed to take no action in the case. Quist shook hands with the jurors as custom demanded, then hastened to leave the courthouse.

Half an hour later when he entered the Shamrock Bar the place was empty, except for Shamus Maguire who was polishing glasses. The interior was cool and dim after the hot sunglare of the street. Maguire gave him a welcoming smile. "Sur-r-re, 'tis good to see you, Mister-r Quist. It's a touch of the Bur-rke's you'd be after, I'm thinkin'. It's the foine, discriminatin' taste, you have. Ther-r-re's none like it in the town —"

"And that's what you Irish call blarney." Quist smiled. "And me with a taste for Scotch."

"It's a proposition I'll make you" — Maguire shoved his face earnestly across the bar — "and one no smart man would be givin' the refusal to. You be takin' of the Irish whisky now, and I'll give you the big glass of Scotch for a chaser."

"God forbid!" Quist laughed. "I just want a drink — not something to put me to sleep —" He paused, as a fresh thought entered his mind. "Irish with a Scotch chaser. Any barkeep that would sell a combination like that, would never need knockout drops."

Maguire stiffened. "You'll be findin' none of the knockout drops in my place, Mister-r Quist," he stated with dignity, and no little belligerence. "I'll be havin' you know that —"

"Take it easy, Shamus," Quist cut in. "I'm not accusing you, or anybody else, of using knockout drops. Hell's-bells! I know you better than that."

"I'm thankin' you for the compliment, Mr. Quist," Maguire said mollified. "At the same time, I'm not denyin' ther-r-re's a spalpeen in this town would not be beyond makin' use of the drops, given the pr-r-roper occasion."

"And who would that be?" Quist inquired.

Maguire shook his head. " 'Tis not Shamus Maguire's place to be belittlin' of his competition, so I'll name no names, Mister-r Quist, and we'll be droppin' of the subject to once. Wild stallions could not be draggin' of the name out of me. I'll say no more on the matter-r-r. So, 'tis finished it is, but Mister-r Quist, should you ever be findin' occasion to be buyin' of the dr-r-rink in another place, you'd do well not to be enterin' of the Red Mustang. And so it's the Irish you'll be takin', to cool the dryness of your gullet?"

"I came in for a beer, Shamus, but you've worn me down. Make it Burke's. And on condition you'll have one on me. I'm buying the drinks now, in case Smoky Hayes hasn't told you yet."

"Somethin' has been said on the matter-r-r," Maguire acknowledged, setting out the flat green bottle and two glasses. Quist poured a modest drink and passed the bottle to Maguire. Maguire lifted his glass. *"Slàinte!"* he toasted, and put back his head.

Quist wiped his lips, replaced his glass on the bar. "What's this 'slawn-gee' word you're always pushing at me, Shamus?"

"Slàinte?" Maguire explained, "It's wishin' you the good health, I am. You'd not be havin' of the Gaelic, now, I suppose?"

"Oh, a sort of toast, eh? And in Gaelic. I see. No, I don't speak anything but English and Mex."

" 'Tis a blessin' a man's not needin' of the Gaelic to have the fine appreciation for Irish *uisge* — whisky."

"Better still," Quist chuckled, "that you can get so much appreciation out of just one drink." He placed some silver on the bar and refused another drink on the house. "Not right now." Drawing out tobacco and papers, he rolled and lighted a cigarette. "Shamus, exactly what happened here, the day Harlan Stewart was shot? Oh, sure, I know it was night when he was shot, but I mean when he came here, drunk, and you had to send for Smoky Hayes —"

"Sure and I was after-r tellin' all I was knowin' at the inquest, Mister-r Quist."

"Yeah, I heard that. But sometimes a man will remember things in a second telling, that he missed the first time. You don't mind?"

"I'm not mindin' at all, at all, but I can see no use to it. Like I told it to the coroner and his jur-r-ry, I spied the poor man come staggerin' from out the Red Mustang." Maguire paused and frowned, then, " 'Twas the wor-r-rst shape ever I saw him in. Weavin' and stumblin', he was, like a beast with the blind staggers, 'til he was like to go down and get run over-r in the dust of the str-r-reet. When he came here, I refused him the drink and got a chair under him. It's glassy his eyes was, and with no focus to them. . . ." The story continued, parallel with the one told at the inquest. Maguire related how he had sent for the sheriff, and of the hot coffee and sandwiches they had endeavored to get him to swallow, and the man's inability to hold down the food, and his jumbled speech.

"You couldn't make out what he was saying, eh?" Quist asked.

" 'Twas nothing but gibberish," Maguire stated. "At the sheriff's request Mr. Stewart's hor-r-rse was brought to the hitchrack. With some trouble we managed of his gettin' to the back of the beast. It could be the coffee he swallowed had done him some good. He asked for a drink. Rather than r-risk more trouble, Smoky told me to get one. I returned to the bar. On the way out again, I spied Mr. Stewart's coat where he'd left it on a table. I picked it up, returned to the hor-r-rse, tossed the garment over the saddlehorn, and gave him the dr-r-rink, which this time he was after-r-r holdin' on his stomach —"

"Burke's Irish, I suppose," Quist said gravely.

"That it was not," Maguire said promptly. "Mister-r Stewart was in no condition to be appreciatin' of the Irish. I had fetched him his usual — the *Old Crow* bourbon — and within a few minutes of his drinkin' that, he and the sher-r-riff got started. So there you have the story, Mister-r Quist, complete as I know it. You'll be now givin' me the solution to the nasty business, I suppose."

Quist sighed. "I'm afraid not, Shamus." The two men talked a time longer, then Quist took his departure. Two customers entered as he was leaving. They spoke to him, and Quist nodded and brushed on past. Outside, in the sunlight, he stood on the sidewalk a moment, thinking. Of only one thing was he certain: he wanted action of some sort, something he could get his teeth into. His brain had whirled madly on various problems connected with the killing of Stewart and Brose Randle, a sort of merry-go-round brain that never stopped running, but spun faster and faster without getting any place. He glanced across the street, his gaze traveling diagonally toward the Red Mustang Saloon. The muscles about his mouth tightened. Impulsively, he crossed the street and pushed through the swinging doors of the entrance.

There was a vast difference between the Red Mustang and Maguire's saloon, the former having the appearance of not having been swept for days, and its 'dobe walls stood badly in need of fresh whitewash. There were cheaply framed pictures, torn from a popular pink-paged periodical of that day, depicting prize fighters, cyclists on high wheels, burlesque actresses and race horses. The short scarred bar ran across the rear of the room, and the mirror behind it was fly-specked. The labels on the bottles arrayed on the back bar were soiled; Quist suspected that Punch Ostrom — proprietor of the place — refilled them all from the same barrel of rotgut. But Ostrom was known to be generous with free drinks, and thus managed to do as much business as any of his competitors.

Witt Auringer was standing at the bar, with half a dozen cowhands also grouped there. Quist, his eyes becoming accustomed to the dim light, after the sunglare of the street, recognized them all as Auringer's D-Bar-A hands. He nodded shortly to them as he approached the bar, spurs clanking on the plank flooring. Auringer returned the greeting, but there was no friendliness in it. Quist took up a position at one end, away from the others. Ostrom, a beetle-browed, unshaven man with a paunch, took his time before approaching Quist, gave him a brief nod and said, "What'll it be, Quist?"

"Bottle of beer, Ostrom. And not too cold."

Quist sipped the beer distastefully after placing a silver dollar on the bar. It tasted like something that had been buried for centuries in a glacier. Ostrom made no move to pick up the money. Auringer said after a minute, with a short laugh, "Am I still under suspicion, Quist?"

Quist stated coldly, "Anybody in this town's under suspicion, until I learn different."

The others stopped talking now. Auringer's face darkened. "Are you crazy," he demanded, "or just trying to give Gaillard a race as town joker? Hell, you ain't got anything on me."

Quist said in a skeptical voice, "I hope you're able to prove that when the showdown comes, Auringer. You and Gaillard both. I'm surprised he's not here with you. Must be he's out buying a cap-and-bells."

Auringer frowned. "What in hell would the Joker do with bells?"

"Let's forget it," Quist sighed. "I made the mistake of overestimating your intelligence." He spoke to Ostrom, "Let me try another beer. This one's too cold."

Ostrom scowled. "Mostly folks like cold beer —"

"Maybe I'm not 'folks' then. I don't," Quist snapped. "Just put out another bottle." Sullenly, Ostrom stooped beneath his bar and produced a second bottle, slid it across the bar to Quist. Quist felt it, frowned. "Look here, I didn't ask you for lukewarm beer. What else you got down there?" A third bottle was set out. Quist shook his head. "That's been on ice too long, too."

Ostrom's features reddened. "I can't be putting out bottles —"

"You'll keep putting 'em out as long as I say," Quist snapped. "I'm paying for 'em —" He broke off, then, "Hell, I'll come around there and pick out what I want." Without giving Ostrom time to refuse, Quist left his position and rounded the end of the bar, ignoring the proprietor's ugly look. He ignored as well the sarcastic comments of Auringer and his followers.

Beer stood in cases beneath the bar; more bottles lay packed in a box of ice, which dripped water at one corner, making sloppy puddles beneath the long duckboard on the floor. Greasy wet rags hung on hooks. Quist's gaze ranged swiftly along the underside of the bar and came to rest on a small shelf, which held a set of brass knuckles, a six-shooter and a small bottle. As he reached for the bottle, Punch Ostrom ripped out an oath and moved to forestall the action. Quist seized the bottle with one hand, then straightened his other arm, fingers spreading widely across Ostrom's face. Then he shoved — hard!

Ostrom's feet made galloping sounds as

he went hurtling back and back, the length of the bar, endeavoring vainly to regain his balance. His right hand grasped at the back bar, jerking it loose on his way. Then bottles, glasses and Ostrom landed with a heavy thud on the floor, accompanied by the tinkling of shattered fragments. There was an instant's silence, then excited exclamations of protest rose on the other side of the bar.

Auringer snarled, "Just like all these lawmen. Give 'em a mite of authority and they start pushing decent folks around."

Quist laughed shortly. "Good thing for you, Auringer, you're not decent." His eyes went back to the label on the bottle he held in his hand. It bore the name of an out-of-town druggist and written in ink, the words: Hydrate of Chloral.

Glass crunched beneath Ostrom's feet as he heaved up from the floor, panting heavily. His face was white, such spaces as weren't streaked with trickling liquor. There was a bruise on one cheekbone and a thin line of crimson ran from one nostril. He stood swaying, one hand supported by the bar, his small eyes showing fright.

". . . and I don't intend," Auringer was saying hotly, "to take any abuse from you, Quist —"

Quist snapped, "You'll take anything I

hand you, Auringer," and added, "That goes for your crew too. Now keep still, I've got business with Ostrom." He turned to the bartender. "How about it? You want me to make this bottle public, or shall we talk it over in private —"

"What's in the bottle?" Auringer wanted to know.

"Sugar water for mewling infants," Quist sneered. "Want some?" Auringer fell silent. Quist swung back to Ostrom. "Make up your mind. Do we talk it up here, or do you want to make it private?"

Ostrom nodded and turned heavily to the men along the bar. "I'm closing up for the day," he said sullenly. "Got to make repairs —"

"Look here, Punch," Auringer started a protest, "you don't have to take orders from this railroad dick. We'll back you up —" The punchers were voicing similar angry words.

"Could be this bottle is a remedy for deafness too," Quist said hard-voiced. "You men heard Ostrom. Now get out!"

"You ain't no authority to —" Auringer commenced.

Quist eyed the man sternly. "You want to see my authority — hear it explode — feel it? It carries weight, Auringer. You wouldn't like it. It hurts like hell too."

Auringer wavered, his eyes shifted uneasily. Then he turned away. "Come on, boys." Speechless, the other men trooped after him. Just as he was departing, Auringer turned, "You think you're pretty damn' smart, Quist. If you ask me, you got another think coming. There's more than me had trouble with Harl Stewart — your own friends fr'instance, Dyke Leigh and Smoky Hayes. Why don't you question them, make them tell what they know? Hell, I saw Stewart really laying the law down to that deputy, six-seven months back, and Dyke wa'n't giving him no back lip, either. Then, later a mite, Hayes and Stewart had a row in the sheriff's office. Has Smoky told you about that? I could hear 'em rowin' when I went past —"

"You're all through?" Quist interrupted icily.

"Hell! Is there anything else to be said?"

"Yeah. Get out of here. *Pronto!*"

Auringer cursed and followed by his hands left the Red Mustang. Quist turned back to the glowering Ostrom. "See how it is, Punch," he said pleasantly. "Get a man mad enough and he starts shooting off his mouth."

Ostrom said whiningly, "Sure, I see, Mr. Quist. Now about them drops. You'll ruin my business, if the boys hears about 'em. Ain't never used 'em, 'cept when some stranger comes in and gets proddy. Anybody knows me, knows I wouldn't —"

"One man in town knew you well enough to know some *hombres* got knocked-out here, from time to time, and rolled for their dough. Don't lie to me, Ostrom. All right, now you're going to talk. The day Harl Stewart was killed, he was in right bad shape when he left here. You gave him a dose of these knockout drops —"

"Gawd, I swear I didn't —"

"Don't lie, I said. I know what I'm talking about." Quist took two quick stops, seized the front of Ostrom's shirt and twisted it, shaking the man. "One more lie and it'll be your neck I'm twisting. Come on now, I want truth."

"Jeez, Quist. The shape he was in from drink, drops wa'n't needed to tip him over — all right, all right" — as Quist tightened his grip — "I'll tell all that happened. But don't blame me. It was Joker Gaillard brought those drops here in the first place. I ain't never used 'em —"

"What about Gaillard?"

"You know how he is," Ostrom whined, "always playing jokes on people. Joker was in here that day, when Stewart came in, already soused to the gills; couldn't hardly hold himself straight at the bar. There wa'n't anybody else in here at the moment. Joker slips around the bar and serves Stewart himself. Stewart never noticed the difference. He drunk up what Joker served him, then goes and sits in a chair. Joker was laughing fit to kill, when he sees Stewart goin' to sleep, sittin' up. I got worried for fear somethin' would happen, so I roused up Stewart and got him started on his way. But them drops couldn't hurt him much. Hell, Joker didn't even give him a full dose —"

"You bustard," Quist said wrathfully, as he released the man, "you unmitigated, lousy —"

Not trusting himself to speak further, he turned and passing around the end of the bar, made for the street, swearing bitterly under his breath.

CHAPTER XV

Jailbird

It was shortly after six o clock that Smoky
Hayes found Quist in the hotel dining room,
eating supper. The place was fairly full; two
waitresses continually negotiated the swinging doors between kitchen and the larger
room. Knives and forks, dishes, clattered.
There was the buzz of conversation. Hayes,
looking slightly concerned, slid into a seat at
Quist's table. Quist offered to buy him a
dinner. The sheriff refused with thanks, saying he had just finished eating at the Chi-
naman's place, near his office. Quist called
to the waitress to bring an extra cup of coffee,
which Hayes accepted.

Quist said, "What's on your mind,
Smoky?"

The sheriff smiled rather ruefully. "You
sure have your mind set on beer being a
certain temperature, don't you?"

"That happens to be a weakness of mine,"
Quist smiled. "Sometimes I'm apt to forget
myself."

Hayes snorted. "My God! Forget yourself!
There's an understatement, if I ever heard

one. Didn't I tell you the Shamrock Bar was the place to go? Did you have to wreck the Red Mustang — ?"

"Maybe it looks that way," Quist said mildly. "Sometimes it's necessary to get rough when you want information out of a man. What's up, did Punch Ostrom make some sort of complaint to you —"

"Not Ostrom, no." Hayes shook his head. "Witt Auringer did though. Auringer is threatening to write the governor. Trouble is, Auringer's word carries some weight in that direction —"

"And there's an election coming up next year," Quist said dryly. In the light from the lamp suspended above, he saw the sheriff wince.

Hayes flushed. "Don't get me wrong, Greg. Anything Auringer says in that direction won't bother me. I'm not sure I'll run next election, even. Dyke's a good man. I'd like to see him get the job. If Eirene and I get married, I'd like to get out of political office, concentrate on my mining interests, or go into stock raising. But Auringer was pretty mad, and I wanted to hear your side of it so I could shut him up."

"What did Auringer tell you?"

"Said he and his hands were in the Red Mustang, drinking peacefully, when you came in. When you couldn't get beer of the right temperature, you walked around the bar and beat up Punch Ostrom, then give Auringer and his men the bum's rush out of the place, claiming you had to have a private talk with Ostrom."

Quist shrugged. "Auringer is partly right. But if he didn't like it, he could have stayed and made his fight. I gave him enough excuse. He had his men with him. What more did he want?"

"Huh!" Hayes snorted. "Auringer didn't want to mix things with you, Greg. That's a cinch. He acted like you've got him scared. I told him I'd look into it, and to go slow with making complaints at the capitol. Then I drifted over to have a talk with Ostrom. The place was locked, but Ostrom let me in. Jeepers! That back bar was a wreck — and Ostrom looked like he'd been in the middle of it. I tried to get out of him what happened, but he just said he had no complaint to make against you — that you two had just had a little misunderstanding and the back bar had fallen down on him. Says if nobody objects he's going to redecorate and open up in a couple of days. Says if I saw you to say he'd try to have the beer just cool enough the next time you came in."

"Apparently." Quist chuckled. "Ostrom

don't hold hard feelings about the 'misunderstanding' — in the hope that I'll say nothing to you." He drained his coffee cup and rolled and lighted a brown-paper cigarette. Next he drew out the small bottle and set it on the table before the sheriff. "Apparently no one has mentioned this," he finished quietly.

Hayes examined the bottle. "What's this?" he frowned.

"Knockout drops. The bottle stood on a convenient shelf beneath Ostrom's bar. Either Ostrom or Gaillard — Ostrom claims it was the Joker — put some drops in Harl Stewart's drink, the last time he was in the Red Mustang. You know what happened later."

Understanding slowly dawned on Hayes' face. "That accounts for it, by God. I thought Harl acted far worse than I'd ever seen him. He'd never been that bad before." Anger contorted the sheriff's features. "By the living shades of Jehovah! I'm going to shut up the Red Mustang and run Ostrom out of town — after he's served a jail sentence. That dirty, lousy, gall-sored, flea-bitten — of all the slimy tricks to pull —"

Quist interrupted. "You keep that bottle for evidence, Smoky. And let Ostrom ride for the present. When this murder business clears up, we may need Ostrom for a witness. He'll talk more willingly, if we just let things ride. Later you can act against him as you see fit."

The sheriff cooled down. "I guess you're right, Greg. You seem to have a habit of looking farther ahead than I do." He paused, "But how did Auringer come into the trouble?"

Quist related the happenings at the Red Mustang exactly as they had taken place. Hayes nodded, "Now I've got something to go on. The next time that hot-headed Auringer says anything to me about me being a servant of the people, I'll tell him just where he stands. And in no uncertain words. He gets right arrogant at times."

Quist nodded. "Now you explain something to me, Smoky. Just before Auringer left the Red Mustang he dropped a nasty hint about investigating my own friends. He suggested I question you about a hot argument you had with Harl Stewart, five or six months back."

"Me? I had a scrap with Stewart? Auringer said that?" The sheriff looked aghast. "Why, that's the craziest thing — hell, Greg, Harl was the closest friend I had —"

"Auringer said the argument took place in your office."

"He's a liar! A double-dyed liar! I never —" Hayes stopped suddenly, then, "Wait — wait! Yeah, I know what he means." A rueful smile crossed Hayes' face. "Auringer's right, in a way, I guess. And the bustard was snooping on us, eh? He's right, though. Harl and I did have a mite of argument, one day. Cripes! I'd just about forgot it. It was right after he'd come back from Tucson with his wife and when he was damn' touchy and irritable. I'd been up to Cripple Creek. I've got an interest in a mine up there. About a year previous I'd persuaded Harl to put some money in it, along with mine. Harl expected some quick profits. So had I for that matter. Well, what I learned when I was up in Colorado didn't look so good. The silver was there all right, and it will still pay off to Harl's estate, but at that time more money was needed for machinery. When I told Harl that, he sort of hit the ceiling for a few minutes. Right after though, he cooled down and realized how things were. I'll be damned! I'd forgotten that. Leave it to Auringer —" He broke off, sobering. "Greg! I'll bet I've been under suspicion too."

Quist smiled. "Everybody's under suspicion in my book, Smoky, until proved innocent. I'm glad you cleared things up for me."

Hayes swallowed hard. "Jeepers! I was beginning to feel scared there for a minute."

Shortly afterward the two men rose. On the street, Hayes said, "I'm going to drift down and see Ostrom. Tell him I know what's been doing in his place, but that we've decided to give him another chance to run decently. As to Gaillard — well, he'll get his comeuppance too, when the time comes right. Want to come with me, Greg?"

"I've seen all I can stand of Punch Ostrom for a spell," Quist stated. "He should be smashed flatter'n a bedbug, but I haven't got the nerve to wipe out that sort of skunk. He's out of my class. Besides, I want to go down to the depot. I'm looking for a telegram to come up, maybe."

"Right. See you later." The sheriff nodded.

At the depot, Quist found a telegram awaiting him, but the Oklahoma operative had had no success digging up the information Quist wanted, and asked for more explicit instructions. Quist swore under his breath and left the depot to tear the telegram into small bits. "More information you'll get when I have it to give," he grunted shortly.

He strolled around town for a spell, dropped into the Shamrock Bar and then out again, after a couple of drinks. "Now why in the devil," he pondered, "should it be necessary to give a man knockout drops, if he's to be shot later?"

He turned his steps toward the sheriff's office. The sheriff wasn't in, and Deputy Leigh was just leaving. "He should be along in a few minutes," Dyke said. "Go on in and wait. I'm heading out to eat now. Got a late start tonight."

"I've been wanting to see you, anyway, Dyke" — Quist had caught at the deputy's sleeve, just outside the doorway — "I won't detain you but a minute. Now you say that you've told me everything you know about anyone who'd ever had trouble with Harl Stewart."

"That's right," Leigh replied promptly.

"You failed to tell me, though, that you'd had quite an argument with Stewart, back about six months ago."

The deputy stiffened. In the light of the lamp from the sheriff's window, Quist could see Leigh's facial muscles go rigid. When he spoke, the words came with an effort, "Don't know where you ever got that idea, Greg —"

Quist said softly, "I never figured you as a liar, Dyke."

Angrily, Leigh flung off Quist's restraining hand. "Right, have it your way, Quist. No, I won't lie about it. I'll just tell you, it's none of your damn' business what we argued about."

"Murder's in my line of business," Quist said pointedly.

"That has nothing to do with Stewart's killing."

"*You* think. Or, say," Quist said caustically. "I hope you don't think I'm fool enough to believe you."

"All right, if you got to know," the deputy said hotly, "Stewart was missing some cows. He wanted that I should come out and ride herd on his range, and I told him I couldn't spare the time —"

Quist interrupted, "Buffalo chips! Do you think I'm fool enough to swallow that. Better tell me what you know, Dyke."

"I've already told you," Leigh half snarled. "If you don't believe me, that's just too damn' bad. Now, Quist, you go ahead. Prove that I'm wrong." He jerked around, stepped down from the porch and strode angrily away.

Quist gazed after the retreating figure. "Well," he mused, "he sure had something get under his skin, one time or another. That boy will stand some more questioning after he cools down." He turned back into the sheriff's office, found a chair and a week-old newspaper and sat down to wait. Maybe Smoky would have some idea regarding Leigh's trouble with Harl Stewart.

A half hour passed. Now and then a rider loped along Main Street, or pedestrians clumped on high-heeled boots along the sidewalk. Saddle-leather creaked at the hitchrack. A moment later there came a step on the sheriff's porch. Jason Randle entered the office. "Know where Smoky is?" he asked through swollen lips.

"I'm expecting him along any minute," Quist replied. With one booted foot he shoved a chair toward Randle, and eyed the man curiously. Randle looked as though he'd been rolling in the dust. His lower lip was cut. The right eye was nearly closed. The left cheekbone was split and caked with dried blood. "What happened to you, Randle?"

Randle jumped to his feet and began pacing back and forth. Three steps, then two across, then three back and two across again. His hands worked nervously. Suddenly he exploded, "That goddamned Chandler!"

"What about Rupe Chandler?" Quist asked quietly.

"That low-life son of a bustard," Randle grated bitterly. "S'help me, I'll put a slug of lead through his guts. Next time —"

"Quit that pacing back and forth, settle down, tell me what happened," Quist prompted.

Randle halted momentarily. "After supper, I saddled up and started to ride in to see if Smoky had seen any sign of my dad's scalp — you didn't, did you?" Quist shook his head. Randle started pacing again. "I'd rode out of the ranchyard and was just turning into the road when I spied Chandler standing under that big oak that marks the turnoff. He'd dismounted and was standing back, so he wouldn't be seen. Damned if the bustard wasn't togged out fit to kill."

"And you got a hunch to kill him?"

Randle ceased his walking momentarily. "No, I just pulled to a halt, and asked what he was doing, or if he'd lost something there. He don't answer at once, just mumbled something I couldn't hear. So I climbed down from my pony to come closer. Then the bustard tells me he'd come to pay a social call of sympathy on Mrs. Stewart, and had stopped for a smoke before going to the house. Imagine the skunk" — Randle resumed his pacing — " 'Course, I knew he was smitten with her. He used to ride out there a lot, when he knew Harl wa'n't there. Harl come home one night and told him to make tracks. A couple of days later, in town, they had words and Harl knocked him down."

"Chandler claimed that was an argument over gambling."

"Gambling hell! Harl knew better than to play that tinhorn's games. Chandler's crookeder than a bent corkscrew. I told him polite as I could that Mrs. Stewart wa'n't ready to receive visitors yet. Does that satisfy him? No. He starts giving me an argument. One word led to another and I could see what was coming. Figured I might's well get in one good wallop, so I swung on him. I could feel his nose bone flatten under my fist. From then on, he was too much for me. I don't know how long I lay there, but when I come to, he was gone. I knew damn' well he wouldn't take that busted nose visitin' though, so I came on into town. I want to ask Smoky if there ain't some law that will keep Chandler away from the house." Randle swore and continued his tireless walking to and fro.

"Likely there is" — Quist nodded — "if Mrs. Stewart don't want visitors. Smoky can handle it. How long did you serve, Randle?"

Quist's words were run so smoothly together that he almost caught Randle off-guard. Randle started to reply, then stopped short, swung around facing Quist, eyes wide, scared. "What — did — you — say — Quist?"

Quist said easily, "I asked how long you'd served in stir, Randle? Never have quite broken yourself of that cell gait, have you? Three steps, then cross over two —"

"You're crazy, Quist!" Randle's eyes looked wild, shifty. "You're crazy as hell. I never been in prison. Don't see where you ever got that idea. Now look here, you . . ."

His words dwindled to silence while Quist looked steadily at him. Finally he said dully, "All right, Quist, you called the turn. But I was innocent. I was framed for a killing down in Mexico, years ago. You know how them Mexes like to pour it on a gringo. So I served my term. The bustards nigh starved me, but I lived through it. I ain't never had any trouble in this country."

"I'm glad to hear that." Quist nodded.

"Nobody 'round here knows anything about that stretch in Mexico. I'd appreciate you keeping it quiet, Quist."

Quist nodded, yawned. "Far be it from me to make trouble for anybody who doesn't deserve it, Randle. Haven't any other confessions to make, have you?"

"Who, me? 'Bout what?"

"Stewart's killing."

"Jeez, no, Quist! I was in town when it happened. You know as much as I do." He hesitated awkwardly a moment, then said, "Guess I'll go out and look for Smoky. S'long, Quist. See you again."

Quist took out his Durham and papers; twisted and put flame to a cigarette, exhaled a long, thoughtful draught of gray smoke. "Mexico, maybe, but I keep remembering that old Brose had come from Oklahoma. Could they have been there together?"

He rose, walked to the depot and sent off another telegram.

CHAPTER XVI

No Churchman

Friday and Saturday passed, with Quist practically gnawing his fingernails in impatience: nothing unusual had happened, nor had he been able to uncover any sort of evidence of the sort he sought. No answers to his telegrams had been received, and he commenced to wonder if the T.N. & A.S. operatives in Oklahoma and Arizona were on strike. Saturday had brought the usual crowd of people to town, some to make weekly purchases at the stores, many to just spend their time at the various saloons; this latter element kept Smoky Hayes and his deputy busy. Over Sunday the jail cells were filled with repentant — sometimes — men with hangovers, who would be released after paying fines to the local J.P. A few fights had been broken up Saturday night; all in all the two law officers had had their hands full, and Quist had seen but little of Smoky Hayes. Dyke Leigh seemed to be avoiding him.

Sunday morning Quist was seated moodily on the hotel gallery. Mostly the people who passed were in their Sunday best. There'd been church bells earlier, and Quist remembered the small frame church with steeple at the east end of town, and the adobe structure with its cross that stood across the railroad tracks, near the cemetery, and was attended largely by the Mexican population. It was peaceful, quiet on the hotel porch, at present. The weather wasn't as hot as it had been the past week. The sky was clear and there was a fresh breeze. "It is," Quist considered moodily, "Sunday weather. I'll be glad when Monday comes. Maybe then, something will turn up."

He glanced along the street, and brightened a trifle, upon seeing Rupe Chandler and Joker Gaillard approaching on the sidewalk. They halted just below the gallery railing, looking up at Quist. Quist grinned upon noticing the broad strip of bandage and court-plaster across Rupe Chandler's nose. Chandler nodded sullenly, while Gaillard laughed. "Lonesome, Quist?"

"Not for some sort of company," Quist said. "Looks like your friend had been sticking his nose in some place where it wasn't wanted."

Chandler growled something unintelligible. Gaillard guffawed, "I figured he was wearing a disguise at first, aiming to sneak into church."

"That's your best joke yet, Gaillard," Quist said. "Chandler in a church?" He laughed. "Chandler wouldn't know how to act in church."

"S'help me, I think he was going in," the Joker said seriously. "I just rescued him in time. Likely he was interested in the weeds in there —"

"Weeds — in church — ?" Quist began, and cursed himself for biting.

"Sure." Gaillard laughed. "Weeds — widow's weeds. The Widow Stewart and her beauteous daughter were driven in, in the surrey, by Jason Randle, this morning —"

"Aw, shut up, Joker," Chandler protested, "I was waiting to see Randle —"

"That's your story," Gaillard interrupted. "If I hadn't come along, you'd have been right up near the pulpit." He spoke to Quist, "I promised him a weed at the nearest saloon, if he'd come along. Get it, Quist? Weed — tobacco — cigar."

"I wouldn't want to get that one," Quist said disgustedly.

Gaillard looked pained. "You don't like me, do you, Quist?"

"Nor anybody else that does," Quist said.

"That makes it mutual." Gaillard grinned. He and Chandler started away, Gaillard saying over one shoulder, "Well, s'long, Quist.

Don't load your gun with wooden ca'tridges. There's no bark left in 'em." He laughed so hard he staggered into Chandler.

Quist scowled after the pair. "So help me, if that bustard isn't the most irritating —" He broke off. "Come to think of it I never saw that pair getting chummy before. Why?" He shrugged his shoulders. "Maybe, like Joker said, he just picked up Chandler. Probably wanted an audience for his horseplay." He shook his head. "Chandler sure must have it bad, when he'll stay up all night with his gambling house, and then get up to hang around the church. Love, or a reasonable facsimile, sure makes a *hombre* do queer things."

People passed along the sidewalk. Some of them spoke to Quist. Lost in thought, he replied absent-mindedly. He sat, head down, scowling, without seeing, the gallery railing before him. When next he looked up, Sheriff Hayes was just escorting Melinda and Eirene Stewart up the gallery steps. Quist got to his feet, doffing his sombrero. He caught his breath a little when he looked at Melinda Stewart, thinking that some widows shouldn't be allowed to wear black. The veil was missing today. There wasn't anything wrong with the pale blue dress Eirene was wearing either.

". . . and, my grief," Eirene was saying, "it was too nice to stay indoors. I just had to get Melinda out. And so Jason drove us into church. I feel very smug and superior now and Christian-like."

"Eirene was right," Melinda Stewart said gravely — and again there was that throaty voice that did things to Quist. "I've decided it doesn't do any good to stay in the house and mope. Harlan was —" She paused, biting her lip; two great tears rolled down her cheeks. One hand reached for a handkerchief.

Smoky Hayes stepped into the breech. "We're eating dinner here at the hotel, Greg. How about joining us?"

"It'll be a pleasure," Quist accepted.

The usual buzz of conversation and clatter of dishes in the dining room allowed them to talk in a normal tone. Quist noticed that Melinda Stewart didn't eat much, though she answered readily when Quist spoke to her. Eirene and Smoky kept up a continual flow of talk. The dinner concluded with pie and additional cups of coffee. The two men lighted cigars. Quist kept talking to Mrs. Stewart just for the pleasure of hearing her voice when she responded, and skirted the death of her husband in all his remarks. Eventually he began to run out of things to talk about.

Melinda Stewart asked finally, "You never did find that scalp that Jason wanted, did you, Mr. Quist? Jason thought so much of his father. I suppose he wants it for a remembrance. He's asked me two or three times if I'd heard anything."

"I have the scalp, Mrs. Stewart," Quist acknowledged. "For one reason and another I'd rather you didn't tell Jason though. He can have it when — well — before I leave town. Right now I'd like to keep it secret. There have been a couple of attempts to steal it —"

"You — you found it?" Melinda Stewart's long-lashed eyes were wide. "Wherever did you find it?"

"I'll tell you all about it, some day," Quist said reluctantly. "Right now, well, it might be rather painful to go into the subject."

She nodded her understanding, and turned to the sheriff. "Smoky, did you know Mr. Quist had found that old Comanche scalp that belonged to Brose?" The sheriff said, rather reluctantly, that he did. Mrs. Stewart said reproachfully, "But you never told me, Smoky."

"Actually," Hayes said, "I didn't feel I had the right to. I know how Greg works. He likes to keep such things under cover."

"Of course," Melinda Stewart said, "I can

understand that. But, please, Mr. Quist don't let anything happen to it. Jason wants it so much, and I'd like to see that he gets it."

"Nothing will happen to it," Quist said.

"But if there've been two attempts to steal it —"

Quist smiled. "I've another hiding place for it now. It will be safe. Don't worry."

The last of the food and coffee was consumed. The sheriff left to find Jason Randle and the surrey. Quist stood talking to the two women on the hotel gallery. Finally, the surrey arrived and Melinda and Eirene got started home, after getting assurances from Quist that he'd come out and pay them a visit soon.

The sheriff and Quist stood talking on the sidewalk when the surrey had rolled down the street, dust sifting from the wheel spokes. Hayes said, "You sure you got that scalp in a safe hiding place now, Greg?"

"It couldn't be safer in a bank vault," Quist said. "By the way, Smoky, did you ever hear of Dyke having any trouble with Harl Stewart?"

"Judas priest, not Dyke! No, I never heard anything about it. Don't tell me Dyke is under suspicion now. Where did you hear this?" Quist told him what he'd learned and of the deputy's reaction to questioning. Hayes frowned, saying, "This is all news to me. If you like, I'll talk to Dyke —" He broke off, swearing. "Dammit, Greg, now that Harl's dead, you wouldn't think he'd had any friends. Seems like everybody's had words with him, one time or another. Actually, I don't think there was a better liked man in all Trastorno County. You saw the turnout for his funeral. I'll speak to Dyke —"

"Not on my account, Smoky. I'd sooner let things ride a mite. Give him a chance to cool down. Eventually, he'll either come through with the truth, or some story we can mix him up on —"

"Just as you say. Hell, I like Dyke; he's a good man —"

"I've seen good men go wrong before this, Smoky. And so have you. They get too ambitious, and the first thing you know, they kill, cheat, rob — God knows what. We'll just hope that Dyke can straighten things out to our satisfaction before long." He changed the subject. "I'm aiming to head out to Borrico Pass this afternoon, Smoky, and see if I can run down any information on those goats and sheep that Auringer lost; so if you don't see me for a spell, you'll know where I am. I've reached the point where

I'm sick of just sitting and waiting."

"Don't blame you," the sheriff said. "It's always tedious to just hang around and wait for something to break." They talked a few minutes more, then parted, Quist to go to his room and get his Winchester and coat. Five minutes later he had saddled up his pony and headed west out of town. He walked the buckskin past Crockett Street, and as he drew abreast of the Golden Spur, saw Joker Gaillard and Rupe Chandler. Gaillard hailed him, "Hi, lawman! Hope you're not leaving us for good."

Quist smiled and slowed pace. "You really mean that, Joker? "

"Sure," Gaillard said with assumed geniality. "I don't know when I've seen anybody that gave me more laughs. You just exercising your hawss, or going hunting?"

"Hunting," Quist responded gravely, "hunting jackasses. You'd better stay in town, Joker."

Gaillard let out a whoop of joy. "Damn, Quist! That ain't bad for a lawman. Sometimes I think you got some good points, if you'll only learn to mind your own business."

"I do. That's why folks like you don't like me," Quist replied. He spoke to the horse and moved on. Chandler hadn't uttered a word.

Gaillard called after Quist, "Well, so long, sucker. And remember, you can't get music out of a saddlehorn." His loud laugh must have sounded the length of Main Street.

At the end of Main Street where it spread out in a wagon-rutted trail, Quist crossed a plank bridge over the south fork of Trastorno Creek, which was flanked on either side by tall cottonwoods, then swerved left to follow the T.N. & A.S. right of way, toward Borrico Pass. The gleaming rails made but few turns, and these were occasioned by high outcroppings of rock which were easier passed than dynamited from the earth.

All around was a vast sea of softly waving mesquite. There was plenty of prickly pear too. Now and then fishhook cactus was seen. The land was rolling and gradually ascending toward the Trastorno Range. Overhead a few clouds pursued each other across the turquoise sky. A half-dozen buzzards had been seen, soaring high, their predatory eyes alert for sign of food of any sort. Quist didn't push the pony hard. Once he stopped and rested it for a few minutes, while he removed his coat and rolled a cigarette. The saddle and saddle-blanket were removed, and the pony's back rubbed dry. Quist seated himself on a flat chunk of rock until the cigarette was finished, and watched a pair of horned toads play in and out through the surrounding brush and grama grass. Finally, he arose, resaddled and continued on.

By five that afternoon, when he looked up, the mountains seemed to tower high overhead and the sun was swinging above their peaks etched sharply against the blue void. He pushed on where the rails led through the foothills. Half an hour later he pulled wide of the tracks while a passenger train rushed past and the engine crew waved to him. A moment more and the speeding caboose was swallowed in a cloud of dust. Once more he swung back to follow the right-of-way. Before long he found himself entering a long canyon, man-carved through a high shoulder of solid rock. Here grew spots of catclaw and manzanita, despite the progress of civilization. The time came when the sun no longer gleamed on the twin rails, and the canyon was deep in shadow.

The breeze was stronger now, too, as it flowed through Borrico Pass, whipping the buckskin's mane and tail, and compelling Quist to settle his sombrero more firmly on his head. He was forced to pull the horse to a walk as it picked its way along the rock-cluttered right-of-way. On either side rose a high jagged escarpment, dotted with straggling bits of plant life which had managed to penetrate their threadlike roots through tiny cracks in the rock. Rounding a high shoulder of jagged rock, Quist found himself passing almost beneath a reddish-brown water tank on its trestlelike support. Water dripped from the tank's sides, furnishing some small nourishment to the wiry grass and sagebrush that had sprung up beneath. A short distance farther on, stood a frame building, painted in the same reddish-brown color, bearing a sign in smudged white that read: Borrico Pass — Texas Northern & Arizona Southern Railroad. There was a small pole corral at the rear of the building, and to one of the poles Quist now tied his horse when he had dismounted. Within the corral was a shaggy burro, which wagged one ear sleepily at Quist and paid him no further attention.

Quist strolled around to the front of the building and entered the open door, where the station-master, if such he could be called, was engaged in sweeping the floor. He was a tall skinny man, with a prominent Adam's-apple and wiry, sand-colored hair which seemed to stand out in all directions. He wore a denim shirt and bibbed overalls, and he was so occupied with his broom that he didn't hear Quist enter. Dust swept up in clouds. Quist said, "Hey! How about giving that broom a rest, mister?"

The man stopped, startled. His jaw dropped, then an interested light entered his pop-eyes. He turned, dropped the broom and went galloping across the floor to get his hat from a hook — an ancient train conductor's hat, faded and with the peak cracked. This he jammed on his head and came galloping back to Quist.

"Whut can I do fer you, mister? Food, drink or a ticket on the next train? Agent Tobias Byrd, at your service!"

CHAPTER XVII

Bounty Money

Quist grinned, the man was so much in earnest. "Well, not a ticket, anyway. My horse is out back. But a feed and water for the pony, if you've got feed. And I could stand a snack myself."

"Jest name 'er, mister."

Quist looked around. At the back of the building was a sort of bar, or counter, contrived by placing a wide plank atop a pair of barrels. On shelves nailed to the back wall were two bottles of whisky, three of catsup and a small supply of canned goods. At one end of the plank stood a keg of water; at the other a tinbox of crackers. A round table with four chairs stood not far from the entrance. Two bunks, one above the other, stood against the far wall. There were windows in three walls. Quist studied the canned goods, then chose tomatoes, sardines, beans and peaches. He got a big fistful of crackers from the tin box. The food was carried to the table. Tobias produced a can opener, knife, fork and spoon, then indicated the small cast-iron stove in one corner. "I could start a fire and bile up some coffee."

"I can do without." Quist started to eat.

"Them bottles of whisky," Byrd stated, "is pers'nal property, but I could sell you a drink. Our road likes to make guests comf'table."

"I don't want any whisky right now."

"I'll give you a drink," Byrd offered hopefully.

"Thanks, no. Now if you only had some beer —"

"Gallopin' gracious, mister! I got beer. Ain't no ice to it though. Warm as all git-out —"

"Now you're talking. Bring on the beer."

Quist continued the conversation while he ate. Byrd was, it appeared, just filling in on this job until there was an opening for a brakeman on the road. His was a twenty-four hour-a-day duty, but there was little to do between trains. Two days a month he had off, on which occasions he saddled the burro and headed for Wolf Springs, to celebrate and lay in fresh stock. People came here only occasionally. He hadn't sold a train ticket in five months. Now and then some sheepherder or rider passed through and stopped off to eat or drink. No, he didn't have a receiving or sending set. If Quist wanted to send a telegram he'd have to catch the next train to Corinth City, or, in the opposite direction, Wolf Springs. It was, Byrd made it clear, downright pleasurable to have a visitor to talk to. Trains just stopped long enough to take on water. To pass time, when he wasn't sleeping or cleaning up, he played tiddly-winks with himself. "You like to play me a game?" he asked wistfully, pop-eyes pleading with Quist. Quist explained gravely that he didn't go in for sports, and Byrd sat back to think that over, while Quist finished his canned peaches. Suddenly the station agent said, "You ain't mentioned your name, mister."

"Name's Quist." A cigarette was rolled, then Quist produced his company credentials and passed them to Byrd.

"In-vest-i-gator," he read from the card, then looked up in alarm. "You ain't a spotter, are you?"

Quist shook his head. "Not the sort you have anything to fear from, anyway, Tobias. I figure to give you a good word in my report."

"That's dang nice of you, Mr. Quist. What can I do for you?" He returned Quist's credentials.

"About two months back," Quist said, "the train coming through here, early one morning, was delayed by a gang of bandits.

A shipment of sheep and Angora goats was taken off and driven away. I want you to tell me what you remember about that."

Byrd's face clouded angrily. "I remember it, all right." He gave the number of the train, the names of the train crew. ". . . comes through here about 3:49 A.M. I was on my job, as usual, outside. Water was bein' took on. Just 'bout startin' time, them bandits come a-swarmin' from behind my depot where they'd been hid. In no time a-tall, the hull train crew was lookin' into gun muzzles. Me, included. There was a stock-tender in each car with the animals. At gunpoint they was forced to open the doors and herd the sheep and goats off the train, then around that rock shoulder, down the tracks a spell. Next, the engineer was told to leave, and he got, and I had to deal with them bandits."

Quist asked how he dealt with them. Byrd said, "I jist fought like hell to loosen up the ropes they tied me to a chair with, but they'd been gone an hour before I got loose. I wa'n't tied very tight, anyway. I figure they jist aimed to fix me till they was gone. After the train pulled out, two of the bandits hung around a spell and et some of my vittles. One of the scuts emptied a bottle of catsup on my head, before he left. Said I could tell my company I got wounded fightin' to save the goats. Then he laughed like hell."

Quist pricked up his ears. That sounded like Joker Gaillard. "But nobody got hurt, eh?" he said. Byrd shook his head; there'd been no shooting at all. "And you didn't recognize anyone, I suppose?"

"They all looked like cowhands with bandanners 'cross their faces. I couldn't tell what they looked like, otherwise."

"Do you remember any names being called out?" Quist asked.

Byrd considered. "Seems like I heard somebody say, 'Tonkawa,' whatever that means. Mebbe I'm mistook." He remembered something else: "This laughin'-hyena feller whut poured catsup on me, he was the one whut told the engineer to pull out, and he says to the engineer, 'S'long, hogger, don't feel sheepish 'cause we took your stock. You still got somethin' tender to your train.' And he burst out fit to kill. The engineer was so mad when he snaked that train off, he nigh flung the caboose plumb to the sky, like a kid playin' at crackin'-the-whip."

"What happened next?"

"Them two that stayed to eat, they left to catch up with their pards, leavin' me to wriggle loose from my ropes. I like to never git that catsup washed outten my hair. It looked like blood too. Must have been 'long 'bout noontime when them two stock-tenders come walkin' in, mad as all-git-out. They told me the sheep and goats had been druv over a bluff. What's more, them bandits had forced 'em to strip down to their underwear. Huh? No, they hadn't been hurt none. They was just sore at havin' that kind of joke played on 'em, and had blisters on their feet and got scratched some from cactus. I fixed 'em up with some burlap sacks so's they'd look decent when the next train come along. But they was sure blushin' when they got on."

It was growing dark now. Byrd lighted a kerosene lamp, then touched the match flame to a lantern which he carried out and hung on a nail. Sometime later, a train rumbled in, stopped for water and snorted off. Quist went out and took care of his pony, then returned to the station. He got another bottle of beer and sat back to consider the matter of the sheep bandits. It sounded like something Joker Gaillard had had a hand in. Well, he'd take that up with Gaillard later. Meanwhile, there were knottier problems for consideration. Byrd's remarks kept intruding on his thoughts.

That Comanche scalp. How did that tie in with things? Quist was wishing he'd had more time to search around the rowboat that day. There might have been further clues. If Brose Randle had flung that scalp where it couldn't be found, he might have left something else. But where? Could he have shoved something beneath the boat perhaps. Quist tensed at the thought. That was an idea!

A train came through, headed west, its vibrations shaking the depot, stopped briefly and then thundered on. Byrd returned to the station. Rather than disappoint the man, Quist allowed himself to be inveigled into a game of tiddly-winks. Quist lost three games straight. On the fourth when Byrd started popping the "undersize poker chips" into the bowl with his eyes shut, Quist surrendered, borrowed a pair of blankets and crawled into the upper bunk, without bothering to remove his trousers.

He lay there while the night drifted on, pretending to be asleep. That damned Comanche scalp! Someone wanted it mighty bad. But why? And had Brose Randle hidden anything beneath the boat before he died? Below Quist, the bunk shook a little, and he realized Byrd had turned in for a sleep between trains, after turning the kerosene lamp low. The hours passed. Quist slept but fitfully.

Shortly before four in the morning, the

humming of distant rails predicted the arrival of the eastbound freight. The station began to quiver. Byrd automatically arose from his bunk and stumbled out to the station platform. Within a few minutes the train departed. Byrd returned to his bunk and almost instantly resumed snoring. Quist waited a minute, then donned his sombrero and climbed down from his bunk. He drew on boots and coat, stuffed crackers into both pockets, left five silver dollars on the plank counter. Outside, he watered the buckskin and saddled up. The stars were fading from the sky now. The morning air was chill. The cigarette Quist rolled, tasted good. He reined the pony away from the station, and after emerging from the pass, struck out toward the southeast.

It was nearing nine that morning when he guided the buckskin pony through the mesquite trees and reached the point where be had found the dead Brose Randle. He dropped reins on the earth and dismounted a few yards from the old boat. Except for the removal of Brose Randle and his sack of tackle, the scene didn't appear to have changed much. The oars lay on the sand. The line still stretched out from the fishpole in the stern, though the boot was now missing from the hook. Tracks of men, horses and wagon-wheels showed on the earth.

Quist straightened up and glanced around. A strong breeze blew down from the Trastornos; the torrid sun painted his shadow in dense black. He stood eyeing the ancient rowboat, already showing the effects of desert suns. Cracks were wider; fresh cracks had appeared; the wood had been water-soaked the last time he'd seen it. Now it was tinder-dry, the boards whitening fast in the daily heat.

"Probably I've just wasted time," Quist muttered. "Now that I'm actually here, I can't believe I'll find anything beneath this skiff. Well, I might as well have a look, anyway."

He lifted the bow from the sand, peered under. Nothing there but some small crushed plant life and the imprint of flat boards. A few sow-bugs moved aimlessly about. He lowered the boat, then moved back to the stern, lifted again. The result was the same. Quist swore in an undertone. "This is what too much thinking will do to a man. I should have known better than to hope for anything."

He was lowering the boat again, when something caught his eye. There was a small round hole in the flat board that ran across the stern. "Well," he mused, "how did I miss that before?"

The small hole looked as though it might have been made by the entrance of a bullet. Quist studied it. "Could be," he speculated, "this wood was so wet when I was here before, that it swelled and closed the hole. Cripes, I'm just trying to find an alibi to excuse my carelessness the other time. Reckon I'll get it out and see what it looks like, anyway."

Lowering the boat the rest of the way to the sand, he got out his knife and set to work, whittling steadily at the dry wood. The bullet, if a bullet was responsible for that hole, had entered at an angle, taking a course that almost paralleled the plane of the heavy board, instead of going straight through. Quist grunted while he toiled, sweating under the hot sun, and finally was rewarded by sight of one end of a chunk of lead. "It's a slug, all right," he muttered, and renewed his carving, working with more care now.

A few moments later he was holding a bullet from a six-shooter in his palm, wondering when it had been fired and by whom. He closed the knife and put it away. After a minute he dropped the leaden slug into a coat pocket. Then he straightened up and glanced around. And tensed suddenly.

Joker Gaillard spoke from the shadow of a mesquite tree, a dozen paces distant. In his right hand he held his drawn six-shooter, bearing on Quist's body. "Playing woodpecker, Quist?" he asked, grinning. "Or just whittling to pass time?"

Quist forced a thin smile. "Looks like I'm getting mighty careless." He didn't raise his hands. "How long you been trailing me?"

"Since yesterday, when you left town. I didn't lose time. Snooping around Borrico Pass station, weren't you? You know what happens to snoopers, Quist." He grinned widely. "Snoopers always get to smell something bad. Powdersmoke, fr'instance. That's your tough luck. I aim to collect me some bounty money on your pelt, Quist. I ain't in a hurry though. Just you keep your hand wide of your hawg-leg. What was you whittlin' out of that boat?"

"A slug from a six-shooter," Quist answered quietly. "Do you want to see it, Joker?"

Gaillard's grin widened. "Not interested, Quist. I'll give you another slug to go with it, though. Maybe a couple of slugs. Ever heard of a man being slugged to death, Quist? You're him! Slugged to death. Not bad, eh?" He started to laugh, his gun-muzzle still bearing on Quist, the barrel tilting slightly.

Abruptly, Quist dropped to his knees, right hand darting within his coat. Flame and smoke was lancing from the .44 barrel even before it swung to cover Gaillard. Quist heard Gaillard's first shot whine over his left shoulder as he dropped. Through the powdersmoke lifting before his eyes, he saw the white flash of Gaillard's second shot, but the gun was dropping now, as Gaillard was swept off his feet by the heavy impact of Quist's forty-four bullets, and went crashing on his side. He struggled a moment and then lay still.

CHAPTER XVIII

One Knot Unraveled

Powdersmoke evaporated on the breeze. For a moment, Quist didn't move, then he rose and strode swiftly across the sand. He stood a moment gazing down on Gaillard, then methodically plugged out five empty shells from his gun and inserted fresh loads in the cylinder. Shoving the gun back in his holster, he knelt at Gaillard's side. He rolled the man on his back. There was blood on the Joker's clothing at various points. Not much blood. Bleeding internally, Quist speculated. He could trace the course his slugs had taken, as the gun-muzzle of the forty-four swung up and across. The first shot had missed, but the other four had found their marks. Grimly, Quist surveyed his work and swore regretfully. "But it was him or me."

Gaillard was still breathing, his eyes closed. Quist stripped off his coat, placed it beneath Gaillard's head and went to his pony for his canteen. He returned and, kneeling, trickled some water into the Joker's open mouth. After a moment, Gaillard moved, though his eyes remained closed.

Quist gave him another drink. He swallowed hard and muttered, "Like you said, lawman, jackasses should stay in town. And this time you did more than shoot off my gun-butt — after me — waiting all night — while you got — your sleep — at Borrico. Last night was — chilly — too. . . ." He opened his eyes and gave Quist a feeble grin. "Can't seem to — think of a — damn' joke — Quist. Maybe, I'm — through joking — eh?"

"It won't be much longer, Joker," Quist said quietly. "You got much pain?"

"Scarce any. Feel — sort of — numb all over. Kind of dopey. Maybe one of your slugs — stiffened my backbone, eh?"

"Could be," Quist said. "You could recover from the other three. Maybe. I'm not sure —"

"Doesn't matter now. It was like you'd — jerked a gatling gun," Gaillard muttered drowsily. "I thought I was fast, but you —"

"Joker," Quist cut in, "you could clear up a lot for me, if you'd talk before you go out."

"Sure, Quist. Anybody outsmarts me — deserves help. Succor from a sucker, eh?" He started to laugh, then winced and caught his breath. "What — you want — to know?"

Quist asked questions. From time to time he gave Gaillard a drink from the canteen. The Joker's voice grew stronger, faded, came better again. ". . . and you see," Gaillard was saying, "there's a heap of things — I don't understand, either."

"You haven't the least idea who killed Harl Stewart?"

"Can't help you a bit, Quist. Auringer or Rupe Chandler, maybe, could be responsible. Hired somebody —" He stopped. Blood trickled from his lips. Quist wiped it away. "What I was thinking — maybe Smoky Hayes —"

"The sheriff?" Quist frowned. "You forget, Joker, Smoky left the Rafter-S and returned to town. He was in town when the news arrived. The ranch is twelve miles out. Pushing steady, that's around an hour for a horse — a good horse."

"I know. But suppose Hayes had a relay. Three hawsses — maybe — waitin' along — the way. Suppose he didn't leave — the Rafter-S when he said — but hung around outside a half hour or so. Then killed Stewart, and started hell bent — for town."

"Even so — three horses —" Quist frowned.

"Three — fast hawsses — poundin' all the way."

"It's hard to believe —"

"Listen, Quist, a spell back I was reading — in a newspaper — a new world's record had been set — for hawss speed. Feller in Arizona rode — better'n forty-eight miles — in a mite over — three hours and a half. On *one* hawss. With *three* fast hawsses, Smoky Hayes could shoot Stewart, then get to town so — fast afterward — it would look — like a good alibi."

"But why should Smoky shoot Stewart?" Quist demanded.

"Ain't got — slightest idea. It's your headache now."

Gaillard didn't last much longer. A fit of coughing brought a great deal of blood to his lips. After a minute he essayed a weak smile and said, "Well, s'long, Quist. Don't ride in — any open hearses. The draught — might give you — a bad cold —" He died, feeble laughter struggling against another flow of blood.

Quist felt for his pulse. It was gone. He rose to his feet. It didn't take long to find Gaillard's pony, tethered back in the mesquite a short distance. He led it back, loaded the dead body across the saddle, lashed it in place. Then mounting the buckskin, he got started, leading behind him Gaillard's horse with its grisly burden. "Anyway," Quist sighed as he rode off, "that's one knot unraveled. But I don't like to see killing for the sake of progress. Maybe" — reluctantly —

"there isn't any other way."

Hours later, when he reached Corinth City, the sun had swung far to the west. Somebody sighted the limp form hanging across the saddle of the led horse. An excited cry went up. A crowd gathered and followed Quist to Barry Lowe's undertaking establishment. Here, Quist dismounted and entering, requested help in carrying Gaillard's body inside. The undertaker assisted Quist, and a few minutes later, Quist emerged from the building and started to mount. Witt Auringer pushed through the crowd, calling angrily, "Just a minute, Quist."

Quist paused, one hand on his bridle reins. "What's on your mind, Auringer?"

Auringer said heatedly, "I understand you killed Gaillard."

"What in hell would you do if Gaillard threw a gun on you and stated he was going to collect a bounty on your pelt?" Quist started to mount.

"I think you're a liar," Auringer stated flatly. He grabbed Quist's arm. "I want to know the right of this business —"

He didn't get any further. Quist wrenched his arm loose, lifted his right fist and swung hard. Auringer staggered back, fell flat, struggled to hands and knees, then suddenly caved forward on his face. Somebody yelled,

"Knocked out, by Gawd!" and the excited voices of the crowd increased.

"Goddam fool." Quist grunted as he swung up on the buckskin's back. "I'm beginning to lose patience." He headed the pony toward the sheriff's office, but saw Hayes approaching before he got there. Without dismounting, Quist swung over to the nearest hitchrack and halted.

"My God, Greg, where have you been? I've been worried. When you said you were going to Borrico Pass, I figured you'd take the train and get back last night —" He broke off, "Say, Rupe Chandler just came running to say you'd shot Gaillard. What —"

"Chandler, eh?" Quist growled. "There's another bustard that's got something coming to him. Yeah, I killed the Joker. He didn't leave me anything else to do. He was set to finish me —"

"Where did this happen?"

"He followed me out of town when I went to Borrico Pass. Later — early this morning — I got to thinking I might pick up some sign or something out there where Brose Randle was shot. Gaillard trailed me there too. Threw a gun on me and was set to pull trigger, when I took a chance and drew my own gun. Gaillard led the gang that stopped the train and ran off those sheep and goats.

Oh, yes, he talked quite a bit before he died." Quist added a few details, then, at a question, "No, he didn't have any idea who killed Harl Stewart. Seemed to feel it might have been Auringer, Chandler or you —"

"Me? For the love of God, Greg. Whatever gave him an idea like that? I was in town when the news was brought —"

"The Joker figured you might have had a relay of horses to get you back to town fast, after you'd pretended to leave the Rafter-S, and then waited a spell to throw a slug through Stewart. His idea was you'd be back to town so soon after the shot was fired, that folks, considering the twelve-mile ride, would never think of suspecting you."

Hayes looked uncomfortable. He scratched his head. "But, Cripes A'mighty, Greg, what would my motive be? Sure, you might even work out a case on me, figuring that way, but why in the devil should I kill Harl?"

"That's what bothered the Joker too. I can't say I put much stock in the idea, Smoky."

The sheriff breathed a sigh of relief. "Lord, Greg, I'm glad to hear that. What else did Gaillard tell you — ?"

"He confessed to killing Brose Randle. Wanted that damnable scalp — no, don't ask me why. Jason Randle hired him to get it. And I don't know the answer to that either. And let's keep that secret for a spell. The Joker didn't know why Jason wanted it — but keep it quiet for now, Smoky." People passing on the street had stopped and were trying to hear what Hayes and Quist were talking about. A crowd began to gather. Quist said, "Where's Doc Wakeman live? I'm going to ride over and tell him to get ready for another inquest. I want him to have my part of the story firsthand, now."

Hayes gave directions for finding the doctor's residence, then Quist pushed off down the street, turning left on Brazos until he came to the corner of Lavaca Street, where the doctor's small residence was surrounded by a whitewashed picket-fence. There was an ancient live-oak in the front yard, and Wakeman was seated on his porch, a bottle of bourbon and a pitcher of cold water by his side. Before Quist had reached the porch, Wakeman rose and stepped within the house. He emerged immediately, bringing an extra glass. He shoved a chair toward Quist and started filling the glass. When Quist had seated himself and had two deep swallows, Wakeman said, "Is this a social call — or trouble?"

Quist said in a reluctant voice, "You've

got another inquest coming up, doc." Wakeman interrupted with a groan of dismay and requested the identity of the guest of honor this time. Quist went on, "Joker Gaillard trailed me out on the range today, and put me in a spot where I couldn't do anything else but kill him. You and your jury will have to take my word for what happened. The point is, I don't want any difficulty with the law now. Things are heading toward a showdown, I think. I don't want to be cramped in any way —"

Wakeman broke in, frowning, "My jury will render the verdict. My job is to see that evidence is presented —"

"True enough — but there are ways and ways of presenting evidence. And of picking a jury. The right sort of jury will be guided by you. For instance, I wouldn't want Randle or Auringer or Rupe Chandler on such a jury. Tell Smoky Hayes the sort of men you want. Later, if you're not satisfied, I'll be ready to stand any sort of investigation you want. I just don't want my hands tied for the next few days," he concluded, adding certain details relative to the shooting of Joker Gaillard.

"All right," Wakeman consented. "I can see your viewpoint. I'll talk to Smoky tonight."

Quist said thanks and the glasses were filled again. Quist shook Durham into a brown paper and lighted a smoke. He said, "There's something else I want to ask you, doc. How close can you — or any doctor — come to determining the minute at which a man died, if you've not seen the body for a time?"

"Depends on the condition of the body, age, health and so on. It definitely can't be determined to the minute, by any medical man I know of. Take Brose Randle, for instance. I couldn't state *definitely* just when he died."

"I suppose if he lingered on for a spell after being shot, that would have to be considered, eh?"

"Naturally. So long as heart beat exists, death is postponed. A man could die twenty-four hours after being shot, but he'd have to stop breathing entirely before he could be considered —"

Quist interrupted, "As I remember it, you stated that Harl Stewart died at about nine o'clock that night —"

"Between eight and nine, and you'll remember I gave it an hour either way. I was prejudiced toward nine because that was about the time both Mrs. Stewart and Deacon Vogel stated they heard the shot. I'd take their words, over my judgment on the condition of the body."

"Let's put it this way. Could Stewart actually have died at a later hour than you gave?" Wakeman interjected a question. Quist said, "All right, later or earlier, then?"

"Yes, that would be possible, if there'd been no one on hand to name the exact hour, Greg. You see, after breathing stops, it is anywhere from two or three hours before *rigor mortis* proper sets in. I made my decision regarding time on the degree to which *rigor mortis* had advanced in Stewart's body. Frankly it didn't agree with the time of death stated by Vogel and Mrs. Stewart, but I could see readily where they could be right. Without their evidence I'd have thought Stewart died even earlier. The rigidity of the muscles was such —" He broke off, then, "There are so many things to be taken into consideration when determining the time of death. If a person's muscles had been weakened by sickness or dissipation, or if he were a very young person, with small muscular development, the body would tend to become rigid quicker than in some husky young buck of twenty-odd. Again, it was very hot that day and evening. Sometimes a body may grow rigid quicker in hot weather than in cold. Strangely enough, an extremely cold temperature could be responsible for a delay in *rigor mortis*. So you see, Greg, there's considerable to take into consideration, when determining a time of death. When you have truthful witnesses on hand when a man dies, I figure it is best to believe them. After all, they're on the job, while the doctor has to depend on a certain amount of speculation."

Quist thanked the doctor for the information and, after a short time, rose and mounted the buckskin. A few lights were coming into being along Main Street, though an afterglow still lingered above the Trastorno Mountains. Quist left his pony at the Bluebonnet Livery, and carrying his rifle, went to the hotel. He stopped a moment at the desk and asked for a small package he had entrusted to the hotel safe. Then he mounted to his room, closed the door and opened the package. A moment later, he was studying the Comanche scalp in his hand. It grew dark in the room while he sat thinking. He rose and after pulling down the shades, lighted his lamp.

He went over the scalp, inch by inch, trying to find some clue that would explain the mystery. Apparently there was nothing out of the ordinary to be seen — just the long braid of blue-black hair, and the circular, decorated piping around the soft doeskin piece sewn to the human skin of the scalp.

The longer he contemplated the Comanche scalp, the more irritated Quist became at his inability to solve the problem. Unconsciously, his fist closed down hard on the beaded scalp, in angry frustration, as though to squeeze the very truth out of it. And then, he abruptly became aware that there was some resistance to his effort: the scalp wasn't crumpling the way it should under such pressure. Something crackled slightly under his hand.

"By the Almighty," Quist exclaimed, "there's something been hidden between those two sections of skin. Quist, you dumb bustard, maybe you've hit on it at last."

His knife came out of his pocket. He opened it, his topaz eyes glinting yellowly with excitement, as they searched for threads to cut. The stitches when he located them, weren't small, but long and far from being neat — like something a man might have been responsible for, if unaccustomed to handling needle and thread. One thread was cut; then the next one snipped through. The knife found a third and the doeskin began to separate from the human scalp piece.

A knock sounded at the door. Quist cursed fervently and thrust the Comanche scalp beneath his bed mattress. He moved quickly toward his gun, hanging in holster on a chair back. The knock sounded again. Quist called, impatiently, "Come on in."

The door opened, closed again. Dyke Leigh stood there. Quist nodded coolly. Leigh said, "I've been looking for you in the dining room."

Quist said quietly. "After what happened today, I can't say I've got much stomach for food."

"Yeah, I guess I understand how you feel. Smoky told me about Joker Gaillard. Those things don't set right, and —"

"Did you come up here to tell me that?"

Dyke Leigh flushed. He said awkwardly, "No, I came up here to do some apologizing and tell you you were right. I shouldn't have refused to tell you what I scrapped with Harl Stewart about. I've been thinking it over —"

"Take a load off your feet." Quist indicated a chair and then seated himself on the bed.

"You see," Leigh spoke earnestly, "it wasn't anything much really, except that every time I think about it, I get mad as hell. The truth is — well, I've been sparkin' Eirene on and off ever since we were kids, and then I got to thinking it was a regular thing. About that time, Smoky started visiting her too. And that was all right. I think a heap of Smoky. Besides I didn't have much to offer her except a deputy's salary —"

"I wouldn't say that," Quist put in quietly.

"It's true, though," Leigh insisted. "Smoky's a lot better fixed. But what made me so damn' mad was one day Harl Stewart came to me in the sheriff's office, and suggested that I quit visiting with Eirene. He pointed out that Smoky was seeing her regular and taking her to dances and such, and that Smoky was far better fixed to take care of her. And he asked that I quit, and added some more stuff about having Eirene's best interests at heart, and if I really cared for her I'd see, too, that Smoky was a better match. With that I hit the ceiling and told him to mind his own business. And then he cut loose at me. I cooled down, but he kept bawling me out, said I was after the money he'd leave her. I kept my temper and didn't hit him, the way I was inclined, and finally he left."

Quist smiled. "That's all there was to it?"

"That's all, but it was sort of a touchy subject I didn't like to discuss. I was afraid you might say something to Smoky, and then Smoky wouldn't feel right — oh, hell, I should have told you in the first place, Greg. I'm sorry."

"Forget it, Dyke." Quist laughed. He rose and stuck out his hand and when the deputy had taken it, subtly drew him out of the chair and maneuvered him toward the door. "I figured it couldn't be serious, Dyke. As for Smoky being a better match for Eirene, why don't you let her decide that. I've talked to Eirene and I think it's possible it may still be an open race." They talked a few minutes longer, then Leigh took his departure.

Quist could scarcely restrain his impatience, until the door had closed, then he strode swiftly to the bed, retrieved the scalp from under the mattress and with feverish fingers once more started cutting threads.

CHAPTER XIX

Fraud and Murder

Despite Auringer's insistence that Quist be jailed and tried for the killing of Joker Gaillard — his first name proved to be Joachim when the inquest got under way the following morning — Quist was held blameless for the man's death, and the inquiry was quickly concluded. Rupe Chandler, too, posing as a close friend of Gaillard, tried to sway the jurors' opinions, but no one took him seriously, nor could anyone, aside from Quist, understand Chandler's vindictiveness, and Quist wasn't talking — yet.

During the remainder of the day, Quist made several trips to the depot to inquire for telegrams. Even when their expected arrival gave him some information he sought, he learned that he'd have to wait for details in pursuant letters. During the evening both Sheriff Hayes and Dyke Leigh encountered him in the Shamrock Bar, or on the street, but as he didn't seem to welcome companions, they quickly left him to his own thoughts.

The letters he awaited arrived about eleven

the following morning and he at once hurried to his hotel room to study them. It was noon when he again descended to the street, whistling softly under his breath. As he reached the sidewalk, Eirene Stewart was just riding past. Seeing him, the girl reined her pony to the hitchrack. It was the first time Quist had seen her in riding togs, and he decided she was a mighty pretty girl. He couldn't blame Dyke Leigh at thought of losing so much loveliness. He doffed his sombrero and they exchanged the usual pleasantries. Eirene explained that she'd come into town to spend the night with her friend Mrs. Emmons, and that she had an engagement to have supper with Smoky.

"I was just thinking" — she laughed — "if I could only find Dyke, I might persuade him to take me to dinner today."

"Playing one man against the other, are you?" Quist chuckled. "Perhaps I'd better get in on the race too."

"I'd like that," the girl said frankly, "but I'm afraid that's hopeless. Hard, ruthless Mr. Quist. Oh, I've heard all about you, you know. Melinda has told me a great deal. We were saying last night that you'd not come to visit yet. It would really do Melinda a lot of good, if you would ride out, sometime."

He talked to the girl a time longer, then she spoke to her pony and rode on. Quist crossed the street, got his buckskin horse from the livery stable and went loping out of Corinth City.

He crossed the plank bridge over Trastorno Creek, then for a time followed the slow-moving shallow river in a northwest direction. Three quarters of an hour later, he reined the pony down to the stream to drink. The shade of the great cottonwoods was welcome after the hot sun, where they bordered the banks. Quist drew his feet from stirrups and held them high while the horse moved into the water to plunge its muzzle deep into the cool depths. Five minutes later, he turned the pony back up the bank and continued on his way. The stream was left behind now, as he headed in a more westerly direction. The way was slightly rolling as it lifted toward the Trastorno Mountains. Now and then he saw small bunches of Hereford cows, branded on the left ribs with the Stewart Rafter-S iron. The bulk of the herds he knew was much farther north at this season, though the stock never strayed too far from the creek.

The clock was pushing toward two when Quist first sighted the Rafter-S ranch buildings. There was the big rambling main house, constructed of adobe and rock, with a wide gallery, raised only slightly from the earth, running the width of the front elevation. Huge old oak trees made moving shadows about the building. There were more trees behind the house and some distance farther on the combination bunkhouse and cook building, corrals, barns, a blacksmith shop; a couple of chuck-wagons and other vehicles stood about. Quist turned from the roadway through a wide open gateway, and headed down toward the corrals. The front door of the house was open when he passed, but he saw no one in sight.

Jason Randle stepped from the bunkhouse as Quist dismounted. Whether Randle was pleased to see him, or not, Quist couldn't decide. At the same time, Quist had to admit that the man's offer to water and rub down the buckskin was pleasant enough. They stood talking a few minutes. All the hands were away, working at one thing or another. Only Randle and Deacon Vogel, the cook, were at the bunkhouse. At that moment, Vogel stuck his head through a window and called a greeting. Quist mentioned that he had come out to see Mrs. Stewart. Randle looked dubious, "Well, I don't know," he said uncertainly. "Mrs. Stewart hasn't been seeing any company yet —"

"I've been invited," Quist said shortly. "Do you object?"

"Hell no, why should I object? It's up to her, I reckon." He instilled a note of cordiality into the tones. "Sure, I reckon she'll be glad to see you. I'd appreciate it if you didn't fret her none, though —"

Quist said sharply, "Why should I?"

"We-ell, I sort of figured you'd be asking questions that had to do with Harl's death, and — and —" He fell silent after a moment and without further speech, turned to remove the saddle from Quist's pony. Quist left him and headed up toward the house, passing the rear door on his way and going around to the front entrance, where he found Melinda Stewart seated on the long gallery, riffling through the pages of *Harper's Weekly*. She looked up startled at his step, then smiled — and Quist caught his breath a trifle.

"Mr. Quist! It's so nice to see you. I didn't hear you ride in." She indicated a chair at her side. "You should give a lady some warning when you come visiting. I'd have fixed up —"

Quist cut in with something appropriate, thinking as he sat down, that she must have dressed very hurriedly in that case. She might have just stepped away from her mirror. Green-and-white checked gingham, he was saying to himself, must have been made to go with that reddish-chestnut hair, falling in soft waves low on her nape. And that white lace at the creamy throat helped along the effect, too. He felt her eyes on him and, looking up, caught the full force of the long lashes and full lips. ". . . and I'm wondering," she was saying in her husky voice, "if this is just a call or are you going to ask me questions?"

Quist scuffed one toe awkwardly on the flagstoned gallery floor. "Well, I'm not sure, if questions would be welcome. Randle gave me to understand you weren't to be bothered —"

"Pshaw! I'm afraid Jason isn't always bright. He's a good man though. His whole life was tied up in Harl's interests." She glanced away a moment, then her eyes again met Quist's and she forced a smile. "And now he appears to be looking after me, as well. You ask me anything you like. I want to help you, oh, so much."

At the end of another fifteen minutes' conversation they were calling each other Melinda and Greg, Melinda saying she'd felt from the first they'd be friends, and she'd heard so much about Gregory Quist. She mentioned various cases he'd been on —

that one in the Thunderbird Country, and that affair on Gunsight Range; then there was the mysterious business over at Dominion City. Her knowledge of Quist's cases was flattering, and Quist didn't deny it. Gradually, he interjected a question here and there, and when he had concluded, had to admit that her story of Stewart's killing agreed with the story as told by Dr. Wakeman on the stand at the Stewart inquest.

"I've been thinking along lines on another theory, Melinda," Quist said at last. "Is it possible, do you suppose, that your husband was killed with a gun you still have on the premises? I mean, here in the house."

The long-lashed eyes widened in perplexity. "You mean, somebody in this house shot Harl? But, Greg, there was no one else but me here at the time."

"I quite understand that," Quist said. "I'm talking about the gun that was used. There are surely a few guns here. Harl Stewart would have more than one." Melinda Stewart admitted this, but looked puzzled. Quist said, "May I see them, please? No, no rifles or shotguns — just the six-shooters that might be around."

She led the way into the house, past a bedroom at the front, where she told Quist in a low voice that Stewart had died, and turned left in the long hall that divided the house, into the main room, a pleasant place with easy chairs, Navajo rugs, animal skins and a huge rock fireplace. Leaving Quist standing by a large oblong table of heavy oak, she went to the back of the house. Presently she returned, weighted down with five six-shooters. Only one of the guns was still loaded. This, Melinda said, was the weapon Stewart had worn on the day he was shot. Quist slipped out the cylinder and examined the barrel. It was clean, apparently having not been fired in some time. He reassembled the gun and placed it on the table.

In succession he examined three other guns — an old cap-and-ball pistol, a double-action, forty-five six-shooter, Colts, and a double-action Smith & Wesson, forty-five six-shooter. None of them showed evidence of recent shooting. The last gun proved to be a thirty-eight Colt's six-shooter. It looked almost brand new and showed signs of small use. Quist squinted through the barrel and then lowered it. "This too, is clean as a whistle." He glanced up to see Melinda smiling at him, and asked, "What's the matter?"

"I think I might have been frightened if you'd found anything significantly wrong about that gun," she admitted. "You see, that's a gun Harl gave to me when we were first married. He insisted that I learn to shoot. We used to have a lot of fun, shooting at tin cans and such. It seems ages since I was last out practicing with him. He insisted that the single-action was better than the double. I don't know why, but he always carried the single-action. The Colt's forty-five, double-action he loaned to Rupe Chandler one time, thinking that Chandler might buy it —"

Quist asked, "How long ago?"

Melinda considered. "A year or more, I guess."

Quist said casually, "Chandler used to be a frequent visitor here, I understand."

A flush entered Melinda's cheeks. She said, "You've been hearing stories, I guess. All right, I'll admit it. Those times when Harl went to town to drink, it was good to have company. I didn't realize at the time that Harl would object. He was a very jealous man, Greg. He objected to nearly any man who came visiting, except Smoky Hayes, and he knew Smoky came to see Eirene." She was standing very close to Quist and he was conscious of some subtle perfume in his nostrils. Quist said something about a good many men being jealous of beautiful wives, and after another run through of the guns, suggested they return to the gallery. She told him she'd be out in a minute, and suggested he go ahead.

Quist again found his seat on the gallery. Within a few minutes, Melinda joined him, carrying a tray with two glasses. Quist's glass contained bourbon and water. He asked her what she was drinking. She confessed, rather sheepishly, that it was sarsaparilla. "I never did like whisky, Greg. Harl used to say I was like a kid when it came to sweet drinks and pop."

Within the house, standing so near to Melinda while he examined the guns, Quist hadn't felt at all sure of himself. Susceptible, as always, to the presence of a beautiful woman, he didn't trust his emotions not to play him false, in such close proximity. There was, he considered, glancing from the gallery out to the oak trees where sunlight filtered through leafy branches, a time for everything; he remembered again what he had come for. The drinks were finally finished. Quist rolled and lighted a cigarette. Blue and gray smoke mingled and disappeared in the warm afternoon air.

Quist cleared his throat. "Eirene said you had a small business in Tucson, Melinda, at the time you met Harl Stewart. I think she said you were a dealer in stationery."

"That's true, Greg."

Quist said quietly, "Could the stationery have been cards — say, playing cards?"

He heard Melinda's sudden gasp. Turning, he saw she had gone white. "Greg — you — you know?"

Quist nodded. "You dealt faro in the Silver Cage gambling house. You were dealing there when Harl Stewart met you."

"Greg, where did you learn this?" Melinda's voice shook.

"It was something one of our operatives ran across in Tucson. It's nothing to be ashamed of, Melinda."

She considered his words a long minute, then raised her chin defiantly. "*I* didn't care. Harl didn't want it known in Corinth City. I took over eight hundred dollars from him one night. The next morning he asked me to marry him." She forced a wan smile. "I asked him if that was the only way he knew to get his money back. And then I married him."

"Melinda, did you love Harl Stewart?"

Her cheeks flamed. "Greg! You have no right —" Then she paused, her slim form slumping a little. "Greg, perhaps I can make you understand. Any normal woman wants a man, but in self-respect she doesn't accept all offerings. All right, I dealt faro, and a good game if I do say so. I didn't like it particularly, but what is there left for a girl in this country? I never had the education to teach school. Would you ask that I work in a restaurant for the small money paid? Oh, yes, I know there was another alternative. It didn't appeal to me. I could support myself dealing faro, better than anything else. I'm not ashamed of it. But I was awful tired of it, just the same. I wanted a husband I could respect. Harl Stewart was that man. Was it love, you ask. I'll say, frankly, no. It wasn't the love I'd have for a young man. But Harl was good and kind. I was so fond of him, Greg, and I appreciated the home he gave me. We were awfully happy, even when he was drinking. And that wasn't so bad, up to about six months back, and then something must have happened."

"You've no idea what it was?"

"Not the slightest. Perhaps something went wrong with his mining interests in Arizona. He refused to talk to me about it, said I mustn't bother my head about business. No, Greg, I didn't love him, but I think I made him a good wife, while it lasted. . . ." Her voice trailed off into silence. She turned her head away, shoulders shaking. Awkwardly, Quist reached across and placed his hand on one of hers. There was a long silence.

Finally, Quist rose to his feet. "Well, I've got to be getting back to town. It was good of you to talk to me."

The girl rose, facing him. "It was good for me, Greg. I wasn't sure how you'd take that faro business, if you ever learned about it. You've been kind, more kind than I deserve, perhaps."

"I could see your side of the faro dealing, too."

"Oh, Greg, if everything else could be cleaned up so simply," she said. Quist told her it would; perhaps the following day. Melinda looked startled. "Greg! You mean you know who killed Harl?"

"I'm pretty certain of it now, Melinda. You've helped me a lot. I hope to have the man who killed your husband, under arrest tomorrow. I'll make my charges then —"

"Greg! Could I be there when it happens?"

Quist stared at her. "Lord, Melinda, I couldn't advise anything like that. It would make pretty rough listening for you — all the stuff about your husband will have to be gone over —"

"I can stand it, Greg. I can! I owe that much to Harl."

He argued against the idea a few minutes more, but finally gave in. "All right, Melinda, if you insist," he said in a reluctant voice. "Have somebody drive you in to the courthouse tomorrow before ten o'clock — probably Jason Randle would do it. Anyway, I'd like to have him there. I want to give him his scalp —"

"Greg, what did that scalp have to do — ?"

Quist smiled. "Don't press me now. I've got to get a few things straightened out in my mind first, before I start talking."

"And you won't even tell me who — who did it?"

"I'll say this much," Quist replied. "I'm having Smoky put Witt Auringer and Rupe Chandler under arrest when I return to town."

Melinda's eyes widened. She started to ask questions, but Quist shook his head and prepared to leave. "I've got to get going, now, Melinda. *Adiós* — until tomorrow."

She didn't answer at once, but came to him, standing very near, and her arms slipped around his shoulders. He held her close, feeling the beating of her heart against his body and her warm lips on his own. He allowed her to go reluctantly, when she drew back. There was a singing in his ears and his breath was coming faster.

"Oh, Greg, please don't get any wrong

impressions of me" — Melinda's voice was almost a sob. "But I've been lonely and you're so — so darn understanding —"

Roughly, he seized her in his arms again. There was a long moment of silence. Finally he stood back. "Maybe that first kiss was for understanding," he said, voice not quite steady, emotion making the tones sound harsh, "that second was just plain me — Greg Quist — who sometimes thinks his control isn't all it should be."

With no further word, he stepped down from the gallery and rounded the house in long strides to reach the corral, muttering savagely over and over. "You bustard, oh, you bustard, Quist —"

Randle was nowhere in sight when Quist saddled up; he even failed to hear the cook's yell of good-bye as he went driving furiously out of the ranchyard. . . .

The buckskin pony was in a lather by the time he reached Corinth City. He pulled it to a long sliding halt, in a shower of dust and gravel before the sheriff's hitchrack. Hayes rose from his desk, as Quist came striding in. "Greg," he commenced, "what — ?"

Quist cut him short. "Smoky, I want you to throw Witt Auringer and Rupe Chandler under arrest, as soon as you can lay hands on 'em. Put 'em in cells. If possible, use your authority to get bail refused. Have their hearing before the justice, at ten, tomorrow."

"Good Lord, Greg! Do you mean — ?"

Again, Quist interrupted. "You'll get the whole story tomorrow. And I want the public excluded from the hearing, too."

Hayes frowned. "That can be arranged with the J.P., I reckon. But I'll have to have warrants —"

"Get 'em. I'll explain the charges at the hearing."

"But what are the charges?" Hayes asked.

"Conspiracy to defraud, conniving to murder," Quist said. Hayes said dubiously it sounded somewhat irregular. Quist half-snarled, "Irregular? How long since things have been regular around here? I'm fed up to the back teeth on the dirty mess. If necessary, I'll use my authority, but I figured you'd want credit in the county."

"Of course, Greg. Whatever you say." Hayes looked strangely at him. "Something seems to have gotten under your skin."

"Yeah," Quist snapped. "Maybe it's a sort of disease, known as hatred for crooks." He swung abruptly around and went out to his horse. The sheriff stared perplexedly after him.

CHAPTER XX

The Price of a Life

Odell Jenkins, Corinth City's Justice of the Peace, frowned at the people sitting before his desk. It wasn't really a desk — just a large scarred table, holding a couple of record books, some papers, an ancient blotter and an inkstand. He moved impatiently in his swivel chair, an elderly man with tousled white hair and lined face, in shiny black serge, white shirt and string tie. He turned his watery blue eyes toward Smoky Hayes. "Sheriff, you asked that these prisoners be given a hearing at ten o'clock, at which time you stated Mr. Quist would be on hand to explain the charges he has made against" — consulting papers on his desk — "Dewitt Auringer and Rupert Chandler. I must ask you again, where is Mr. Quist? It is ten — fifteen now."

Smoky Hayes looked uncomfortable. "I'm sure he'll be here in a few minutes, judge. Something must have detained him."

"That's fairly evident," Jenkins said crustily.

The Justice of the Peace's office — most

people called Jenkins "judge" was situated in an old building, on the southeast corner of Main and Brazos Streets, just across Brazos from the sheriff's office. It was a fairly large room, the rear half of which had been partitioned off to make a storeroom for county records. There was a double-doored entrance. At either side was a window with the shade, drawn from the bottom halfway to the top. Jenkins sat at the table with his back to the left-hand wall. A filing case stood at his rear.

Nearest the entrance sat Smoky Hayes, then came Auringer and Chandler. Neither of the prisoners had been handcuffed, though their guns had been taken away. They sat sullen and resigned, as though long since weary of protesting their innocence of wrongdoing. Chandler looked frightened with no fight left in him. Beyond these two sat Deputy Dyke Leigh, with Eirene Stewart at his right. Then came Melinda and Jason Randle. The straight-backed chairs had been placed in a sort of half circle before the justice; their occupants awaited Quist's arrival with an impatience that matched Jenkins'.

One of the entrance doors opened, and Quist came in, closing it behind him. Heads swiveled in his direction. Jenkins started to speak, but Quist cut him short: "My apologies for being late. Something went haywire with the hotel safe, and it took a few minutes to work the combination. I had to have this" — indicating a newspaper wrapped parcel under his arm. He placed the parcel on Jenkins' table and nodded greetings to the others.

Auringer leaped to his feet. "Quist, this is an outrage! I'm going to sue your railroad for false arrest —"

"Better go slow," Quist snapped. "I'm not through with you yet."

Smoky Hayes pressed Auringer back in the chair. Chandler swallowed hard; he didn't say anything. Justice Jenkins said irritably, "I'll point out to you, Mr. Quist, that this proceeding seems highly irregular. It is not usual for me to conduct closed hearings. The citizens of this country have the right to know what their public servants are doing. And yet you have reserved the privilege of having only certain people here, this morning —"

"I don't remember," Quist interrupted, "that Miss Stewart was invited to be present."

Eirene spoke from her chair. "So long as Melinda was coming, I thought it would be all right if I came too."

Quist sighed and shrugged his shoulders. "All right, but don't blame me if your feelings get hurt. This won't be pleasant."

Jenkins cleared his throat. "Mr. Quist, you have made charges, mentioning fraud and plotting murder. Are you charging both these men with the same crimes?"

"My mistake," Quist said tersely. "I should have made myself clearer to Sheriff Hayes, last night, but I had a lot on my mind. I wasn't thinking straight at the time. I was mad. No, judge, don't fill in any papers yet" — as the justice drew a form toward him. "There're a few things I want to say first. Later, you can do as you see fit about such information as I place before you."

Jenkins smoothed his tobacco-stained mustache, and said crustily, "Let us hope you're thinking straighter this morning."

"I agree with you," Quist conceded. "The conniving to murder charge, I lay against Rupe Chandler." Chandler started a protest, but Dyke Leigh pushed him back in his chair. Quist continued, "Auringer I charge with an attempt to defraud the T.N. & A.S. Railroad —"

"I've done nothing of the sort," Auringer shouted angrily, leaping to his feet. "Where did you ever get such an idea — ?"

"You've entered a claim against my company for the loss of fifty sheep and fifty goats —"

"My Gawd," Auringer exclaimed, righteously indignant. "Those animals were mine. They were destroyed while in the care of your —"

"Destroyed by your own men," Quist interrupted sharply, "led by Joker Gaillard. Your own men, with one exception — Tonkawa Talbert, and he's beyond prosecution, as is Gaillard. Before he died, Gaillard confessed the whole business to me. D-Bar-A hands held up that train, Auringer, and destroyed the stock — men on your payroll."

Auringer's jaw sagged. He dropped weakly back in his chair. "I — I swear I didn't know that —" he started.

"I'll give you the benefit of the doubt, Auringer. I don't think you did. But it was done by men in your pay. You should exercise a certain control there. I think you'd best withdraw that claim."

"But why," Auringer asked, bewildered, "should *my* men —"

Quist cut in, "Because they're cowmen, Auringer. They didn't want sheep brought into this country. You can't shove sheep down a cowman's throat. He'll do almost anything to keep them out —"

"That's Gawd's own truth," Jason Randle

exclaimed. "Dirty, woolly, stinkin', blattin' critters! They ruin the range, after the cowmen came in and cleared it of danger —"

Quist swung savagely on Randle. "And who cleared the way for the cowmen?" he demanded. "The buffalo hunters fought the Indians too, and the mountain men and the army. I'm pretty sick of hearing the cowmen take all the credit for cleaning up the range."

Randle fell silent and Quist swung back to Auringer. "Knowing that sheep weren't wanted in this country, you still insisted on bringing them in. You expected trouble, too. You hired Joker Gaillard, a professional killer and gunman, for your protection. That could have resulted in a range war, and that sort of thing lends to murder. Can you deny it, Auringer?"

Auringer was wilting under the attack. "I had rights to come in with sheep if I wanted —" he began weakly.

"I do not think any man has the right to push in where he's not wanted," Quist stated, "if his coming leads to trouble. But for the sake of profits, you were willing to risk that. Gaillard told me, before he died, that the thought of a range war didn't bother you, so long as your interests prevailed. You blamed Harl Stewart's hatred of sheep for the train hold-up. Even when Stewart denied having anything to do with it, you tried to force a showdown to get the matter settled once and for all. What the people around here want to do with you, I'll leave them to determine. If the law in this county doesn't take action against your hands, my company will institute an action. I'll make no further charges against you personally; just don't press the claim against the railroad, that's all."

Quist moved over to the justice's table and sat down on one corner, his right foot supporting him on the floor. The J.P. looked about to protest such familiarity, but only said, "What about Rupert Chandler, Mr. Quist?"

Quist shoved his hands in his coat pockets. "I'll get to Chandler in a minute. Let's go back to Brose Randle's murder. Yes, it was murder. Gaillard confessed to the killing." He drew a deep breath. "There's an old Comanche scalp has figured largely in the skulduggery hereabouts, a scalp that Brose Randle had owned since he was a young man. Jason knew his father had it, and for a particular reason, Jason wanted to lay hands on it. The night news was brought to town that Stewart had been killed and Brose Randle had fled, Jason had a moment to talk with Gaillard. Remember, Randle, the night

Gaillard dropped the dead mouse in your beer? You pretended to be bawling him out, but you offered him twenty-five dollars to get on Brose's trail and get the scalp. Isn't that right, Randle?"

"Gaillard must have been filling you with hot air." Randle growled, but he looked uneasy. "But go ahead. It's a good story."

Quist said coldly, "You won't like it so well by the time I'm through. So Gaillard took after the old man's wagon, with its rutty old skiff. The trail looked like it was leading down into Mexico, when Gaillard finally found it. When the Joker was drawing near, Brose happened to look back and saw him. He whipped up his team. Doubtless he realized what Gaillard had in mind, because he tossed the Comanche scalp into a clump of mesquite trees, before the Joker overtook him. Gaillard didn't know that. He finally stopped the old man and demanded the scalp. Old Brose had courage and he went for his gun. He didn't have a chance against Gaillard, of course. So that accounts for Brose Randle's murder, which I think should be laid at his son's door —"

An anguished exclamation came from Randle. "Gaillard always denied he killed my father. I couldn't prove otherwise, but I —"

"You didn't dare bring your deal with

Gaillard into the open either," Quist cut in. "You didn't want that scalp brought into prominence." Smoky Hayes asked a question. Quist replied, "Gaillard had a macabre sense of humor. It was he who unloaded that boat, and propped the old man in it, as though he were fishing. The Joker assumed the sheriff and others would be on Brose's trail, too. He laughed when he thought how startled they'd be. I'll admit that I —"

The justice asked curiously, "What's so precious about that scalp?"

"Be patient," Quist said, "I'll get around to telling you. Gaillard next drove the team off, then took his own leave before the sheriff could arrive and find him in the neighborhood. Later, he spied me from a hilltop. I'd found the scalp by sheer accident. Gaillard saw me with it, and started shooting, figuring no doubt if he killed me, Jason would get the scalp and Gaillard the credit. A short time later, Smoky and his men arrived and I was taken to town."

"Regardless of the truth of your yarn," Randle said nervously. "That should be my scalp now, and I want it."

Quist turned to the newspaper-wrapped package, unrolled it part way and removed the Comanche scalp which he tossed to Randle. "And you can have it," Quist said. "I'm through with it." Randle caught the scalp and examined it. His face tightened. He whispered something to Melinda who was eagerly looking at it. She stiffened and bit her lip, but made no comment. Quist went on:

"Two attempts have been made to steal that scalp from me. Gaillard offered Tonkawa Talbert money — not much I'm sure — to get it. The second time I was forced to kill Tonkawa. There was a check in his pocket for one thousand dollars, with Harl Stewart's name forged to it. That bothered me for a while." Quist uttered a short disgusted laugh. "That was due to more of Gaillard's twisted humor. He'd written the check, knowing that Tonkawa could neither read nor write. Gaillard told me before he died, that he shook with laughter every time he thought what would have happened if Tonkawa had presented the check for payment at the bank. I've a hunch there was something wrong with Gaillard's mind. He was ready to kill for anyone who'd pay. Sunday, on my way to Borrico Pass, I rode by Gaillard and Rupe Chandler on the street. Chandler made a remark that he'd pay a hundred dollars to see me dead. Gaillard wasn't the man to turn down a job like that. He took up my trail. When he finally caught up with me, we shot it out. I guess I was lucky —"

"That's a lie." White-faced, Chandler found his voice. "I never offered the Joker a hundred dollars. He lied to you —"

Quist shrugged careless shoulders. "Not a very big price for a life, at that. But, Chandler, I know you'd like me out of the way. I know too much about your former life. You're afraid I may run you out of Corinth City as I did out of El Paso. Well, Gaillard's not here to stuff the words down your throat, Chandler, but I prefer his dying words to your live ones."

Chandler muttered a feeble denial again, and slumped down on his chair. Quist turned to his audience, shifting his seat slightly on the table, hands in coat pockets. "So it's a dead man's word against a live crook's. If I haven't actual proof of Gaillard's words, for other things I have to say I have the telegrams and letters of my company's investigators in Colorado, Arizona and Oklahoma. We cooperate with each other in digging up information." Abruptly, he spoke to Jason Randle: "Randle, you didn't serve time in any Mexican prison. It was in the Oklahoma Penitentiary, wasn't it?"

Randle gave a start of alarm. "Where'd you ever get that crazy idea, Quist? You won't find my name on the Oklahoma Pen's records. What sort of a frame are you — ?"

"No," Quist conceded, "your name wasn't found on the prison records. You'd managed to get tried under an assumed name — an alias. The charge was murder. You suspected your wife, I believe, of being too chummy with another man. So you shot him. There were extenuating circumstances, so your sentence wasn't severe. Maybe you got wondering about your wife. I don't know. Anyway, prison life irked, and you managed an escape. You came back to Texas and got a job with Harl Stewart. You didn't tell anyone you'd been in prison —"

"What a story," Randle jeered. "You can sure cook 'em up, Quist." But he was commencing to look more unsure of himself.

Quist smiled thinly and went on, "There are people up in Chotokee, Oklahoma, who remember an old codger that used to visit you at prison. His name was Brose Randle, though because of your prison records, he claimed to be only a friend of yours. He liked to fish. And later he came to the Rafter-S, with his old wagon and boat, when he thought enough time had elapsed, so he wouldn't lead lawmen to you, Randle. Isn't all this so?" Randle didn't reply. He had gone paper-white and fidgeted nervously with his hands. Melinda spoke to him, and he began to shake.

Smoky Hayes said, "It looks as if I'll have to get in touch with the prison authorities in Oklahoma. Jason, you should have known better than try anything like that. Sooner or later, you were bound to be found out." Randle lifted his head, then dropped it again.

Quist continued, "It was in Chotokee you were married, a few months before you had that prison trouble, wasn't it, Randle? Too bad the courthouse there burned down, destroying the record of your marriage. Whatever happened to your wife, Randle? I understand she cleared out for parts unknown, after you went to prison —"

"Quit it, for Gawd's sake, quit it!" Randle leaped frantically to his feet, eyes wild. "I'll tell you about it, myself, Quist. Quit stabbing at me that way. I can't stand it!" Melinda spoke low voiced to him; her long-lashed eyes went reproachfully to Quist, when Randle failed to listen, and shook off her restraining hand. "Yes, I'll talk, Quist," words tumbled from his mouth in a torrent. "You got that scalp. Took out the stitches. You found what was hidden between the layers of skin. All right, all right. Tell it — tell what you found. It doesn't matter now." He dropped, shaking, back in

300

his chair, head lowered in his hands.

Melinda spoke to Dyke Leigh. The deputy rose and went to a tin water cooler in one corner and returned with a glass which Randle accepted. Quist drew a long breath. "So you all think I'm being pretty hard about this business. All right. Sometimes people make me that way. Yes, I ripped out the stitches that held a section of doeskin to the human scalp. Between them was a folded marriage certificate, all the proof that Randle possessed that he'd been married. According to the certificate, Randle had married someone named Melinda Powell." He handed Jenkins a paper. "Look for yourself, judge."

He spoke now to the woman named Melinda Stewart. "I believe that was your name, wasn't it?"

CHAPTER XXI

Conclusion

Surprised exclamations rose on the air. Justice Jenkins pounded on the table, with his clenched fist, demanding quiet. Little attention was paid him. Smoky Hayes had risen from his chair, a shocked expression on his face. "Melinda! You never told me."

"She didn't tell a lot of other men, either," Jason Randle half snarled, fighting for self-control again. Melinda said something low-voiced to him. Randle spat a single word at her, and she sank back, red-faced, in her chair. Jenkins pounded on the table again, and said he'd have no such language in his court. Randle appeared not to hear him. He went on, "There were always men coming visiting, whenever Harl Stewart was away, and when he was there too. Chandler was one." He named a couple of other men. Hayes darted a nasty look at Chandler. Randle said, "Yeah — and you too, Smoky Hayes."

Hayes stiffened. He hadn't sat down again. "Don't talk like a fool, Randle. Everyone knew I was there to visit Eirene —"

Randle rushed on, infuriated. "Double-crossed, that's what I was. I'd not seen Melinda for years, didn't even know where she was. And then one day, Stewart brought her home and announced they were married. I reckon it was a shock for her to see me there. I was supposed to still be in the pen. Neither of us dared tell on the other. Soon's possible, we had a talk. She told me to keep my mouth shut. She said Stewart was old and couldn't live much longer, and then she'd have the Rafter-S and his money. And she'd go through another marriage with me. I was a damn' fool to ever trust her —"

"Greg! Justice Jenkins!" Melinda's husky tones cut through Randle's revelations. Bright pink burned in her cheeks and her head was high. "Is it fair to me for you to listen to such nonsense? He's twisting facts for his own purposes. You've got to listen to my side of the story."

Melinda held everyone's interest now. Eirene gazed at her with a sort of horror in her features. Auringer and Chandler appeared to have forgotten their own troubles momentarily. The sheriff's face had taken on a cold, implacable look. Melinda went on, "It's true to some extent what Jason says. I was at one time married to him. We quarreled from the first. I was young and foolish

303

those days. I couldn't bear the thought of leaving him. I wanted our marriage to stand up. Later I came to my senses. I went to Arizona to make my own way, as Greg Quist knows. I got a divorce —"

Quist interrupted dryly, "I know you were making your own way, but I didn't know all of the story. I suppose you've a paper to prove your divorce." Melinda bit her lip, seeking a reply. Before she could speak, he said, "Let's hear Jason's story first."

Randle said skeptically, "If she got a divorce, that's the first I ever heard of it. Would she have asked me to keep my mouth shut, if she was in the clear? Don't believe a word she says, Quist. She'll double-cross you, too, as she did me, time after time. My father always said she couldn't be trusted and that some day she'd deny our marriage. So one day when she was away from the ranch, he went to her room and stole the marriage certificate. Said if I didn't have sense enough to hold on to the proof, he'd take care of it for me. He sewed it inside that old Comanche scalp. Then one day she got around me and like a fool I told her where it was. From then on she was after the both of us to get it, but my father had it hid. He knew her better'n I, Dad did — always predicted that some day she'd commit murder to get what she wanted. He was afraid of her. If I'd had sense I'd have listened. He was always after me to leave and get shet of her —"

"Look here, Greg," Smoky Hayes interrupted, "aren't we just wasting time hearing all this rot about Randle and his woman — ?"

"Yaah!" Randle raged. "And she double-crossed you, too. Did you figure I was blind? I knew what was going on —"

"Shut your dirty mouth, Randle," Hayes snapped. "Greg, not one word we've heard gives us any clue as to Harl Stewart's death. That's what I'm after. Can't we just skip these domestic squabbles —"

"Smoky — !" Melinda wailed a protest.

"— and get on with the business?" Hayes said, as though he'd not heard Melinda's voice. "I'm waiting to learn who killed Harlan Stewart."

"Smoky" — Quist eyed the sheriff reproachfully — "I shouldn't have to tell you. It was you —"

He stopped. Hayes had drawn his six-shooter, covering Quist and the rest of the room. He backed a few steps, gun-muzzle moving in a short arc to cover Quist and the other men. "Greg, I was afraid of this," Hayes said regretfully. "You're just too

305

damn' smart. And don't try reaching for that hideout gun. You wouldn't have a chance. Dyke! Randle! Draw your guns easy and toss 'em out to the middle of the floor. *Pronto!* You know me, Dyke. I don't miss. Hurry it up!"

The guns were tossed out, to land with a clatter in the center of the floor. "Me, too?" Quist asked quietly.

Hayes shook his head. "I don't trust your hand near that gun, Greg. I'll take care of it." He approached carefully, until his gun-barrel was pressed against Quist's middle, then with one hand reached to Quist's underarm holster, drew out the short-barreled forty-four. Backing away again, he tossed Quist's six-shooter with the others on the floor. Justice Jenkins was excitedly protesting Hayes' actions, but Hayes ignored the old man's words. Those in the chairs gazed at Hayes as though hypnotized, as he backed slowly toward the entrance doors, reached behind him and shot the bolt, never once lowering his gun. He came back into the room a few paces to stand near his chair.

Quist said tonelessly, "So, I've had another lesson in carelessness. But you'll never make it far, Smoky. I'm telling you."

Hayes laughed harshly. "Farther than you think, Greg. Figured on a contingency of this sort. My pony's outside, saddled. All right, I'll admit to being double-crossed by a — a witch, shall we say? — but that's no sign I'm going to swing for playing her game. I'll be leaving in a minute or so, but I'm curious to know how you found out, Greg. Feel like talking?"

"Cripes, yes." Quist smiled thinly. "Y'know, Smoky, I've sort of had suspicions about you since the first day we met. I was right sure you recognized my name — as a known railroad dick — but you weren't certain. You had to go slow. For all you knew I had been called here on Stewart's death. You acted too apologetic for a sheriff —"

"All right, I slipped there," Hayes acknowledged.

"And then, after you'd talked to Jay Fletcher, you realized you'd best go easy. You already knew my record. You passed that on to Melinda. No woman could have known so much about my past cases, otherwise. I suppose you planned to marry her and get control of Stewart's holdings. It could be you'd have had to murder Randle, too, before you got far, but you didn't know before today he was her husband —"

"Correct as hell, Greg," Hayes said coolly. "But talk fast. How did you figure out I did it?"

"You told certain lies that weren't borne out by my brother investigators. At the time Stewart went to Arizona to bring Melinda home from her visit, you told me you were in Cripple Creek, looking into your mining properties. The Colorado Mining Association never heard of you. But investigators in Arizona heard of you. Instead of visiting friends, there, Melinda was staying at a hotel. And a man named Bert Haynes was registered at that same hotel. Bert Haynes and Melinda Stewart saw a great deal of each other there. Haynes' description fits you, Smoky. And then, Stewart arrived unexpectedly to take Melinda home. And found her with you. He knew then that your pretending to be interested in Eirene was just a cover-up."

"Yes, I guess I played the wrong filly," Hayes admitted brazenly. "I doubt that Eirene is a double-crosser, anyway."

Quist cast a glance at Eirene. She was listening, white-faced. Then, with a certain contempt for the susceptibility of his own sex, Quist saw Melinda weeping on Randle's shoulder, while Randle tried to comfort her. Quist slowly shook his head in unbelief and muttered, "Sucker." Then his gaze came back to face Hayes' six-shooter.

". . . and so," Hayes mockingly took up

the story, "when we got back, Stewart brooded over — well, Melinda's infidelity, let's say — and started drinking heavily. Sure, we quarreled, but not about mining profits. I thought I convinced him that he was mistaken about Melinda and me, while I continued to call on Eirene. Stewart by that time didn't know just what to believe. We pretended to patch up our quarrel, but I figured he was planning out some sort of revenge."

"I'm glad to have you confirm my ideas, Smoky," Quist said dryly. "And so you and Melinda decided to get rid of Stewart. I don't know whether you planned it a long way ahead, or if things just happened right that day you escorted Stewart home from the Shamrock Bar. That's where you slipped again. Sick as Stewart was that day, no real friend would have started him on that ride. He should have been put to bed. And so you shot him a few miles from the ranch, and with Melinda's connivance —"

"You're smart, Greg," Hayes said with reluctant admiration, "too smart to go on living much longer. How did you figure that out?"

"Melinda claimed," Quist explained, "that Stewart was shot while he was turning away from the doorway, then staggered in and fell face down across the bed. If that had been so, the blood from the wound would likely have spread evenly on his shirt, instead of running in a streak down his back." He reached behind him, still facing Hayes' gun, drew from the newspaper package, Stewart's shirt which he had taken from the undertaker's. Holding the shirt with both hands, he displayed the back with its long streak of brownish color running to the tail from the bullet hole. "And so I knew," Quist went on, "that Stewart had been held in an erect position after being shot. That's when you lashed him to the saddle."

Hayes' eyes narrowed. "You're smart all right."

Eirene was crying softly. There was no other sound in the room.

Quist continued, "I figured that sometime during that ride to the ranch, Smoky, the horses were halted. Perhaps you pretended to fix Stewart's stirrup or something. Anyway, you dismounted, got behind him and fired. The course the bullet took shows that the shot came from below Stewart. If he had been shot in his own doorway, the bullet would have entered straighter, even if shot by a man who was mounted. Here's another point: Shamus Maguire remembers carrying Stewart's coat out to him, before you left the Shamrock Bar, and tossing it across Stewart's saddlehorn. Deacon Vogel, the ranch cook, testified at the inquest that Stewart wore the coat when he arrived — drunk as Vogel thought — at the rear door of the ranchhouse. It was pretty hot that day, Smoky. Why should you put that coat on Stewart, except to hide that blood on the back of his shirt?"

"Got it all figured out, haven't you, Greg?" Hayes said with cool nonchalance.

Quist smiled thinly. "Just about. You knew the cowhands were away from the ranch that day. Only Vogel and Brose Randle were there. Two old men. Eyes not too good maybe. And one of them on the verge of senility. And it was getting dark. Instead of taking Stewart to the front door as would be natural, being nearer the bedroom, you took him around to the back, where Vogel or Randle could see you helping him down from the saddle. You'd called to Melinda as you passed the front of the house — asked her to meet you at the rear. At the back, after loosening Stewart's ropes you helped him down — for Vogel's benefit. You gripped him tightly by one arm, held him erect — almost, anyway. Melinda helped from behind, and thus cut off some of Vogel's view. Once you got him into the house,

311

you carried him to the front bedroom, stripped off the coat and placed him face down on the bed as though he had fallen there —"

"Just a minute, Mr. Quist," the justice broke in. "Do I understand you to say the sheriff — Hayes — held that body erect with one hand? That would require a mighty strong arm —"

"Which Smoky has," Quist said over his shoulder, still watching Hayes' gun. He slid his left hand into his coat pocket again. "I've seen Smoky lift Gaillard bodily from the sidewalk, with only one hand." He shifted position slightly on the table.

"Easy, Greg," Hayes warned sharply. "No fast moves. I don't like it. I'm remembering that you tricked Gaillard. That won't work with me —"

"There's a number of things haven't worked with you," Quist pointed out, his topaz eyes steady on Hayes. "And so, after leaving Stewart on the bed, you gave Melinda directions, mounted and headed fast toward town. Giving you a proper length of time, Melinda took her thirty-eight six-shooter, stepped to the open front door, and fired a shot at random into the darkness. The sound of the shot brought Vogel out of the bunkhouse instantly. He didn't stop to distinguish the difference between a thirty-eight report and a forty-five. He'd have no reason to. And at the moment, Brose Randle was whipping his team into action, hurtling the wagon away from the house. Vogel said he drove like he was scared. Maybe he was. Maybe he'd learned what happened to Stewart and feared a similar dose for himself. I imagine he had drawn rein some place in the shadows before the house for a few minutes, about the time that Melinda stepped out and fired the thirty-eight. Likely Brose thought she was firing at him, and he took off like a bat out of hell. By chance the shot from her gun came mighty close to the wagon. I know because I dug the thirty-eight slug from the stern board of the skiff." Quist paused and looked toward Melinda, expecting contradictions.

She appeared to be in a half-fainting condition and protested only feebly, supported by Randle's left arm. "I've examined certain six-shooters at the Rafter-S, among them Stewart's Colt and Melinda's thirty-eight. Neither, Melinda said, had been fired in some time. Both had been cleaned after the last shooting, but there was a difference. Stewart's gun had dust in the barrel. Melinda's was as clean as a whistle. It had been cleaned very recently." He glanced at Melinda, saying harshly, "That could be an act. She seems able to turn on the weeps at will." Randle glared angrily at him, but said nothing.

Hayes laughed in self-contempt. "She was actress enough to fool me. But only a dumb idiot would fall more than once. All right, Greg. I'll hand it to you. I admit everything. You've called the turn at every point —"

What more he might have said was never spoken. Quist's index finger had tightened about the trigger of the forty-four six-shooter in his left coat pocket, and he shot through the cloth. A grimace of agonized surprise swept across Hayes' features. He staggered back, fighting to bring his gun to bear on Quist. Quist jerked the gun from his pocket, fired a second time. The impact of the heavy forty-four swung Hayes sidewise, even as he started shooting. Fire and flame spurted from the gun-muzzle as he strove doggedly to stay erect, but his shots were flying wild, even as he was falling, the bullets slashing sharp paths through the swirling powder-smoke.

Through the detonations shaking the building, Quist heard Randle shout excitedly to Melinda something about making a getaway. The man scrambled toward his six-shooter on the floor, then jerked Melinda to her feet. Quist shifted aim. The forty-four roared a third time. Randle sat down abruptly. Melinda was already slumped on the floor. Two chairs crashed over as Auringer and Chandler scurried to get out of line of the gunfire.

Eirene screamed, "Greg! Dyke! Stop the guns — stop — stop —" then dropped to her knees beside Melinda. Dyke had his gun by this time, but the shooting was all over. He stammered, "My God, Greg! Smoky — of all people —"

Quist said grimly to no one in particular. "Smoky's not the only one to prepare for contingencies. I reckon he forgot I had a mate to my underarm gun." He smothered the smoldering cloth about the hole in his coat pocket, then crossed the floor to gaze down a minute at the dead sheriff. He turned back, reloading his forty-four, then got his other gun from the floor. His nose was still stinging from the acrid odor of burned powder. He said tersely to Justice Jenkins who sat as though petrified in his chair, "Now do you understand why I didn't want many people to attend this hearing?" Jenkins nodded dumbly. Quist heard Dyke Leigh's voice at his shoulder:

"Greg! Melinda's dead. I —"

Quist swallowed hard. "I saw her go

down. I think she caught that last wild shot from Smoky's gun." He glanced toward Randle who was sitting on the floor, moaning, clutching his right thigh. Quist muttered bitterly, "The poor woman-ridden fool. Well, he'll make a witness. . . ."

Auringer and Chandler were standing before him now, fawning, making apologies, saying anything that might get them into Quist's good graces. Quist snarled, "Get out of my sight, you bustards!" then turned to Dyke Leigh, saying, "Take charge, Dyke. You're sheriff now. Do as you see fit about things. I'll be at the hotel."

He was conscious suddenly of excited yelling from the street. Somebody was pounding on the door. He walked over and unbolted it. Men swarmed into the room. A babel of voices rose. Quist spoke over his shoulder to Justice Jenkins. "You'd better send somebody for Doc Wakeman, then get Eirene Stewart out of here. Dyke's going to be busy for some time."

Without waiting for a reply, he turned and forced his way through the crowd. On the sidewalk he turned in the direction of the hotel, ignoring the queries that greeted him on every hand. He reached the hotel, got his key and ascended to his room. Sitting down at his table, he rolled and lighted a brown-paper cigarette. Reaching for paper and pencil, he started a letter to Jay Fletcher:

Dear Jay, it read, *why do beautiful women have to get mixed up in murder business? And why do I have to be such an awful bustard — ?*

He paused, stared at what he had written, then slowly, deliberately, he tore the paper to bits. Then he commenced a second letter, one worded in the more stilted phrases of modern civilization.

We hope you have enjoyed this Large Print book. Other Thorndike Press or Chivers Press Large Print books are available at your library or directly from the publishers.

For more information about current and upcoming titles, please call or write, without obligation, to:

Thorndike Press
P.O. Box 159
Thorndike, Maine 04986 USA
Tel. (800) 257-5157

OR

Chivers Press Limited
Windsor Bridge Road
Bath BA2 3AX
England
Tel. (0225) 335336

All our Large Print titles are designed for easy reading, and all our books are made to last.